"It surpasses most of the books in which experience of terror and physical cruelty are told because by the great beauty of its style it lifts the entire experience to the philosophic, mythological realms of knowledge."

—Anaïs Nin

"Perhaps the book which has impressed me the most. More than realism, this book is a trip into the world of nightmare and anxiety, through a world of injustice which is our own."

—Luis Buñuel

"To me, the Nazi experience is the key one of this century—they merely carried to the final extreme what otherwise lies within so-called normal social existence and normal man. You have made the normality of it all apparent, and this is a very important and difficult thing to have done."

—Arthur Miller
(in a letter to the author)

"One of the grimmest and yet most beautiful books . . . One which will rank with *The Diary of Anne Frank* as a testament not only to the atrocities of the war, but to the failings of human nature. A book of striking intensity, written with a luminous apprehension of the natural and supernatural worlds."

—*Chicago Daily News*

"Of all the remarkable fiction that emerged from World War II, nothing stands higher than Jerzy Kosinski's *The Painted Bird*. A magnificent work of art, and a celebration of the individual will. No one who reads it will forget it; no one who reads it will be unmoved by it. *The Painted Bird* enriches our literature and our lives."

—Jonathan Yardley,
Miami Herald

THE
PAINTED
BIRD

Jerzy Kosinski

BANTAM BOOKS
TORONTO · NEW YORK · LONDON · SYDNEY

THE PAINTED BIRD

*A Bantam Book / published by arrangement with
Houghton Mifflin Company*

PRINTING HISTORY

*Houghton Mifflin edition published October 1965
4 printings through January 1966
Revised Houghton Mifflin edition published March 1976*

*Bantam edition / September 1972
8 printings through August 1977
Revised Bantam edition / September 1978*

10th printing .... May 1979	12th printing ...... August 1980
11th printing . November 1979	13th printing ...... August 1981

ISBN 0–553–20554–4

Printed simultaneously in the United States and Canada

PRINTED IN THE UNITED STATES OF AMERICA

22 21 20 19 18 17 16 15 14

*To the memory of my wife Mary Hayward Weir
without whom even the past would
lose its meaning*

and only God,
                    omnipotent indeed,
knew they were mammals
                        of a different breed.

MAYAKOVSKY

This new edition of The Painted Bird *incorporates some material that did not appear in the first edition.*

THE
PAINTED
BIRD

1

In the first weeks of World War II, in the fall of 1939, a six-year-old boy from a large city in Eastern Europe was sent by his parents, like thousands of other children, to the shelter of a distant village.

A man traveling eastward agreed for a substantial payment to find temporary foster parents for the child. Having little choice, the parents entrusted the boy to him.

In sending their child away the parents believed that it was the best means of assuring his survival through the war. Because of the prewar anti-Nazi activities of the child's father, they themselves had to go into hiding to avoid forced labor in Germany or imprisonment in a concentration camp. They wanted to save the child from these dangers and hoped they would eventually be reunited.

Events upset their plans, however. In the confusion of war and occupation, with continuous transfers of population, the parents lost contact with the man who had placed their child in the village. They had to face the possibility of never finding their son again.

In the meantime, the boy's foster mother died within two months of his arrival, and the child was left alone to wander from one village to another, sometimes sheltered and sometimes chased away.

The villages in which he was to spend the next four years differed ethnically from the region of his birth. The local peasants, isolated and inbred, were fair-skinned with blond hair and blue or gray eyes. The boy was olive-skinned, dark-haired, and black-eyed. He spoke a language of the educated class, a language barely intelligible to the peasants of the east.

He was considered a Gypsy or Jewish stray, and harboring Gypsies or Jews, whose place was in ghettos and extermination camps, exposed individuals and communities to the harshest penalties at the hands of the Germans.

The villages in that region had been neglected for centuries. Inaccessible and distant from any urban centers, they were in the most backward parts of Eastern Europe. There were no schools or hospitals, few paved roads or bridges, no electricity. People lived in small settlements in the manner of their great-grandfathers. Villagers feuded over rights to rivers, woods, and lakes. The only law was the traditional right of the stronger and wealthier over the weaker and poorer. Divided between the Roman Catholic and the Orthodox faiths, the people were united only by their extreme superstition and the innumerable diseases plaguing men and animals alike.

They were ignorant and brutal, though not by choice. The soil was poor and the climate severe. The rivers, largely emptied of fish, frequently flooded the pastures and fields, turning them into swamps. Vast marshlands and bogs cut into the region, while dense forests traditionally sheltered bands of rebels and outlaws.

The occupation of that part of the country by the Germans only deepened its misery and backwardness. The peasants had to deliver a large part of their meager crops to the regular troops on the one hand, and to the

*partisans on the other. Refusal to do so could mean
punitive raids on the villages, leaving them in smoldering ruins.*

I lived in Marta's hut, expecting my parents to come
for me any day, any hour. Crying did not help, and
Marta paid no attention to my sniveling.

She was old and always bent over, as though she
wanted to break herself in half but could not. Her
long hair, never combed, had knotted itself into innumerable thick braids impossible to unravel. These
she called elflocks. Evil forces nested in the elflocks,
twisting them and slowly inducing senility.

She hobbled around, leaning on a gnarled stick,
muttering to herself in a language I could not quite understand. Her small withered face was covered with a
net of wrinkles, and her skin was reddish brown like
that of an overbaked apple. Her withered body constantly trembled as though shaken by some inner wind,
and the fingers of her bony hands with joints twisted
by disease never stopped quivering as her head on its
long scraggy neck nodded in every direction.

Her sight was poor. She peered at the light through
tiny slits embedded under thick eyebrows. Her lids were
like furrows in deeply plowed soil. Tears were always
spilling from the corners of her eyes, coursing down her
face in well-worn channels to join glutinous threads
hanging from her nose and the bubbly saliva dripping
from her lips. She looked like an old green-gray puff-
ball, rotten through and waiting for a last gust of wind
to blow out the black dry dust from inside.

At first I was afraid of her and closed my eyes
whenever she approached me. All I could sense then
was the foul smell of her body. She always slept in her
clothes. They were, according to her, the best defense
against the danger of the numerous diseases which fresh
air might waft into the room.

To insure health, she claimed, a person should

wash no more than twice a year, at Christmas and Easter, and even then very lightly and without undressing. She used hot water only to relieve her countless corns, bunions, and the ingrown toenails on her gnarled feet. That is why she soaked them once or twice a week.

Often she stroked my hair with her old, trembling hands that were so like garden rakes. She encouraged me to play in the yard and make friends with the household animals.

Eventually I realized that they were less dangerous than they appeared. I remembered the stories about them which my nurse used to read to me from a picture book. These animals had their own life, their loves and disagreements, and they held discussions in a language of their own.

The hens crowded the chicken house, jostling one another to reach the grain I threw to them. Some strolled in pairs, others pecked weaker ones and took solitary baths in puddles after the rain or foppishly ruffled their feathers over their eggs and quickly fell asleep.

Strange things happened in the farmyard. Yellow and black chicks hatched out of the eggs, resembling little live eggs on spindly legs. Once a lonely pigeon joined the flock. He was clearly unwelcome. When he made a landing in a flurry of wings and dust amidst the chickens, they scurried away, frightened. When he began to court them, cooing gutturally as he approached them with a mincing step, they stood aloof and looked at him with disdain. They invariably ran away clucking as soon as he drew closer.

One day, when the pigeon was trying as usual to consort with the hens and chicks, a small black shape broke away from the clouds. The hens ran screaming toward the barn and the chicken coop. The black ball fell like a stone on the flock. Only the pigeon had no place to hide. Before he even had time to spread his wings, a powerful bird with a sharp hooked beak pinned him to the ground and struck at him. The pigeon's feathers were speckled with blood. Marta came running out of the hut, brandishing a stick, but the hawk flew off smoothly, carrying in its beak the limp body of the pigeon.

Marta kept a snake in a special small rock garden, carefully fenced in. The snake slithered among the leaves sinuously, waving its forked tongue like a banner at a military review. It seemed quite indifferent to the world; I never knew if it noticed me.

On one occasion the snake hid itself deep under the moss in its private quarters, staying there for a very long time without food or water, participating in strange mysteries about which even Marta preferred to say nothing. When it finally emerged, its head glistened like an oiled plum. An incredible performance followed. The snake sank into immobility with only very slow shivers running along its coiled body. Then calmly it crawled out of its skin, looking suddenly thinner and younger. It did not wave its tongue any more but seemed to wait for its new skin to harden. The old, semitranslucent skin had been completely discarded and was marched upon by disrespectful flies. Marta lifted the skin with reverence and hid it in a secret place. A skin like this had valuable remedial properties, but she said I was too young to understand their nature.

Marta and I had watched this transformation with amazement. She told me that the human soul discards the body in a similar manner and then flies up to God's feet. After its long journey God picks it up in His warm hands, revives it with His breath, and then either turns it into a heavenly angel or casts it down into hell for eternal torture by fire.

A small red squirrel often visited the hut. After a meal it would dance a jig in the yard, beating its tail, uttering tiny squeaks, rolling, jumping, and terrorizing the chickens and pigeons.

The squirrel visited me daily, sitting on my shoul-

der, kissing my ears, neck, and cheeks, teasing my hair
with its light touch. After playing it would vanish, returning to the wood across the field.

One day I heard voices and ran to the nearby rise.
Hiding in the bushes, I was horrified to see some village
boys chasing my squirrel through the field. Running
frantically, it tried to reach the safety of the forest.
The boys threw rocks in front of it to cut it off. The
tiny creature weakened, its leaps shortened and slowed.
The boys finally caught it, but it bravely continued to
struggle and to bite. Then the boys, bending over the
animal, poured some liquid from a can on it. Feeling
that something horrible was about to be done, I tried
desperately to think of some way to save my little
friend. But it was too late.

One of the boys took a piece of smoldering wood
out of the can slung over his shoulder and touched the
animal with it. Then he threw the squirrel to the
ground where it immediately burst into flames. With a
squeal that stopped my breath it leapt up as if to escape
from the fire. The flames covered it; only the bushy tail
still wagged for a second. The small smoking body
rolled on the ground and was soon still. The boys
looked on, laughing and prodding it with a stick.

With my friend dead I no longer had anyone to wait
for in the morning. I told Marta what had happened,
but she did not seem to understand. She muttered
something to herself, prayed, and cast her secret en-
chantment over the household to ward off death, which,
she maintained, was lurking close by and trying to
enter.

Marta became sick. She complained about a sharp
pain under the ribs, where the heart flutters caged
forever. She told me that either God or the Devil had
sent a disease there to destroy yet another being and
thus put an end to her sojourn on earth. I could not
understand why Marta did not discard her skin like
the snake and start life all over again.

When I suggested this to her she grew angry and cursed me for being a blasphemous Gypsy bastard, kin to the Devil. She said that disease enters a person when he least expects it. It might be sitting behind you in a cart, jump on your shoulders as you bend down to pick berries in the woods, or crawl out of the water as you cross the river in a boat. Disease sneaks into the body invisibly, cunningly, through the air, water, or by contact with an animal or another person, or even—and here she gave me a wary look—from a pair of black eyes set close to a hawk nose. Such eyes, known as Gypsy or witches' eyes, could bring crippling illness, plague, or death. That is why she forbade me to look directly into her eyes or even those of the household animals. She ordered me to spit quickly three times and cross myself if I ever accidentally looked into an animal's eyes or her own.

She often became enraged when the dough she kneaded for bread turned sour. She blamed me for casting a spell and told me I would get no bread for two days as punishment. Trying to please Marta and not to look into her eyes, I walked about the hut with my eyes closed, stumbling over furniture, overturning buckets, and trampling flower beds outside, knocking against everything like a moth blinded by sudden brightness. In the meantime Marta collected some goose down, and scattered it over burning coals. She blew the resulting smoke all over the room to the accompaniment of incantations designed to exorcise the evil spell.

She would announce, finally, that the spell was lifted. And she was right, for the next baking always produced good bread.

Marta did not succumb to her sickness and pain. She waged a constant, wily battle against them. When her pains started bothering her, she would take a chunk of raw meat, chop it up finely, and place it in an earthenware jar. Then she would pour water over it that was drawn from a well just before sunrise. The jar was then buried deep in a corner of the hut. This would bring her relief from the aches for a few days, she said, until the meat decomposed. But later, when the pains returned, she went through the whole painstaking procedure once again.

Marta never drank any fluids in my presence, and she never smiled. She believed that if she did so, it could give me a chance to count her teeth, and that each tooth so counted would subtract one year from her life. It is true that she did not have many teeth. But I realized that at her age every year was very precious.

I tried to drink and eat without showing my teeth, and I practiced looking at my own reflection in the blue-black mirror of the well, smiling at myself with unopened mouth.

I was never allowed to pick up any of her lost hairs from the floor. It was well known that even a single lost hair, if spied by an evil eye, could be the cause of serious throat trouble.

In the evenings Marta sat by the stove, nodding and mumbling prayers. I sat nearby thinking of my parents. I recalled my toys, which now probably belonged to other children. My big teddy bear with glass eyes, the airplane with the turning propellers and its passengers whose faces were visible through the windows, the small easy-moving tank, and the fire engine with its extending ladder.

Suddenly Marta's hut would become warmer as the pictures grew sharper, more real. I could see my mother sitting at the piano. I heard the words of her songs. I recalled my fear before an appendix operation when I was only four years old, the glossy hospital floors, the gas mask the doctors placed on my face which prevented me from even counting to ten.

But this past of mine was rapidly turning into an illusion like one of my old nanny's incredible fables. I wondered whether my parents would ever find me again. Did they know that they should never drink or smile in the presence of evil-eyed people who might count their teeth? I would remember my father's broad, relaxed smile and begin to worry; he showed so many teeth that if an evil eye were to count them, he would most certainly die very soon.

One morning when I awoke the hut was cold. The fire in the stove was out and Marta was still sitting in the middle of the room, her many skirts tucked up and her bare feet resting in a bucket full of water.

I tried to speak to her, but she did not answer. I tickled her cold, stiff hand, but the knobby fingers did not move. The hand hung down from the arm of the chair like wet linen from a clothesline on a still day. When I lifted her head, her watery eyes seemed to be staring up at me. I had seen such eyes only once before, when the stream threw up the bodies of dead fish.

Marta, I concluded, was waiting for a change of skin and, like the snake, she could not be disturbed at such a time. Though uncertain what to do, I tried to be patient.

It was late fall. The wind was cracking the brittle twigs. It tore off the last of the wrinkled leaves, tossing them into the sky. Hens perched owlishly on their roosts, sleepy and depressed, opening with distaste one eye at a time. It was cold, and I did not know how to kindle a fire. All my efforts to talk to Marta failed to elicit any response. She sat there motionless, staring fixedly at something I could not see.

I went back to sleep, having nothing else to do, confident that when I woke up Marta would be scurrying around the kitchen humming her mournful psalms. But when I awoke in the evening she was still soaking her feet. I was hungry and frightened of the darkness.

I decided to light the oil lamp. I began to search for the matches Marta kept safely hidden. I carefully took the lamp off the shelf, but it slipped in my hand and spilled some kerosene on the floor.

The matches refused to light. When one finally flared up, it broke off and fell on the floor into the pool of kerosene. At first the flame timidly stopped there, casting off a puff of blue smoke. Then it boldly leapt into the middle of the room.

It was no longer dark, and I could plainly see Marta. She did not appear to notice what was happening. She did not seem to mind the flame, which had by then moved to the wall and up the legs of her wicker chair.

It was not cold any more. The flame was now close to the bucket in which Marta was soaking her feet. She must have felt the heat, but she did not move. I admired her endurance. After having sat there all night and all day, she still did not stir.

It became very hot in the room. Flames climbed up the walls like clinging vines. They flapped and crackled like dried pods underfoot, especially by the window where a meager draft managed to penetrate. I stood by the door, ready to run, still waiting for Marta to move. But she sat stiffly, as though unaware of anything. The flames started to lick her dangling hands as might an affectionate dog. They now left purple marks on her hands and climbed higher toward her matted hair.

The flames sparkled like a Christmas tree, and then burst into a high blaze, forming a peaked hat of fire on Marta's head. Marta became a torch. Flames circled her tenderly from all sides, and the water in the bucket hissed when shreds of her ragged rabbit-fur jacket fell into it. I could see under the flames patches of her wrinkled, sagging skin and whitish spots on her bony arms.

I called out to her for the last time as I ran outside into the yard. The hens were cackling furiously and beating their wings in the coop adjoining the house. The usually placid cow was mooing and butting the barn door with her head. I decided not to wait for

Marta's permission, and set about freeing the hens on my own. They rushed out hysterically, and tried to take flight on desperate, beating wings. The cow succeeded in breaking down the barn door. She took up an observation point at a safe distance from the fire, pensively chewing her cud.

By now the inside of the hut was a furnace. Flames jumped through the windows and holes. The thatched roof, catching fire from below, was smoking ominously. I marveled at Marta. Was she really so indifferent to all this? Had her charms and incantations granted her immunity against a fire that turned everything else about her into ashes?

She still had not come out. The heat was becoming unbearable. I had to move to the far end of the yard. The chicken coops and the barn were now on fire. A number of rats, frightened by the heat, scurried wildly across the yard. The yellow eyes of a cat, reflecting the flames, gazed from the dark edges of the field.

Marta failed to appear, though I was still convinced that she could emerge unscathed. But when one of the walls collapsed, engulfing the charred interior of the hut, I began to doubt that I would ever see her again.

In the clouds of smoke rising to the sky I thought I detected a strange oblong shape. What was it? Could it be Marta's soul making its escape to the heavens? Or was it Marta herself, revived by the fire, relieved of her old crusty skin, leaving this earth on a fiery broomstick like the witch in the story my mother told me?

Still staring into the spectacle of sparks and flame, I was jolted out of my reverie by the sound of men's voices and barking dogs. The farmers were coming. Marta always warned me about the village people. She said if they ever caught me alone they would drown me like a mangy kitten or kill me with an ax.

I started running as soon as the first human figures

appeared within the circle of light. They did not see me. I ran madly, hitting unseen tree stumps and thorny bushes. I finally fell into a ravine. I heard the faint voices of people and the crash of the falling walls, and then I fell asleep.

I woke up at dawn, half frozen. A shroud of mist hung between the edges of the ravine like a spider's web. I scrambled back to the top of the hill. Wisps of smoke and an occasional flame rose over the pile of scorched wood and ashes where Marta's hut had stood.

Everything around was silent. I believed that now I would meet my parents in the ravine. I believed that, even far away, they must know all that had happened to me. Wasn't I their child? What were parents for if not to be with their children in times of danger?

Just in case they should be coming near, I called out to them. But no one answered.

I was weak and cold and hungry. I had no idea what to do or where to go. My parents were still not there.

I trembled and vomited. I had to find people. I had to go to the village.

I limped on my bruised feet and legs, cautiously making my way over the yellowing autumn grass toward the distant village.

2

My parents were nowhere. I began to run across the field toward the peasants' huts. A rotting crucifix, once painted blue, stood at the crossroads. A holy picture hung at the top, from which a pair of barely visible but seemingly tear-stained eyes gazed into the empty fields and the red glow of the rising sun. A gray bird sat on an arm of the cross. On catching sight of me, it spread its wings and vanished.

The wind carried the charred smell of Marta's hut over the fields. A narrow thread of smoke drifted from the cooling ruins upward into the wintry sky.

Chilled and terrified, I entered the village. The huts, sunk halfway into the earth, with low-slung thatched roofs and boarded-up windows, stood along both sides of the packed dirt road.

The dogs tied to the fences noticed me and began to howl and strain against their chains. Afraid to move, I halted in the middle of the road, expecting one of them to break free at any moment.

The monstrous idea that my parents were not here and would not be here passed through my mind. I sat down and began to cry again, calling for my father and mother and even nanny.

13

A crowd of men and women was gathering around me, talking in a dialect unknown to me. I feared their suspicious looks and movements. Several were holding dogs which snarled and strained toward me.

Someone jabbed me from behind with a rake. I jumped aside. Someone else pricked me with a sharp prong. Again I sprang away, crying loudly.

The crowd became more lively. A stone struck me. I lay down, face to the earth, not wishing to know what might happen next. My head was being bombarded with dried cow dung, moldy potatoes, apple cores, handfuls of dirt, and small stones. I covered my face with my hands and screamed into the dust which covered the road.

Someone yanked me up from the ground. A tall red-headed peasant held me by the hair and dragged me toward him, twisting my ear with his other hand. I resisted desperately. The crowd shrieked with laughter. The man pushed me, kicking me with his wood-soled shoe. The mob roared, the men clasped their bellies, shaking with laughter, and the dogs struggled closer toward me.

A peasant with a burlap sack pushed his way through the crowd. He grabbed me by the neck and slipped the sack over my head. Then he threw me to the ground and tried to knead the rest of my body into the stinking black soil.

I lashed out with my feet and hands, I bit and scratched. But a blow on the back of my neck quickly made me lose consciousness.

I awoke in pain. Crammed into the sack, I was being carried on someone's shoulders, whose sweaty heat I felt through the rough cloth. The sack was tied with a string above my head. When I tried to free myself the man put me down on the ground and knocked me breathless and groggy with several kicks. Afraid to move, I sat hunched as though in a stupor.

We arrived at a farm. I smelled manure and heard

the bleating of a goat and the mooing of a cow. I was dumped on the floor of a hut and someone whacked the sack with a whip. I leapt out of the sack, bursting through the tied-up neck as if burned. The peasant stood there with a whip in his hand. He brought it down on my legs. I hopped around like a squirrel while he continued whipping me. People entered the room: a woman in a stained, pulled-up apron, small children who crawled out like cockroaches from the feather bed and from behind the oven, and two farmhands.

They surrounded me. One tried to touch my hair. When I turned toward him he quickly withdrew his hand. They exchanged remarks about me. Although I could not understand very much I heard the word "Gypsy" many times. I tried to tell them something, but my language and the manner in which I spoke it only made them giggle.

The man who had brought me began to whack my calves again. I jumped higher and higher, while the children and adults howled with laughter.

I was given a piece of bread and locked in the firewood closet. My body burned from the slashes of the whip and I could not fall asleep. It was dark in the closet and I heard rats scampering near me. When they touched my legs I cried out, scaring the hens sleeping behind the wall.

During the next few days peasants with their families came to the hut to stare at me. The owner whipped my welt-encrusted legs so I would hop like a frog. I was nearly naked but for the sack I was given to wear, with the two holes cut in the bottom for my legs. The sack often fell off when I jumped up and down. The men would roar and the women would titter, looking at me while I tried to cover my little tassel. I stared at a few of them straight in the eye, and they would rapidly avert their eyes or spit three times and drop their gaze.

One day an elderly woman called Olga the Wise One came to the hut. The owner treated her with obvious respect. She looked me all over, scrutinized my eyes and teeth, felt my bones, and ordered me to urinate in a small jar. She examined my urine.

Then, for a long time, she contemplated the long scar on my belly, the souvenir of my appendectomy, kneading my stomach with her hands. After the inspection she haggled fiercely and at length with the peasant, until finally she tied a string round my neck and led me away. I had been bought.

I began to live in her hut. It was a two-room dugout, full of piles of dried grasses, leaves, and shrubs, small oddly shaped colored stones, frogs, moles, and pots of wriggling lizards and worms. In the center of the hut caldrons were suspended over a burning fire.

Olga showed me everything. Henceforth I had to take care of the fire, bring faggots from the forest, and clean the stalls of the animals. The hut was full of varied powders which Olga prepared in a large mortar, grinding up and mixing the different components. I had to help her with this.

Early in the morning she took me to visit the village huts. The women and men crossed themselves when they saw us but otherwise greeted us politely. The sick waited inside.

When we saw a moaning woman clutching her abdomen, Olga ordered me to massage the woman's warm moist belly and to stare at it without pausing, while she muttered some words and made various signs in the air over our heads. One time we attended a child with a rotting leg, covered with wrinkled brown skin, from which a bloody yellow pus oozed. The stench from the leg was so strong that even Olga had to open the door every few moments and let in a draft of fresh air.

All day long I stared at the gangrenous leg while the child alternately sobbed and fell asleep. Its terrified family sat outside praying loudly. When the child's attention flagged, Olga applied to his leg a red-hot rod that was held ready in the fire, carefully burning out the entire wound. The child lashed out to all sides, screamed wildly, fainted and regained consciousness. A smell of charred flesh filled the room. The wound sizzled, as though pieces of bacon were being seared in a skillet. After the wound was burned out Olga covered it with gobs of wet bread into which were kneaded mold and freshly gathered cobwebs.

Olga had a treatment for nearly every disease, and my admiration for her steadily grew. People came to her with an enormous range of complaints and she could always help them. When a man's ears hurt, Olga washed them with caraway oil, inserted into each ear a piece of linen wound into a trumpet shape and soaked in hot wax, and set fire to the linen from outside. The patient, tied to a table, shrieked with pain while the fire burned out the remainder of the cloth inside the ear. Then she promptly blew out the residue, "sawdust" as she called it, from the ear and then coated the burned area with an ointment made from the juice of a squeezed onion, the bile of a billygoat or rabbit, and a dash of raw vodka.

She could also cut out boils, tumors, and wens, and pull out decayed teeth. She kept the excised boils in vinegar until they became marinated and could be used as medicines. She carefully drained the pus that suppurated from the wounds into special cups and left it to ferment for several days. As for extracted teeth, I pulverized them myself in the large mortar, and the resulting powder was dried over pieces of bark on top of the oven.

Sometimes in the dark of the night a frightened peasant would rush in for Olga and off she would go to attend to a childbirth, covering herself with a large wrap and shuddering from the chill and lack of sleep. When she was asked to one of the neighboring villages and did not return for several days, I watched over the hut, feeding the animals and keeping the fire burning.

Although Olga spoke in a strange dialect, we came to understand each other quite well. In the winter when a storm raged and the village was in the tight embrace of impassable snows, we would sit together in the warm hut and Olga would tell me of all God's children and of all Satan's spirits.

She called me the Black One. From her I learned for the first time that I was possessed by an evil spirit, which crouched in me like a mole in a deep burrow, and of whose presence I was unaware. Such a darkling as I, possessed of this evil spirit, could be recognized by his bewitched black eyes which did not blink when they gazed at bright clear eyes. Hence, Olga declared, I could stare at other people and unknowingly cast a spell over them.

Bewitched eyes can not only cast a spell but can also remove it, she explained. I must take care, while staring at people or animals or even grain, to keep my mind blank of anything other than the disease I was helping her remove from them. For when bewitched eyes look at a healthy child, he will immediately begin to waste away; when at a calf, it will drop dead of a sudden disease; when at grass, the hay will rot after the harvest.

This evil spirit which dwelled in me attracted by its very nature other mysterious beings. Phantoms drifted around me. A phantom is silent, reticent, and is rarely seen. Yet it is persistent: it trips people in fields and forests, peeks into huts, can turn itself into a vicious cat or rabid dog, and moans when enraged. At midnight it turns into hot tar.

Ghosts are attracted to an evil spirit. They are persons long dead, condemned to eternal damnation, returning to life only at full moon, having super-human powers, with eyes always turned mournfully eastward.

Vampires, perhaps the most harmful of these intangible threats because they often assume human form, are also drawn to a possessed person. Vampires are people who were drowned without having first been baptized or who were abandoned by their mothers. They grow to the age of seven in water or in the forests, whereupon they take human form again and, changing into vagabonds, insatiably try to gain access to Catholic or Uniate churches whenever they can. Once they have taken nest there they stir restlessly around the altars, maliciously soil the pictures of the saints, bite, break, or destroy the holy objects and, when possible, suck blood from sleeping men.

Olga suspected me of being a vampire and now and then told me so. To restrain the desires of my evil spirit and prevent its metamorphosis into a ghost or phantom, she would every morning prepare a bitter elixir which I had to drink while eating a chunk of garlicked charcoal. Other people also feared me. Whenever I attempted to walk through the village alone, people would turn their heads and make the sign of the cross. What is more, pregnant women would run away from me in panic. The bolder peasants unleashed dogs on me, and had I not learned to flee quickly and always keep close to Olga's hut, I would not have returned alive from many of these excursions.

I usually remained in the hut, preventing an albino cat from killing a caged hen, which was black and of great rarity, and much valued by Olga. I also looked at the blank eyes of toads hopping in a tall pot, kept the fire burning in the stove, stirred simmering brews, and peeled rotten potatoes, gathering carefully in a cup the greenish mold which Olga applied to wounds and bruises.

Olga was highly respected in the village, and when I accompanied her I did not fear anyone. She was often asked to come and sprinkle the eyes of cattle, to protect them from any malicious spell while they were

being driven to market. She showed the peasants the
manner in which they should spit three times when
purchasing a pig, and how to feed a heifer with spe-
cially prepared bread containing a sanctified herb before mating it with a bull. No one in the village would
buy a horse or cow until Olga had decreed that the
animal would remain healthy. She would pour water
over it, and, after seeing how it shook itself, would give
the verdict on which the price and often the very sale
depended.

Spring was coming. Ice was breaking up on the
river and low rays of the sun penetrated the slippery
coils and eddies of the rushing water. Blue dragonflies
hovered above the current, struggling with the sudden
bursts of cold, wet wind. Wraiths of moisture rising
from the sun-warmed surface of the lake were seized
upon by the gusts and eddies of the wind and then
teased out like wisps of wool and drawn up into the
turbulent air.

Yet when the eagerly expected warmer weather
came at last, it brought along a plague. The people
whom it struck wriggled with pain like transfixed earth-
worms, were shaken by a ghastly chill, and died without regaining consciousness. I rushed with Olga from
hut to hut, stared at the patients in order to drive the
sickness out of them, but all to no avail. The disease
proved too strong.

Behind the tightly shut windows, inside the half-
dark huts, the dying and suffering groaned and cried
out. Women pressed the small tightly swaddled bodies
of their babies, whose life was swiftly ebbing, against
their breasts. Men, in despair, covered their fever-
wracked wives with feather mattresses and sheepskins.
Children gazed tearfully at the blue-spotted faces of
their dead parents.

The plague persisted.

The villagers would come to the thresholds of
their huts, raise their eyes from the earthly dust, and

search for God. He alone could assuage their bitter sorrow. He alone could bestow the mercy of serene sleep on these tormented human bodies. He alone could change the horrible enigmas of the disease into ageless health. He alone could deaden the pain of a mother mourning for her lost child. He alone . . .

But God, in His impenetrable wisdom, waited. Fires burned around the huts, and the paths and gardens and yards were fumigated with smoke. The ringing strokes of axes and the crash of falling trees could be heard from the neighboring forests as the men hewed the wood needed to keep the fires alive. I heard the crisp, sharp sounds of ax blade on trunk coursing through the clear, still air. As they reached the pastures and the village they became strangely muffled and faint. As a fog hides and dims a candle flame, so the silent brooding air, heavy with disease, absorbed and enmeshed these sounds in a poisoned net.

One evening my face began to burn and I shook with uncontrollable throbs. Olga looked for a moment into my eyes and placed her cold hand on my brow. Then rapidly and wordlessly she dragged me toward a remote field. There she dug a deep pit, took off my clothes, and ordered me to jump in.

While I stood at the bottom, trembling with fever and chill, Olga pushed the earth back into the pit until I was buried up to my neck. Then she trampled the soil around me and beat it with the shovel until the surface was very smooth. After making sure there were no anthills in the vicinity, she made three smoky fires of peat.

Thus planted in the cold earth, my body cooled completely in a few moments, like the root of a wilting weed. I lost all awareness. Like an abandoned head of cabbage, I became part of the great field.

Olga did not forget me. Several times during the day she brought cool drinks which she poured into my mouth and which seemed to drain right through my body into the earth. The smoke from the fires, which she stoked with fresh moss, misted my eyes and stung my throat. Seen from the earth's surface when the wind occasionally cleared the smoke away, the world looked like a rough rug. The small plants growing round about loomed as tall as trees. When Olga approached she cast an unearthly giant's shadow over the landscape.

Having fed me at twilight for the last time, she threw fresh peat on the fires and went to her hut to sleep. I remained in the field, alone, rooted into the earth which seemed to draw me down deeper and deeper.

The fires burned slowly and the sparks jumped like glow-worms into the infinite blackness. I felt as though I were a plant straining toward the sun, unable to straighten its branches, restrained by the earth. Or again, I felt that my head had acquired a life of its own, rolling faster and faster, picking up dizzying speed until it finally struck the disk of the sun which had graciously warmed it during the day.

At times, feeling the wind on my brow, I went numb with horror. In my imagination I saw armies of ants and cockroaches calling to one another and scurrying toward my head, to some place under the top of my skull, where they would build new nests. There they would proliferate and eat out my thoughts, one after another, until I would become as empty as the shell of a pumpkin from which all the fruit has been scraped out.

Noises woke me. I opened my eyes, uncertain of my surroundings. I was fused with the earth, but thoughts stirred in my heavy head. The world was graying. The fires had gone out. On my lips I felt the cold of streaming dew. Drops of it settled on my face and in my hair.

The sounds returned. A flock of ravens circled over my head. One of them landed nearby on broad rustling wings. It approached my head slowly while the others began to alight.

In terror I watched their shining black-feathered tails and darting eyes. They stalked around me, nearer and nearer, flicking their heads toward me, uncertain whether I was dead or alive.

I did not wait for what would come next. I screamed. The startled ravens leapt back. Several rose a few feet into the air, but touched ground again not far off. Then they glanced suspiciously at me and began their circuitous march.

I shouted once more. But this time they were not frightened, and with increasing boldness advanced ever more closely. My heart thudded. I did not know what to do. I screamed again but now the birds showed no fear. They were only two feet from me. Their shapes loomed larger and larger in my eyes, their beaks grew more and more vicious. The curved widespread claws of their feet resembled huge rakes.

One of the ravens halted in front of me, inches from my nose. I yelled right into its face, but the raven only gave a slight jerk and opened its beak. Before I could shout again, it pecked at my head and several of my hairs appeared in its bill. The bird struck again, tearing out another tuft of hair.

I turned my head from side to side, loosening the earth around my neck. But my movements only made the birds more curious. They surrounded me and pecked at me wherever they could. I called loudly, but my voice was too weak to rise above the earth and only seeped back into the soil without reaching the hut where Olga lay.

The birds played with me freely. The more furiously I swiveled my head to and fro, the more excited and bold they became. Seeming to avoid my face, they attacked the back of my head.

My strength ebbed. To move my head each time

seemed like shifting a huge sack of grain from one
place to another. I was crazed and saw everything as
through a miasmal fog.

I gave up. I was myself now a bird. I was trying
to free my chilled wings from the earth. Stretching my
limbs, I joined the flock of ravens. Borne abruptly up
on a gust of fresh, reviving wind, I soared straight into
a ray of sunshine that lay taut on the horizon like a
drawn bowstring, and my joyous cawing was mimicked
by my winged companions.

Olga found me in the midst of the swarming flock
of ravens. I was nearly frozen and my head was deeply
lacerated by the birds. She quickly dug me out.

After several days my health returned. Olga said
that the cold earth had driven the sickness out of me.
She said that the disease was picked up by a throng of
ghosts transformed into ravens which tasted my blood
to make sure that I was one of them. This was the
only reason, she asserted, they did not peck my eyes
out.

Weeks passed. The plague subsided and fresh
grass grew on the many new graves, grass that one
could not touch because it surely contained poison from
the plague victims.

One fair morning Olga was summoned to the
riverbank. The peasants were pulling from the water a
huge catfish with long whiskers stiffly sprouting from its
snout. It was a powerful-looking, monstrous fish, one of
the largest ever seen in that region. While catching it
one of the fishermen had a vein cut by his net. While
Olga was applying a tourniquet to his arm to stem the
gushing blood, the others disemboweled the fish and, to
everyone's joy, extracted the air bladder, which was un-
damaged.

Suddenly, at a moment when I was completely relaxed and unsuspecting, a fat man raised me high in
the air and shouted something to the others. The crowd
applauded and I was swiftly passed from hand to hand.

Before I realized what they were doing, the large bladder was thrown into the water and I was flung on top of it. The bladder sank a little. Someone shoved it with a foot. I began to float away from the riverbank, feverishly hugging the buoyant balloon with my legs and hands, plunging now and again into the cold brownish river, screaming and begging for mercy.

But I was drifting farther and farther away. The people ran along the riverbank and waved their hands. Some hurled rocks which splashed at my side. One almost hit the bladder. The current was fast carrying me into the middle of the river. Both banks seemed unreachable. The crowd disappeared behind a hill.

A fresh breeze, which I had never felt on land, rippled over the water. I moved smoothly downstream. Several times the bladder sank almost completely under the light waves. But it bobbed up again, sailing on slowly and majestically. Then abruptly I was swept into a whirlpool. Round and round the bladder swirled, pulling away from and returning to the same spot.

I tried to swing it up and down to throw it out of the circuit by the movements of my body. I was agonized at the thought that I would have to spend all night in this manner. I knew that if the bladder should burst, I would immediately drown. I could not swim.

The sun was slowly setting. Every time the bladder turned, the sun shone straight into my eyes and its dazzling reflections danced on the shimmering surface. It grew chilly and the wind became more turbulent. The bladder, pushed by a new gust, glided out of the eddy.

I was miles from Olga's village. The current carried me toward a shore obscured by a deepening shadow. I began to discern the marshes, the tall swaying clumps of rushes, the hidden nests of sleeping ducks. The bladder moved slowly through the scattered tufts of grass. Waterflies hovered nervously on every side of me. The yellow chalices of lilies rustled, and a frightened frog belched from a ditch. Suddenly a reed pierced the bladder. I stood on the spongy bottom.

It was completely still. I could hear vague voices, human or animal, in the alder groves and dank swamps. My body was doubled up with cramp and covered with gooseflesh. I listened intently, but the stillness was everywhere.

3

I was frightened to find myself entirely alone. But I remembered the two things which, according to Olga, were necessary for survival without human help. The first was a knowledge of plants and animals, familiarity with poisons and medicinal herbs. The other was possession of fire, or a "comet" of one's own. The first was harder to obtain—it required a great deal of experience. The second consisted merely of a one-quart preserve can, open at one end and with a lot of small nail holes punched in the sides. A three-foot loop of wire was hooked to the top of the can by way of a handle, so that one could swing it either like a lasso or like a censer in church.

Such a small portable stove could serve as a constant source of heat and as a miniature kitchen. One filled it with any kind of fuel available, always keeping some sparks of fire at the bottom. By swinging the can energetically, one pumped air through the holes, as the blacksmith does with his bellows, while centrifugal force kept the fuel in place. A judicious choice of fuel and an appropriate swinging motion permitted the building up of heat suitable for various purposes, while steady stoking prevented the "comet" from going out.

For example, the baking of potatoes, turnips, or fish required a slow fire of peat and damp leaves, and the roasting of a freshly killed bird required the live flame of dry twigs and hay. Birds' eggs freshly plucked from their nests were best cooked on a fire of potato stalks.

To keep the fire alight through the night, the comet had to be tightly packed with damp moss collected from the bases of tall trees. The moss burned with a dim glow, producing smoke which repelled snakes and insects. In case of danger it could be brought to white heat with a few swings. On wet snowy days the comet had to be refilled frequently with dry resinous wood or bark and required a lot of swinging. On windy or hot dry days the comet did not need much swinging, and its burning could be further slowed down by adding fresh grass or by sprinkling in some water.

The comet was also indispensable protection against dogs and people. Even the most vicious dogs stopped short when they saw a wildly swinging object showering sparks which threatened to set their fur on fire. Not even the boldest man wanted to risk losing his sight or having his face burned. A man armed with a loaded comet became a fortress and could be safely attacked only with a long pole or by throwing rocks.

That is why the extinction of a comet was an extremely serious thing. It could happen through carelessness, oversleeping, or a sudden downpour. Matches were very scarce in that area. They were costly and hard to obtain. Those who had any matches got into the habit of splitting each match in half for economy.

Fire was therefore preserved most scrupulously in kitchen stoves or in the fireboxes of ovens. Before retiring for the night women would bank up ashes to make certain that the embers would keep glowing until morning. At dawn they reverently made the sign of the cross before blowing the fire back to life. Fire, they said, is no natural friend to man. That is why one must humor it. It was also believed that sharing fire, especially borrowing it, could only result in misfortune. After all, those who borrow fire on this earth might have to return it in hell. And carrying fire out of the house might make the cows dry or go barren. Also, a fire that went out could produce disastrous consequences in cases of childbirth.

Just as fire was essential to the comet, the comet was essential to life. A comet was necessary for approaching human settlements, which were always guarded by packs of savage dogs. And in the winter an extinguished comet might lead to frostbite as well as to the lack of cooked food.

People always carried small sacks on their backs or at their belts for collecting fuel for the comets. In the daytime, peasants working in the fields baked vegetables, birds, and fish in them. At night, men and boys coming home would swing them with all their strength and let them fly into the sky, burning fiercely, like soaring red disks. The comets flew in a wide arc, and their fiery tails traced their courses. That is how they got their name. They did really look like comets in the skies with their flaming tails, whose appearance, as Olga explained, signified war, plague, and death.

It was very difficult to obtain a can for a comet. These were found only along the railroad tracks which carried military transports. The local peasants prevented outsiders from collecting them, exacting a high price for the cans they found themselves. Communities on each side of the tracks fought over the cans. Every day they sent out teams of men and boys equipped with sacks for any cans they could find, and armed with axes to ward off any competitors.

I was given my first comet by Olga, who had received it in payment for treating a patient. I took very good care of it, hammering over the holes that threatened to become too large, flattening dents, and polishing the metal. Anxious not to be robbed of my only important possession, I wrapped some of the wire at-

tached to the handle around my wrist and never parted
from my comet. The brisk, sparkling fire filled me with
a feeling of security and pride. I never missed an opportunity to fill my sack with the right kinds of fuel.
Olga often sent me to the woods for certain plants and
herbs with curative properties, and I felt perfectly safe
as long as I had my comet with me.

But Olga was now far away and I was without the
comet. I shivered with cold and fear and my feet were
bleeding from cuts of the sharp blades of water reeds. I
brushed off from my calves and thighs the leeches
which swelled visibly as they sucked my blood. Long,
crooked shadows fell over the river and muffled sounds
crept along the murky banks. In the creaking of the
thick beech branches, in the rustling of the willows trailing their leaves in the water, I heard the utterances of
the mystic beings of whom Olga had spoken. They
took on peculiar shapes, serpentine and peaked of face,
having a bat's head and a snake's body. And they
coiled themselves around a man's legs, drawing his will
to live out of him until he sat down on the ground, in
search of a slumber from which there was no awakening. I had sometimes seen such strange-shaped snakes
in barns, where they terrified the cows into agitated
mooing. They were said to drink the cows' milk or, even
worse, to crawl inside the animals and consume all the
food they ate until the cows starved to death.

Cutting through the reeds and tall grasses, I
started running away from the river, forcing through
barricades of tangled weeds, bending low to squeeze
under walls of overhanging branches, almost impaling
myself on sharp reeds and thorns.

A cow mooed far away. I quickly climbed a tree
and after scanning the countryside from its height I
noticed the twinkle of comets. People were coming
home from the pastures. Cautiously I made my way in
their direction, listening for the sound of their dog,
which came toward me through the undergrowth.

The voices were quite close. There was obviously a path behind the thick wall of foliage. I heard the shuffle of the walking cows and the voices of young herdsmen. Now and then some sparks from their comets lit up the dark sky and then zigzagged down into oblivion. I followed them along the bushes, determined to attack the herdsmen and to seize a comet.

The dog they had with them picked up my scent several times. It dashed into the bushes, but evidently did not feel too secure in the dark. When I hissed like a snake it withdrew to the path, growling from time to time. The herdsmen, sensing danger, grew silent and listened to the sounds of the forest.

I approached the lane. The cows almost rubbed their flanks against the branches behind which I was hiding. They were so close I could smell their bodies. The dog tried another attack, but hissing drove it back to the road.

When the cows moved closer to me I jabbed two of them with a sharp stick. They bellowed and started trotting, followed by the dog. Then I screamed with a long, vibrating banshee howl and struck the nearest herder in the face. Before he had time to realize what was happening, I grabbed his comet and sped back into the bushes.

The other boys, frightened by the eerie howl and the panic of the cows, ran toward the village, dragging the dazed herder with them. Then I went deeper into the forest, dampening the bright fire of the comet with some fresh leaves.

When I was far enough, I blew at the comet. Its light lured scores of odd insects out of the dark. I saw witches hanging from the trees. They stared at me, trying to lead me astray and confuse me. I distinctly heard the shudders of wandering souls which had escaped from the bodies of penitent sinners. In the rusty glow of my comet I saw trees bending over me. I heard the plaintive voices and strange movements of ghosts

and ghouls trying to bore their way out from inside
their trunks.

Here and there I saw ax cuts on tree trunks. I remembered that Olga had told me that such cuts were
made by peasants trying to cast evil spells on their
enemies. Striking the juicy flesh of the tree with an ax,
one had to utter the name of a hated person and
visualize his face. The cut would then bring disease and
death to the enemy. There were many such scars on
the trees around me. People here must have had many
enemies, and they were quite busy in their efforts to
bring them disaster.

Frightened, I swung the comet wildly. I saw unending rows of trees bowing obsequiously to me, inviting
me to step deeper and deeper into their closing ranks.

Sooner or later I had to heed their invitation. I
wanted to stay away from the riverside villages.

I went ahead, firmly convinced that Olga's spells
would eventually bring me back to her. Didn't she always say that if I tried to run away, she could bewitch
my feet and make them walk me back to her? I had
nothing to fear. Some unknown force, either from above
or within myself, was leading me unerringly back to
old Olga.

4

I was now living at the miller's, whom the villagers had nicknamed Jealous. He was more taciturn than was usual in the area. Even when neighbors came to pay him a visit, he would just sit, taking an occasional sip of vodka, and drawling out a word once in a while, lost in thought or staring at a dried-up fly stuck to the wall.

He abandoned his reverie only when his wife entered the room. Equally quiet and reticent, she would always sit down behind her husband, modestly dropping her gaze when men entered the room and furtively glanced at her.

I slept in the attic directly above their bedroom. At night I was awakened by their quarrels. The miller suspected his wife of flirting and lasciviously displaying her body in the fields and in the mill before a young plowboy. His wife did not deny this, but sat passive and still. Sometimes the quarrel did not end. The enraged miller lit candles in the room, put on his boots, and beat his wife. I would cling to a crack in the floorboards and watch the miller lashing his naked wife with a horsewhip. The woman cowered behind a feather quilt tugged off the bed, but the man pulled it away, flung it on the floor, and standing over her

33

with his legs spread wide continued to lash her plump
body with the whip. After every stroke, red blood-
swollen lines would appear on her tender skin.

The miller was merciless. With a grand sweep of
the arm he looped the leather thong of the whip over
her buttocks and thighs, slashed her breasts and neck,
scourged her shoulders and shins. The woman weakened and lay whining like a puppy. Then she crawled
toward her husband's legs, begging forgiveness.

Finally the miller threw down the whip and, after
blowing out the candle, went to bed. The woman remained groaning. The following day she would cover
her wounds, move with difficulty, and wipe away her
tears with bruised, cut palms.

There was another inhabitant of the hut: a well-
fed tabby cat. One day she was seized by a frenzy. Instead of mewing she emitted half-smothered squeals.
She slid along the walls as sinuously as a snake, swung
her pulsating flanks, and clawed at the skirts of the
miller's wife. She growled in a strange voice and
moaned, her raucous shrieks making everyone restless.
At dusk the tabby whined insanely, her tail beating her
flanks, her nose thrusting.

The miller locked the inflamed female in the cellar
and went to his mill, telling his wife that he would
bring the plowboy home for supper. Without a word
the woman set about preparing the food and table.

The plowboy was an orphan. It was his first season
of work at the miller's farm. He was a tall, placid
youth with flaxen hair which he habitually pushed back
from his sweating brow. The miller knew that the villagers gossiped about his wife and the boy. It was said
that she changed when she gazed into the boy's blue
eyes. Heedless of the risk of being noticed by her husband, she impulsively hiked her skirt high above her
knees with one hand, and with the other pushed down
the bodice of her dress to display her breasts, all the
time staring into the boy's eyes.

The miller returned with the young man, carrying in a sack slung over his shoulder, a tomcat borrowed from a neighbor. The tomcat had a head as large as a turnip and a long, strong tail. The tabby was howling lustingly in the cellar. When the miller released her, she sprang to the center of the room. The two cats began to circle one another mistrustfully, panting, coming nearer and nearer.

The miller's wife served supper. They ate silently. The miller sat at the middle of the table, his wife on one side and the plowboy on the other. I ate my portion squatting by the oven. I admired the appetites of the two men: huge chunks of meat and bread, washed down with gulps of vodka, disappeared in their throats like hazelnuts.

The woman was the only one who chewed her food slowly. When she bowed her head low over the bowl the plowboy would dart a glance faster than lightning at her bulging bodice.

In the center of the room the tabby suddenly arched her body, bared her teeth and claws, and pounced on the tomcat. He halted, stretched his back, and sputtered saliva straight into her inflamed eyes. The female circled him, leaped toward him, recoiled, and then struck him in the muzzle. Now the tomcat stalked around her cautiously, sniffing her intoxicating odor. He arched his tail and tried to come at her from the rear. But the female would not let him; she flattened her body on the floor and turned like a millstone, striking his nose with her stiff, outstretched paws.

Fascinated, the miller and the other two stared silently while eating. The woman sat with a flushed face; even her neck was reddening. The plowboy raised his eyes, only to drop them at once. Sweat ran down through his short hair and he continually pushed it away from his hot brow. Only the miller sat calmly eating, watching the cats, and glancing casually at his wife and guest.

The tomcat suddenly came to a decision. His movements became lighter. He advanced. She moved playfully as if to draw back, but the male leapt high and flopped onto her with all fours. He sank his teeth in her neck and intently, tautly, plunged directly into her without any squirming. When satiated and exhausted, he relaxed. The tabby, nailed to the floor, screamed shrilly and sprang out from under him. She jumped onto the cooled oven and tossed about on it like a fish, looping her paws over her neck, rubbing her head against the warm wall.

The miller's wife and the plowboy ceased eating. They stared at each other, gaping over their food-filled mouths. The woman breathed heavily, placed her hands under her breasts and squeezed them, clearly unaware of herself. The plowboy looked alternately at the cats and at her, licked his dry lips, and got down his food with difficulty.

The miller swallowed the last of his meal, leaned his head back, and abruptly gulped down his glass of vodka. Though drunk, he got up, and grasping his iron spoon and tapping it, he approached the plowboy. The youth sat bewildered. The woman hitched up her skirt and began puttering at the fire.

The miller bent over the plowboy and whispered something in his reddened ear. The youth jumped up as if pricked with a knife and began to deny something. The miller asked loudly now whether the boy lusted after his wife. The plowboy blushed but did not answer. The miller's wife turned away and continued to clean the pots.

The miller pointed at the strolling tomcat and again whispered something to the youth. The latter, with an effort, rose from the table, intending to leave the room. The miller came forward overturning his stool and, before the youth realized it, suddenly pushed him against the wall, pressed one arm against his throat, and drove a knee into his stomach. The boy could not move. Terror stricken, panting loudly, he babbled something.

The woman dashed toward her husband, imploring and wailing. The awakened tabby cat lying on the oven looked down on the spectacle, while the frightened tomcat leapt onto the table.

With a single kick the miller got the woman out of his way. And with a rapid movement such as women use to gouge out the rotten spots while peeling potatoes, he plunged the spoon into one of the boy's eyes and twisted it.

The eye sprang out of his face like a yolk from a broken egg and rolled down the miller's hand onto the floor. The plowboy howled and shrieked, but the miller's hold kept him pinned against the wall. Then the blood-covered spoon plunged into the other eye, which sprang out even faster. For a moment the eye rested on the boy's cheek as if uncertain what to do next; then it finally tumbled down his shirt onto the floor.

It all had happened in a moment. I could not believe what I had seen. Something like a glimmer of hope crossed my mind that the gouged eyes could be put back where they belonged. The miller's wife was screaming wildly. She rushed to the adjoining room and woke up her children, who also started crying in terror. The plowboy screamed and then grew silent covering his face with his hands. Rivulets of blood seeped through his fingers down his arms, dripping slowly on his shirt and trousers.

The miller, still enraged, pushed him toward the window as though unaware that the youth was blind. The boy stumbled, cried out, and nearly knocked over a table. The miller grabbed him by the shoulders, opened the door with his foot, and kicked him out. The boy yelled again, stumbled through the doorway, and fell down in the yard. The dogs started barking, though they did not know what had happened.

The eyeballs lay on the floor. I walked around them, catching their steady stare. The cats timidly moved out into the middle of the room and began to play with the eyes as if they were balls of thread. Their own pupils narrowed to slits from the light of the oil lamp. The cats rolled the eyes around, sniffed them, licked them, and passed them to one another gently with their padded paws. Now it seemed that the eyes were staring at me from every corner of the room, as though they had acquired a new life and motion of their own.

I watched them with fascination. If the miller had not been there I myself would have taken them. Surely they could still see. I would keep them in my pocket and take them out when needed, placing them over my own. Then I would see twice as much, maybe even more. Perhaps I could attach them to the back of my head and they would tell me, though I was not quite certain how, what went on behind me. Better still, I could leave the eyes somewhere and they would tell me later what happened during my absence.

Maybe the eyes had no intention of serving anyone. They could easily escape from the cats and roll out of the door. They could wander over the fields, lakes, and woods, viewing everything about them, free as birds released from a trap. They would no longer die, since they were free, and being small they could easily hide in various places and watch people in secret. Excited, I decided to close the door quietly and capture the eyes.

The miller, evidently annoyed by the cats' play, kicked the animals away and squashed the eyeballs with his heavy boots. Something popped under his thick sole. A marvelous mirror, which could reflect the whole world, was broken. There remained on the floor only a crushed bit of jelly. I felt a terrible sense of loss.

The miller, paying no attention to me, seated himself on the bench and swayed slowly as he fell asleep.

I stood up cautiously, lifted the bloodied spoon from the floor and began to gather the dishes. It was my duty to keep the room neat and the floor swept. As I cleaned I kept away from the crushed eyes, uncertain what to do with them. Finally I looked away and quickly swept the ooze into the pail and threw it in the oven.

In the morning I awoke early. Underneath me I heard the miller and his wife snoring. Carefully I packed a sack of food, loaded the comet with hot embers and, bribing the dog in the yard with a piece of sausage, fled from the hut.

At the mill wall, next to the barn, lay the plowboy. At first I meant to pass him by quickly, but I stopped when I realized that he was sightless. He was still stunned. He covered his face with his hands, he moaned and sobbed. There was caked blood on his face, hands, and shirt. I wanted to say something, but I was afraid that he would ask me about his eyes and then I would have to tell him to forget about them, since the miller had stamped them into pulp. I was terribly sorry for him.

I wondered whether the loss of one's sight would deprive a person also of the memory of everything that he had seen before. If so, the man would no longer be able to see even in his dreams. If not, if only the eyeless could still see through their memory, it would not be too bad. The world seemed to be pretty much the same everywhere, and even though people differed from one another, just as animals and trees did, one should know fairly well what they looked like after seeing them for years. I had lived only seven years, but I remembered a lot of things. When I closed my eyes, many details came back still more vividly. Who knows, perhaps without his eyes the plowboy would start seeing an entirely new, more fascinating world.

I heard some sound from the village. Afraid that the miller might wake up, I went on my way, touching my eyes from time to time. I walked more cautiously now, for I knew that eyeballs did not have strong roots. When one bent down they hung like apples from a tree and could easily drop out. I resolved to jump across fences with my head held up; but on my first try I stumbled and fell down. I lifted my fingers fearfully to my eyes to see whether they were still there. After carefully checking that they opened and closed properly, I noticed with delight the partridges and thrushes in flight. They flew very fast but my sight could follow them and even overtake them as they soared under the clouds, becoming smaller than raindrops. I made a promise to myself to remember everything I saw; if someone should pluck out my eyes, then I would retain the memory of all that I had seen for as long as I lived.

5

My duty was to set snares for Lekh, who sold birds in several neighboring villages. There was no one who could compete with him in this. He worked alone. He took me in because I was very small, thin, and light. Thus I could set traps in places where Lekh himself could not reach: on slender branches of trees, in dense clumps of nettle and thistle, on the waterlogged islets in the bogs and swamps.

Lekh had no family. His hut was filled with birds of all varieties, from the common sparrow to the wise owl. The peasants bartered food for Lekh's birds, and he did not have to worry about essentials: milk, butter, sour cream, cheeses, bread, hunter's sausage, vodka, fruits, and even cloth. He would collect all this from the nearby villages while carrying around his caged birds and hawking their beauty and singing abilities.

Lekh had a pimpled, freckled face. The peasants claimed that such faces belong to those who steal eggs from swallows' nests; Lekh himself asserted that this was due to his spitting carelessly into fire in his youth, claiming that his father was a village scribe who wanted him to become a priest. But he was drawn to the forests. He studied the ways of birds and envied them their ability to fly. One day he escaped from his father's hut and began to wander from village to village, from forest to forest, like a wild and abandoned bird. In time he began to catch birds. He observed the wondrous habits of quail and larks, could imitate the carefree call of the cuckoo, the screech of the magpie, the hooting of the owl. He knew the courting habits of the bullfinch; the jealous fury of the landrail, circling a nest abandoned by its female; and the sorrow of the swallow whose nesting place was wantonly destroyed by young boys. He understood the secrets of the hawk's flight and admired the stork's patience in hunting for frogs. He envied the nightingale its song.

Thus he passed his youth amidst the birds and trees. Now he was rapidly growing bald, his teeth were rotting, the skin of his face was sagging into folds, and he was becoming slightly shortsighted. So he settled down for good in a hut he built himself, in which he occupied one corner and filled the others with birdcages. At the very bottom of one of these cages a narrow space was found for me.

Lekh spoke often of his birds. I listened avidly to everything he had to say. I learned that flocks of storks always came from beyond distant oceans on St. Joseph's day and remained in the village until St. Bartholomew drove all the frogs into the mud with hop poles. The mud would plug the frogs' mouths and the storks, unable to hear their croaking, would not be able to catch them and would therefore have to leave. The storks brought good luck to the houses on which they nested.

Lekh was the only man in the area who knew how to prepare a stork's nest in advance, and his nests were never without tenants. He charged high prices for building such nests, and only the wealthiest farmers could afford his services.

Lekh set about nest building with great deliberation. On the selected roof he first placed a harrow at the halfway point, providing a framework for the structure. It was always slanted slightly toward the west, so that the prevailing winds could not damage the nest badly. Then Lekh drove long nails halfway into the harrow, thus providing anchorage for the twigs and straw which the storks gathered themselves. Just before their arrival he placed a large piece of red cloth in the middle of the harrow to attract the storks' attention.

It was known that it brought good luck to see the first springtime stork in flight; but seeing the first springtime stork sitting down was an augury of a year of trouble and misfortune. The storks also provided clues as to what went on in the village. They would never return to a roof under which some misdeed had been committed in their absence or under which people lived in sin.

They were strange birds. Lekh told me how he had been pecked by a female sitting on her eggs when he tried to correct the position of the nest. He took revenge by placing one goose egg among the other stork eggs. When the chicks hatched, the storks looked with amazement at their offspring. One of them was misshapen, on short bowlegs, with a flat beak. Father Stork charged his wife with adultery and wanted to kill the bastard chick on the spot. Mother Stork felt that the baby should be kept in the nest. Family argument continued for several days. Finally the hen decided on her own to save the gosling's life, and she carefully rolled it onto the thatched roof, from which it fell harmlessly into some straw.

It would seem that this closed the matter and that matrimonial harmony would be restored. But when the time came for flying away, all the storks held a conference as usual. After debate it was decided that the hen was guilty of adultery and did not deserve to accompany the husband. Sentence was duly passed. Before the birds took off in their faultless formation, the

faithless wife was attacked with beaks and wings. She
fell down dead, close to the thatched house on which
she had lived with her husband. Next to her body the
peasants found an ugly gosling shedding bitter tears.

The swallows also led interesting lives. The favorite birds of the Virgin Mary, they came as harbin-
gers of spring and joy. In the fall they were supposed
to fly far away from human life, to perch, tired and
sleepy, on the reeds growing in distant marshes. Lekh
said that they rested on a reed until it broke under their
weight, plunging them into the water. They were supposed to remain underwater all through the winter, secure in their icy home.

The voice of the cuckoo could mean many things.
A man hearing it for the first time in the season should
immediately start jangling coins in his pockets and
counting all his money, in order to secure at least the
same amount for the whole year. Thieves should be
careful to remember when they heard their first cuckoo
of the year. If it was before there were leaves on the
trees, it was better to abandon their plans of robbery,
which would be unsuccessful.

Lekh had a special affection for cuckoos. He regarded them as people turned into birds—noblemen,
begging God in vain to turn them back into humans.
He perceived a clue to their noble ancestry in the manner in which they raised their young. The cuckoos, he
said, never undertook the education of their young
themselves. Instead, they hired wagtails to feed and
look after their young, while they themselves continued
flying around the forest, calling upon the Lord to
change them back into gentlemen.

Lekh viewed bats with disgust, regarding them as
half birds and half mice. He called them the emis-
saries of evil spirits, looking for fresh victims, capable
of attaching themselves to a human scalp and infusing
sinful desires into the brain. Even bats, however, had
their uses. Lekh once caught a bat in the attic. He

captured it with a net and placed it on an anthill outside the house. By the next day only white bones remained. Lekh meticulously collected the skeleton and took out the wishbone, which he wore on his chest. After grinding the rest of the bones to dust, he mixed them in a glass of vodka and gave it to the woman he loved. This, he said, would assure him of her increased desire for him.

Lekh taught me that a man should always watch birds carefully and draw conclusions from their behavior. If they were seen flying in a red sunset in large numbers, and were of many different breeds, then it was obvious that evil spirits on the lookout for damned souls rode on their wings. When crows, rooks, and jackdaws assembled together in a field, the meeting was usually inspired by an Evil one, who tried to instill in them hate for other birds. The appearance of long-winged white crows signaled a cloudburst; low-flying wild geese in the springtime meant a rainy summer and a poor harvest.

At dawn when the birds were sleeping we would venture out to stalk up to their nests. Lekh strode ahead, carefully jumping over bushes and shrubs. I followed directly behind. Later on, when daylight reached even the most shaded corners of the forest and fields, we would take the terrified, thrashing birds from the traps we had set the day before. Lekh removed them carefully, either speaking soothingly to them or threatening them with death. Then he would put them into a large bag slung over his shoulder, in which they would struggle and stir until their strength waned and they calmed down. Every new prisoner pushed down into the bag brought new life, causing the bag to quiver and swing against Lekh's back. Above our heads the friends and family of the prisoner would circle, twittering curses. Lekh would then look up from under his gray eyebrows and hurl insults at them. When the birds persisted, Lekh put the bag down, took out a

sling, placed a sharp stone in it, and, aiming it carefully, shot it at the flock. He never missed; suddenly a
motionless bird would hurtle from the sky. Lekh would
not bother to look for the corpse.

When noon approached, Lekh hastened his steps
and wiped the perspiration from his brow more often.
The most important hour of his day was nearing. A
woman locally nicknamed Stupid Ludmila was waiting
for him in some distant forest clearing known only to
the two of them. I would proudly trot behind him,
the bag of twitching birds slung over my shoulder.

The forest became increasingly dense and forbidding. The slimy striped trunks of snake-colored hornbeams shot straight up into the clouds. The linden
trees, all of which, according to Lekh, remembered the
very beginnings of the human race, stood broadshoul-
dered, their trunks resembling coats of mail festooned
with the gray patina of mosses. The oaks stretched out
of their trunks like the necks of starving birds looking
for food, and obscured the sun with gloomy branches,
casting the pines and poplars and lindens into shadow.
Sometimes Lekh would stop and silently look at some
spoors in the crannies of decaying bark, and in tree
knots and gallnuts full of black, curious holes from
whose interior shone bare white wood. We would pass
through groves of young birches with lean, fragile
shoots, diffidently flexing their thin, small branches and
buds.

Through the gauzy curtain of foliage we were
noticed by perching flocks of birds who became frightened and would soar away with beating wings. Their
chirping mixed with the chorus of bees murmuring
around us like a moving, gleaming cloud. Lekh protected his face with his hands and fled from the bees to
a denser thicket, while I ran at his heels holding on to
the bag of birds and basket of traps, waving my hand
to drive off the harassing and vengeful swarm.

Stupid Ludmila was a strange woman and I feared

her increasingly. She was well built and taller than the other women. Her hair, seemingly never cut, cascaded down her shoulders. She had large breasts, which hung nearly to her belly, and strong muscular calves. In the summer she went around dressed only in a faded sack which revealed her breasts and a clump of red hair at her crotch. Men and boys would tell of the pranks they played with Ludmila when she was in the mood. The village women often tried to trap her but, as Lekh said with pride, Ludmila's tail was windblown and no one could catch her against her will. She would disappear in the undergrowth like a starling and creep out when no one was around.

No one knew where her lair was. Sometimes at dawn when peasants walked to the fields, scythes on their shoulders, they saw Stupid Ludmila waving to them amorously from afar. They would halt and wave back to her, stretching their arms lazily as their will to work weakened. Only the calls of their wives and mothers, approaching with sickles and hoes, brought them back to their senses. Women often set dogs on Ludmila. The largest and most dangerous one ever sent to attack her decided not to return. After that she would always appear holding the animal by a rope. The other dogs would flee with their tails between their legs.

It was said that Stupid Ludmila lived with this huge dog as with a man. Others predicted that someday she would give birth to children whose bodies would be covered with canine hair and who would have lupine ears and four paws, and that these monsters would live somewhere in the forest.

Lekh never repeated these stories about Ludmila. He only mentioned once that when she was very young and innocent her parents ordered her to get married to the son of the village psalmist, notorious for his ugliness and cruelty. Ludmila refused, infuriating her fiancé so much that he enticed her outside the village where an entire herd of drunken peasants raped the

girl until she lost consciousness. After that she was a
changed woman; her mind had become addled. Since
no one remembered her family and she was considered
not too bright, she was nicknamed Stupid Ludmila.

She lived in the forests, lured men into the bushes
and pleased them so much with her voluptuousness
that afterwards they could not even look at their fat
and stinking wives. No one man could satisfy her; she
had to have several men, one after another. And yet
she was Lekh's great love. He made up tender songs
for her in which she figured as a strange-colored bird
flying to faraway worlds, free and quick, brighter and
more beautiful than other creatures. To Lekh she
seemed to belong to that pagan, primitive kingdom of
birds and forests where everything was infinitely abun-
dant, wild, blooming, and royal in its perpetual decay,
death, and rebirth; illicit and clashing with the human
world.

Every day at noon Lekh and I would walk toward
the clearing where he hoped to meet Ludmila. When
we arrived Lekh hooted in imitation of an owl. Stupid
Ludmila would rise above the tall grass, bluebottles and
poppy flowers intertwined in her hair. Lekh rushed
eagerly toward her and they stood together, swaying
slightly like the grasses around them, almost growing
into each other like two tree trunks rising up from a
single root.

I watched them from the edge of the clearing,
behind the leaves of ferns. The birds in my bag were
disturbed by the sudden stillness and chirped and floun-
dered and excitedly beat their wings against each other.
The man and woman kissed each other's hair and
eyes, and rubbed cheek against cheek. They were in-
toxicated by the touch and smell of their bodies and
slowly their hands became more playful. Lekh moved
his big, calloused paws over the smooth arms of the
woman while she drew his face closer to hers. Together
they slid down into the tall grass which now shook

above their bodies, partly concealing them from the
curious gaze of the birds gyrating over the clearing.
Lekh would say afterwards that while they lay in the
grass Ludmila told him stories of her life and her sufferings, disclosing the quirks and kinks of her strange
untamed feelings, all the byways and secret passages
that her frail mind wandered through.

It was hot. There was not a breath of wind and
the treetops stood rigid. The grasshoppers and dragonflies buzzed; a butterfly suspended on an invisible
breeze hovered over the sun-whitened clearing. The
woodpecker ceased pecking, the cuckoo grew silent. I
dozed off. Then I was awakened by voices. The man
and the woman stood clinging to each other as if grown
into the soil, saying words to each other I did not understand. They separated reluctantly; Stupid Ludmila
waved her hand. Lekh strode toward me, repeatedly
turning to look at her as he stumbled, a wistful smile on
his lips.

On the way home we set more traps; Lekh was
tired and withdrawn. In the evening, when the birds
fell asleep in their cages, he cheered up. Restless, he
spoke of Ludmila. His body trembled, he giggled, closing his eyes. His white pimply cheeks grew flushed.

Sometimes days passed and Stupid Ludmila did
not appear in the forest. Lekh would become possessed
by a silent rage. He would stare solemnly at the birds
in the cages, mumbling something to himself. Finally,
after prolonged scrutiny, he would choose the strongest
bird, tie it to his wrist, and prepare stinking paints of
different colors which he mixed together from the most
varied components. When the colors satisfied him, Lekh
would turn the bird over and paint its wings, head, and
breast in rainbow hues until it became more dappled
and vivid than a bouquet of wildflowers.

Then we would go into the thick of the forest.
There Lekh took out the painted bird and ordered me
to hold it in my hand and squeeze it lightly. The bird

would begin to twitter and attract a flock of the same species which would fly nervously over our heads. Our prisoner, hearing them, strained toward them, warbling more loudly, its little heart, locked in its freshly painted breast, beating violently.

When a sufficient number of birds gathered above our heads, Lekh would give me a sign to release the prisoner. It would soar, happy and free, a spot of rainbow against the backdrop of clouds, and then plunge into the waiting brown flock. For an instant the birds were confounded. The painted bird circled from one end of the flock to the other, vainly trying to convince its kin that it was one of them. But, dazzled by its brilliant colors, they flew around it unconvinced. The painted bird would be forced farther and farther away as it zealously tried to enter the ranks of the flock. We saw soon afterwards how one bird after another would peel off in a fierce attack. Shortly the many-hued shape lost its place in the sky and dropped to the ground. When we finally found the painted bird it was usually dead. Lekh keenly examined the number of blows which the bird had received. Blood seeped through its colored wings, diluting the paint and soiling Lekh's hands.

Stupid Ludmila did not return. Lekh, sulking and glum, removed one bird after another from the cages, painted them in still gaudier colors, and released them into the air to be killed by their kin. One day he trapped a large raven, whose wings he painted red, the breast green, and the tail blue. When a flock of ravens appeared over our hut, Lekh freed the painted bird. As soon as it joined the flock a desperate battle began. The changeling was attacked from all sides. Black, red, green, blue feathers began to drop at our feet. The ravens flew amuck in the skies, and suddenly the painted raven plummeted to the fresh-plowed soil. It was still alive, opening its beak and vainly trying to move its wings. Its eyes had been pecked out, and fresh blood streamed over its painted feathers. It made yet another attempt to flutter up from the sticky earth, but its strength was gone.

Lekh grew thin and stayed in the hut more often, swigging homemade vodka and singing songs about Ludmila. At times he would sit astride his bed, leaning over the dirt floor, and drawing something with a long stick. Gradually the outline became clear: it was the figure of a full-breasted, long-haired woman.

When there were no more birds to be painted, Lekh began to roam the fields with a bottle of vodka sticking out from under his jacket. Sometimes as I rambled along nearby, afraid that something might happen to him in the swamps, I would hear him singing. The man's deep, sorrowful voice rose and spread grief over the bogs like a heavy winter fog. The song soared along with the flocks of migrating birds but grew remote as it reached the abysmal depths of the forests.

In the villages people laughed at Lekh. They said that Stupid Ludmila had cast a spell over him and put fire in his loins, a fire that would drive him insane. Lekh protested, hurling the most vile curses at them and threatening to send birds against them that would peck out their eyes. Once he rushed at me and struck me in the face. He shouted that my presence scared his woman off because she was afraid of my Gypsy eyes. For the next two days he lay ill. When he arose he packed his knapsack, took along a loaf of bread, and went into the forest, ordering me to keep setting new snares and catching new birds.

Weeks passed. The traps that I set according to Lekh's orders more often than not caught only the tenuous, filmy gauze of cobwebs that drifted in the air. The storks and swallows had flown away. The forest was becoming deserted; only the snakes and lizards increased in numbers. The birds perched in their cages puffed up, their wings graying and still.

Then came an overcast day. Clouds of barely discernible shapes screened the skies like a thick feather
bed, hiding the anemic sun. The wind whipped over
the fields, wilting the blades of grass. The huts, cowering against the earth, were surrounded by vacant stubble, blackened and brown with mildew. In the undergrowth, where careless birds once thrashed, the wind
ruthlessly scourged and sheared the gray shagginess of
the tall thistles and shifted the rotting stalks of potato
plants from place to place.

Suddenly Stupid Ludmila appeared, leading her
huge dog on a rope. Her behavior was odd. She kept
asking about Lekh; and when I told her that he had
left many days ago and that I did not know where he
was, she alternately sobbed and laughed, walking from
one corner of the cabin to another, watched by the dog
and the birds. She noticed Lekh's old cap, pressed it
against her cheeks and burst into tears. Then she
abruptly threw the cap on the floor and trampled it
with her feet. She found a bottle of vodka which Lekh
had left under the bed. She drained it, then turned and,
looking furtively at me, ordered me to go with her to
the pasture. I tried to escape, but she set her dog on
me.

The pastures stretched directly beyond the cemetery. A few cows were foraging not far off, and several
young peasants warmed themselves at a fire. To avoid
being noticed we quickly crossed through the cemetery and climbed over a high wall. On the other side,
where we could not be seen, Stupid Ludmila tied the
dog to a tree, threatened me with a belt and commanded me to take off my pants. She herself wriggled
out of her sack and, naked, pulled me toward her.

After a moment of struggling and squirming, she
drew my face closer to her and ordered me to lie down
between her thighs. I tried to free myself but she
whipped me with the belt. My screams attracted the
other shepherds.

Stupid Ludmila noticed the approaching group of peasants and spread her legs wider. The men came over slowly, staring at her body.

Without a word they surrounded her. Two of them immediately began to let down their pants. The others stood undecided. No one paid any attention to me. The dog was struck by a rock and lay licking its wounded back.

A tall shepherd mounted the woman while she writhed below him, howling at his every move. The man struck open-handed blows at her breasts, leaned over and bit her nipples and kneaded her belly. When he finished and rose, another man took his place. Stupid Ludmila moaned and shuddered, drawing the man to her with her arms and legs. The other men crouched nearby, looking on, snickering and jesting.

From behind the cemetery appeared a mob of village women with rakes and shovels. It was led by several younger women who shouted and waved their hands. The shepherds hitched up their pants but did not flee; instead, they held on to the desperately struggling Ludmila. The dog strained at the leash and snarled, but the thick rope did not loosen. The women came closer. I sat down at a safe distance near the cemetery wall. Only then I noticed Lekh running across the pastures.

He must have returned to the village and learned what was going to happen. The women were quite close now. Before Stupid Ludmila had time to get up, the last of the men fled to the cemetery wall. The women now grabbed her. Lekh was still far away. Exhausted, he had to slow down. His pace was shambling and he stumbled several times.

The women held Stupid Ludmila down flat against the grass. They sat on her hands and legs and began beating her with the rakes, ripping her skin with their fingernails, tearing out her hair, spitting into her face. Lekh tried to push through, but they barred his way.

He tried to fight, but they knocked him down and hit him brutally. He ceased to struggle and several women turned him over on his back and straddled him. Then the women killed Ludmila's dog with vicious shovel blows. The peasants were sitting on the wall. When they moved closer toward me I edged away, ready at any moment to flee into the cemetery, where I would be safe among the graves. They feared the spirits and ghouls which were said to reside there.

Stupid Ludmila lay bleeding. Blue bruises appeared on her tormented body. She groaned loudly, arched her back, trembled, vainly trying to free herself. One of the women now approached, holding a corked bottle of brownish-black manure. To the accompaniment of raucous laughter and loud encouragements from the others, she kneeled between Ludmila's legs and rammed the entire bottle inside her abused, assaulted slit, while she began to moan and howl like a beast. The other women looked on calmly. Suddenly with all her strength one of them kicked the bottom of the bottle sticking out of Stupid Ludmila's groin. There was the muffled noise of glass shattering inside. Now all the women began to kick Ludmila; the blood spurted round their boots and calves. When the last woman had finished kicking, Ludmila was dead.

Their fury spent, the women went to the village chattering loudly. Lekh rose, his face bleeding. He swayed on his weak legs and spat out several teeth. Sobbing, he threw himself on the dead woman. He touched her mutilated body, crossing himself, babbling through his swollen lips.

I sat, huddled and chilled, on the cemetery wall, not daring to move. The sky grayed and darkened. The dead were whispering about the wandering soul of Stupid Ludmila, who was now asking mercy for all her sins. The moon came up. Its cold, pale, drained light illuminated only the dark shape of the kneeling man and the fair hair of the dead woman lying on the ground.

I slept and woke by turns. The wind raged over the graves, hanging wet leaves on the arms of the crosses. The spirits moaned, and the dogs could be heard howling in the village.

When I awoke, Lekh was still kneeling by Ludmila's body, his hunched back shaken by sobs. I spoke to him, but he paid no attention. I was too frightened to go back to the hut. I resolved to leave. Above us wheeled a flock of birds, chirping and calling from all directions.

6

The carpenter and his wife were convinced that my black hair would attract lightning to their farm. It was true that on hot dry nights when the carpenter touched my hair with a flint or a bone comb bluish-yellow sparks jumped over my head like "the Devil's lice." In the village rapturous storms came often and abruptly, causing fires and killing people and cattle. The lightning was always described as a great fiery bolt hurled from the heavens. Therefore the villagers made no attempt to put out such fires, believing that no human power could extinguish them, just as a person struck by lightning could not be saved. It was said that when lightning strikes a house it hurtles deep into the earth, where it crouches patiently, growing in power, and every seven years attracts a new lightning bolt to the same spot. Even objects saved from a burning house that had been struck by lightning were similarly possessed and could attract new lightning.

Often at dusk when the meager flames of candles and kerosene lamps began to flicker in the huts, the skies would become veiled by heavy sagging clouds that sailed obliquely over the thatched roofs. The villagers would grow silent, fearfully looking out from behind the windows, listening to the growing rumble. Old women squatting on cracked tiled ovens ceased their prayers and deliberated as to who would be rewarded this time by the Almighty or who would be punished by ubiquitous Satan, on whom fire and destruction, death or a crippling malady would fall. The groans of creaking doors, the sighing of trees bent by the storm, and the whistle of the wind would sound to the villagers like the curses of long-dead sinners, tormented by the uncertainty of limbo or slowly roasting in the neverending fires of hell.

At such moments the carpenter jerkily threw a thick jacket over his shoulders and, while he crossed himself many times, looped an ingenious padlocked chain around my ankle, fastening the other end of the chain to a heavy worn harness. Then in a roaring gale, amidst flashing thunderbolts, he placed me on a cart and, beating his ox frantically, drove me outside the village to a distant field and left me there. I was far from trees and human habitation, and the carpenter knew that the chain and harness would prevent me from returning to the hut.

I remained alone, afraid, listening to the noise of the receding cart. Lightning flashed close by, suddenly revealing the contours of the faraway huts, which then vanished as though they had never existed.

For a time a marvelous lull would prevail and the life of the plants and animals would be at a standstill. Yet I could hear the moans of the desolated fields and tree trunks, and the grunt of the meadows. Around me the forest werewolves would slowly creep forth. Translucent demons would come flying on their beating wings from steaming swamps, and stray graveyard ghouls would collide in the air with a clatter of bones. I felt their dry touch on my skin, the shuddering brushes and the icy breezes of their frozen wings. Terrified, I ceased to think. I threw myself on the earth, into the spreading puddles, dragging the rain-soaked harness by its chain. Above me, God Himself stretched, suspended in space, timing the horrendous spectacle with His perpetual clock. Between Him and me the murky night deepened.

By now the dark could be touched, grasped like a clot of coagulated blood, smeared over my face and body. I drank it in, gulped it, smothered in it. It outlined new roads around me and transformed the flat field into a bottomless chasm. It erected impassable mountains, leveled hills, filled up the rivers and valleys. In its embrace perished villages, forests, road shrines, human bodies. Far beyond the boundaries of the known the Devil was sitting and hurling sulphur-yellow lightning, loosing reverberating thunderbolts from behind the clouds. Every bolt of thunder shook the earth to its base and caused the clouds to sink lower and lower, until the wall of downpour changed everything into one watery swamp.

Hours later at dawn, when the bone-white moon had given way to the bleak sun, the carpenter would drive to the fields and take me back to the hut.

One stormy afternoon the carpenter fell ill. His wife fluttered around him preparing bitter juices and could not bother to drive me outside the village. When the first thunderbolts resounded, I hid myself in the barn under the hay.

In an instant the barn was jarred by an uncanny peal of thunder. A short while later a wall burst into fire, the tall flame glowing through the resin-soaked planks. Fanned by the wind, the fire raged loudly, the tips of its long wings extending to the hut and cow barn.

I darted into the courtyard in complete confusion. In the surrounding huts people tossed in the darkness. The village was astir; shouting could be heard in every direction. A dazed clustering throng, carrying axes and rakes, ran toward the carpenter's burning barn. The dogs howled, and the women with babies in their arms struggled to keep their skirts down which the wind was lifting up shamelessly over their faces. Every living creature had rushed outside. Their tails raised, furious, bellowing cows, jabbed by ax handles and shovel blades, were running, while calves on lean, quivering legs tried in vain to cling to the udders of their mothers. Trampling down the fences, breaking off the barn doors, colliding in a stupor with invisible walls of houses, the oxen lunged with their heavy heads hung low. Frenzied hens spattered into the air.

After a moment I ran away. I believed that my hair had attracted the lightning to the barn and huts and that the mob would surely kill me if it saw me.

Fighting with the squalling gale, stumbling over stones, falling into trenches and waterlogged pits, I reached the forest. By the time I had run as far as the railroad track in the forest, the storm had passed and was superseded by a night full of the loud sounds of splashing raindrops. In a thicket nearby I found a protected hole. Crouching in it, I listened to the confessions of the mosses and waited there the night through.

A train was due to pass here at dawn. The track served mainly to transport timber from one station to another, a dozen miles apart. The cars carrying the logs were pulled by a small, slow locomotive.

When the train approached I ran for a while alongside the end car, jumped a low-slung step, and was carried away into the safe interior of the forest. After some time I noticed a flat part of the embankment and jumped down, plunging into the thick undergrowth, unnoticed by the guard on the locomotive.

As I walked through the forest, I discovered a cobblestone road overgrown with weeds, and evidently long abandoned. At its end stood a deserted military bunker with massive reinforced-concrete walls.

There was utter silence. I hid behind a tree and threw a stone at the closed door. It rebounded. The echo came back quickly, and then there was silence again. I walked around the bunker, stepping over broken ammunition crates, scraps of metal, and empty tin cans. I climbed to an upper terrace of the mound, and then to the very top, where I found bent cans and, somewhat farther off, a wide opening. When I leaned over the opening I smelled a foul odor of decay and dampness; from within I heard some muffled squeaking. I picked up an old helmet and dropped it through the opening. The squeaks multiplied. I began quickly to throw clods of earth into the hole, followed by pieces of metal hoops from the crates and lumps of concrete. The squeaks grew louder; there were animals living and floundering inside.

I found a piece of smooth sheet metal and reflected a beam of sunlight into the interior. I saw clearly now: several feet below the opening there surged, billowing and receding, a black churning sea of rats. This surface twitched in an uneven rhythm, glittering with countless eyes. The light revealed wet backs and hairless tails. Time and again, like the spray of a wave, dozens of long scrawny rats assaulted with spasmodic leaps the smooth inner wall of the bunker, only to fall back onto the spines of others.

I gazed at this rippling mass and saw how the rats were murdering and eating one another, pouncing on one another, furiously biting out chunks of flesh and shreds of skin. The spurts of blood enticed more rats to fight. Each rat tried to scramble out of this living mass, competing for a place at the top, for yet another attempt to climb the wall, for yet another torn piece of rump.

I quickly covered the opening with a tin panel and hastened on my journey through the forest. On the way I ate my fill of berries. I hoped to reach a village before dusk.

In the late afternoon, as the sun was setting, I saw the first farm buildings. When I approached, some dogs leapt out from behind a fence and rushed at me.

I crouched before the fence, waving my hands vigorously, hopping like a frog, howling, and throwing stones. The dogs halted astonished, uncertain of who I was and how to act. A human being had suddenly acquired dimensions unknown to them. While they stared at me, dumfounded, their snouts bent sideways, I jumped over the fence.

Their barking and my shrieks brought out the owner of the hut. When I saw him I immediately realized that by an unhappy quirk of fortune I had returned to the same village from which I had fled the night before. The peasant's face was familiar, too familiar: I had seen him often at the carpenter's hut.

He recognized me at once and shouted something to a farmhand, who rushed in the direction of the carpenter's hut, while another farmhand kept watch over me, restraining the dogs at their leashes. The carpenter came, followed by his wife.

The first blow pitched me off the fence directly at his feet. He raised me and held me so I would not fall and slapped me again and again. Then, holding me like a cat by the neck, he dragged me to his farm, toward the charred smell of the smoldering ruins of the barn. Once there he threw me down on a pile of manure. He delivered one more blow to my head and I fainted.

When I came to, the carpenter was standing nearby preparing a sizable sack. I remembered that he used to drown sick cats in sacks like this. I flung myself at his feet, but the peasant kicked me away without a word and calmly continued preparing the sack.

Suddenly I recalled that the carpenter had once told his wife about partisans who hid their war trophies and supplies in old bunkers. I crawled toward him again, this time swearing that if he would not drown me, I would show him a pillbox full of old boots, uniforms, and military belts, which I had discovered during my escape.

The carpenter was intrigued, though he feigned disbelief. He squatted at my side, gripping me hard. I repeated my offer, trying as dispassionately as I could to assure him of the great value of the objects.

At dawn he harnessed an ox to his cart, tied me by a string to his hand, took along a large ax, and, saying nothing to his wife or neighbors, set off with me.

On the way I racked my brains for a way to tear myself loose; the string was strong. After we had arrived, the carpenter halted the cart and we walked toward the bunker. We climbed onto the hot roof; for a while I acted as if I had forgotten the direction of the opening. Finally we reached it. The carpenter avidly pushed aside the tin panel. The stench hit our nostrils, and from the interior the rats squeaked, blinded by the light. The peasant leaned over the opening, but he could not see for the moment because his eyes were not accustomed to the darkness.

I slowly moved to the opposite side of the opening, which now separated the carpenter from me, pulling taut the string by which I was tied. I knew that unless I succeeded in escaping in the next few seconds, the peasant would kill me and throw me into the depths.

Horror-stricken, I tugged suddenly at the string, so hard that it cut my wrist to the bone. My abrupt leap pulled the carpenter forward. He tried to rise, yelled, waved his hand, and dropped into the maw of the pillbox with a dull thud. I pressed my feet against the uneven concrete flange over which the slab had rested. The string grew tauter, scraped against the rough edge of the opening, and then snapped. At the same time I heard from below the scream and the broken, babbling cry of a man. A fine shudder shook the concrete walls of the bunker. I crept, terrified, toward the opening, directing into the interior a beam of daylight reflected from a piece of tin sheet.

The massive body of the carpenter was only partly visible. His face and half of his arms were lost under the surface of the sea of rats, and wave after wave of rats was scrambling over his belly and legs. The man completely disappeared, and the sea of rats churned even more violently. The moving rumps of the rats became stained with brownish red blood. The animals now fought for access to the body—panting, twitching their tails, their teeth gleaming under their half-open snouts, their eyes reflecting the daylight as if they were the beads of a rosary.

I observed this spectacle as if paralyzed, unable to tear myself away from the edge of the opening, lacking sufficient will power to cover it with the tin panel. Suddenly the shifting sea of rats parted and slowly, unhurrying, with the stroke of a swimmer, a bony hand with bony spreadeagled fingers rose, followed by the man's entire arm. For a moment it stood immobile above the rats scuttling about below; but suddenly the momentum of the surging animals thrust to the surface the entire bluish-white skeleton of the carpenter, partly defleshed and partly covered with shreds of reddish skin and gray clothing. In between the ribs, under the armpits, and in the place where the belly was, gaunt rodents fiercely struggled for the remaining scraps of dangling muscle and intestine. Mad with greed, they tore from one another scraps of clothing, skin, and formless chunks of the trunk. They dived into the center of the man's body only to jump out through another chewed hole. The corpse sank under renewed thrusts. When it next came to the surface of the bloody writhing sludge, it was a completely bare skeleton.

Frantically I grabbed the carpenter's ax and fled. I reached the cart breathlessly; the unsuspecting ox was grazing calmly. I leapt onto the box seat and pulled the reins, but the animal did not want to move without its master. Looking behind, convinced that at any moment the swarm of rats would rush out in pursuit, I jabbed the ox with the whip. It turned around in disbelief, hesitated, but the next few blows convinced it that we would not wait for the carpenter.

The cart jerked furiously over the ruts of the long untraveled road; the wheels tore the bushes and crushed the weeds growing across the trail. I was unfamiliar with the road and was only trying to get as far away as possible from the bunker and the carpenter's village. I drove at a frenzied pace through the forests and clearings, avoiding roads with any fresh traces of peasant vehicles. When night fell I camouflaged the cart in the bushes and went to sleep on the box seat.

The next two days I spent traveling, once just missing a military outpost at a sawmill. The ox grew lean and its flanks narrowed. But I rushed on and on, until I was certain I was far enough away.

We were approaching a small village; I rode into it calmly and halted at the first hut I came to, where a peasant crossed himself immediately on beholding me. I offered him the cart and ox, in return for shelter and food. He scratched his head, consulted his wife and neighbors, and finally agreed, after looking suspiciously at the ox's teeth—and at mine.

7

The village lay far from the railroad line and river. Three times a year detachments of German soldiers would arrive to collect the foodstuffs and materials which the peasants were obliged to provide for the army.

I was being kept by a blacksmith who was also the head peasant of the village. He was well respected and esteemed by the villagers. For this reason I was better treated here. However, now and then when they had been drinking the peasants would say that I could only bring misfortune to the community and that the Germans, if they found out about the Gypsy brat, would punish the entire village. But no one dared to say such things directly to the blacksmith's face, and in general I was not bothered. True, the blacksmith liked to slap my face when he was tipsy and I got in his way, but there were no other consequences. The two hired hands preferred to thrash each other rather than me, and the blacksmith's son, who was known in the village for his amorous feats, was almost never on the farm.

Early each morning the blacksmith's wife would give me a glass of hot borscht and a piece of stale bread, which, when soaked in the borscht, gained flavor as rapidly as the borscht lost it. Afterwards I would light the fire in my comet and drive the cattle toward the pasture ahead of the other cowherds.

In the evening the blacksmith's wife said her prayers, he snored against the oven, the hired hands tended the cattle, and the blacksmith's son prowled the village. The blacksmith's wife would give me her husband's jacket to delouse. I would sit in the brightest spot in the room, folding the jacket at various places along the seams and hunting the white, lazily moving blood-filled insects. I would pick them out, put them on the table, and crush them with my fingernail. When the lice were exceptionally numerous the blacksmith's wife would join me at the table and roll a bottle over the lice as soon as I put several of them down. The lice would burst with a crunching sound, their flattened corpses lying in small pools of dark blood. Those that fell onto the dirt floor scurried away in every direction. It was almost impossible to squash them underfoot.

The blacksmith's wife did not let me kill all the lice and bedbugs. Whenever we found a particularly large and vigorous louse, she would carefully catch it and throw it into a cup set aside for this purpose. Usually, when the number of such lice reached a dozen, the wife would take them out and knead them into a dough. To this she added a little human and horse urine, a large amount of manure, a dead spider, and a pinch of cat excrement. This preparation was considered to be the best medicine for a bellyache. When the blacksmith suffered his periodic bellyache, he had to eat several balls of this mixture. This led to vomiting and, as his wife assured him, to the total conquest of the disease, which promptly fled his body. Exhausted by vomiting and trembling like a reed, the blacksmith would lie on the mat at the foot of the oven and pant like a bellows. He would then be given tepid water and honey, which calmed him. But when the pain and fever did not die down, his wife prepared more medicines. She would pulverize horses' bones to fine flour, add a cup of mixed bedbugs and field ants, which would start fighting with each other, mix it all with several hen's eggs, and add a dash of kerosene. The patient had to gulp it all down in one big swallow and was then rewarded with a glass of vodka and a piece of sausage.

From time to time the blacksmith was visited by mysterious mounted guests, who carried rifles and revolvers. They would search the house and then sit down at a table with the blacksmith. In the kitchen the blacksmith's wife and I would prepare bottles of home-brewed vodka, strings of spiced hunter's sausages, cheeses, hard-boiled eggs, and sides of roast pork.

The armed men were partisans. They came to the village very often, without warning. What is more, they fought each other. The blacksmith explained to his wife that the partisans had become divided into factions: the "whites," who wanted to fight both the Germans and the Russians, and the "reds," who wanted to help the Red Army.

Varied rumors circulated in the village. The "whites" wanted also to retain the private ownership of property, leaving the landlords as they were. The "reds," supported by the Soviets, fought for land reform. Each faction demanded increasing assistance from the villages.

The "white" partisans, cooperating with the landlords, took revenge on all who were suspected of helping the "reds." The "reds" favored the poor and penalized the villages for any help they gave to the "whites." They persecuted the families of the rich peasants.

The village was also searched by German troops, who interrogated the peasants about the partisan visits and shot one or two peasants to set an example. In such cases the blacksmith would hide me in the potato

cellar while he himself tried to soften the German
commanders, promising them punctual deliveries of
foodstuffs and extra grain.

Sometimes the partisan factions would attack and
kill each other while visiting the village. The village
would then become a battlefield; machine guns roared,
grenades burst, huts flamed, abandoned cattle and
horses bellowed, and half-naked children howled. The
peasants hid in cellars embracing their praying women.
Half-blind, deaf, toothless old women, babbling prayers
and crossing themselves with arthritic hands, walked
directly into machine-gun fire, cursing the combatants
and appealing to heaven for revenge.

After the battle the village would slowly return to
life. But there would be fights among the peasants and
boys for the weapons, uniforms, and boots abandoned
by the partisans, and also arguments about where to
bury the dead and who should dig the graves. Days
would pass in argument as the corpses decomposed,
sniffed by dogs in the daytime and chewed by rats at
night.

I was awakened one night by the blacksmith's
wife who urged me to flee. I barely had time to leap
out of bed before male voices and rattling weapons
could be heard surrounding the hut. I hid in the attic
with a sack thrown over my body, clinging to a crack
in the planks, through which I could see a large part
of the farmyard.

A firm male voice ordered the blacksmith to come
out. Two armed partisans dragged the half-naked
blacksmith into the yard, where he stood, shivering
from cold and hitching up his falling trousers. In a
tall cap with star-spangled epaulets on his shoulders,
the leader of the band approached the blacksmith and
asked him something. I caught a fragment of a sentence: ". . . you helped enemies of the Fatherland."

The blacksmith threw up his hands, swearing in
the name of the Son and the Holy Trinity. The first

blow felled him. He continued his denials, rising slowly
to his feet. One of the men tore out a pole from the
fence, swung it through the air and clouted the blacksmith in the face. The blacksmith fell, and the partisans began to kick him all over with their heavy boots.
The blacksmith groaned, writhing with pain, but the
men did not stop. They leaned over him twisting his
ears, stepping on his genitals, breaking his fingers with
their heels.

When he ceased to groan and his body sagged, the
partisans hauled out the two hired hands, the blacksmith's wife, and his struggling son. They opened wide
the doors of the barn and threw the woman and the
men across the shaft of a cart in such a way that,
with the shaft under their bellies, they hung over it
like upset sacks of grain. Then the partisans tore the
clothing off their victims and tied their hands to their
feet. They rolled up their sleeves and, with steel canes
cut from track signal wire, began to beat the squirming
bodies.

The crack of the blows rebounded loudly off the
taut buttocks while the victims twisted, shrinking and
swelling, and howled like a pack of abused dogs. I
quivered and sweated with fear.

The blows rained one after another. Only the
blacksmith's wife continued to wail, while the partisans exchanged witticisms over her lean, crooked
thighs. Since the woman did not stop moaning, they
overturned her, face to the sky, her whitening breasts
hanging down at both sides. The men struck her heat-
edly, the rising crescendo of blows slashing the woman's
body and belly, now darkened by streams of blood.
The bodies on the shaft drooped. The torturers put
on their jackets and entered the hut, demolishing the
furniture and plundering all in sight.

They entered the attic and found me. They held
me up by the neck, turning me around, punching me
with their fists, pulling me by the hair. They had im-

mediately assumed I was a Gypsy foundling. They
loudly deliberated what to do with me. Then one of
them decided I should be delivered up to the German
outpost about a dozen miles from the hut. According
to him, this would make the commander of the outpost
less suspicious of the village, which was already tardy
in its compulsory deliveries. Another man agreed, adding rapidly that the whole village might be burned
down because of a single Gypsy bastard.

My hands and feet were tied and I was carried
outside. The partisans summoned two peasants, to
whom they carefully explained something while pointing at me. The peasants listened obediently, with ob-
sequious nods. I was placed on a cart and lashed to a
crosstie. The peasants climbed onto the box seat and
drove off with me.

The partisans escorted the cart for several miles,
swaying freely in their saddles, sharing food from the
blacksmith. When we entered the denser part of the
forest, they again spoke to the peasants, struck their
horses, and vanished in the thicket.

Tired by the sun and by my uncomfortable position, I dozed off into half-sleep. I dreamed I was a
squirrel, crouching in a dark tree hole and watching
with irony the world below. I suddenly became a
grasshopper with long, springy legs, on which I sailed
across great tracts of land. Now and then, as if through
a fog, I heard the voices of the drivers, the neighing of
the horse, and the squeaking of the wheels.

We reached the railroad station at noon and were
immediately surrounded by German soldiers in faded
uniforms and battered boots. The peasants bowed to
them and handed them a note written by the partisans.
While a guard went off to call an officer, several soldiers approached the cart and stared at me, exchanging
remarks. One of them, a rather elderly man, clearly
fatigued by the heat, was wearing spectacles fogged by
sweat. He leaned against the cart and watched me

closely, with dispassionate, watery-blue eyes. I smiled at him but he did not respond. I looked straight into his eyes and wondered if this would cast an evil spell on him. I thought he might fall sick but, feeling sorry for him, I dropped my gaze.

A young officer emerged from the station building and approached the cart. The soldiers quickly straightened their uniforms and stood at attention. The peasants, not quite sure what to do, tried to imitate the soldiers and also drew themselves up servilely.

The officer tersely said something to one of the soldiers, who came forward from the file, approached me, patted my hair roughly with his hand, looked into my eyes while pulling back my lids, and inspected the scars on my knees and calves. He then made his report to the officer. The officer turned to the elderly bespectacled soldier, issued an order and left.

The soldiers moved away. From the station building a gay tune could be heard. On the tall watchtower with its machine-gun post the guards were adjusting their helmets.

The bespectacled soldier approached me, wordlessly untied the rope with which I had been tied to the cart, looped one end of the rope around his wrist, and with a movement of his hand ordered me to follow him. I glanced back at the two peasants; they were already on the cart, whipping the horse.

We passed the station building. On the way the soldier stopped at a warehouse, where he was handed a small can of gasoline. Then we walked along on the railroad track toward the looming forest.

I was certain that the soldier had orders to shoot me, pour the gasoline over my body and burn it. I had seen this happen many times. I remembered how the partisans had shot a peasant who was accused of being an informer. In that case the victim was ordered to dig a ditch into which his dead body later dropped. I remembered the Germans shooting a wounded partisan who was fleeing into the forest, and the tall flame rising later over his dead body.

I dreaded pain. The shooting would certainly be very painful, and the burning with gasoline even more so. But I could do nothing. The soldier carried a rifle, and the rope tied to my leg was looped over his wrist.

I was barefoot and the crossties, hot from the sun, scorched my feet. I hopped about on the sharp particles of gravel lying between the crossties. I tried several times to walk on the rail, but the rope tied to my leg somehow prevented me from keeping my balance. It was difficult to adjust my small steps to the large, measured stride of the soldier.

He watched me and smiled faintly at my attempt at acrobatics on the rail. The smile was too brief to signify anything; he was going to kill me.

We had already left the station area and now passed the last switchpoint. It was darkening. We drew nearer to the forest and the sun was setting behind the treetops. The soldier halted, put down the gasoline can, and transferred the rifle to his left arm. He sat down on the edge of the track and, heaving a deep sigh, stretched his legs down the embankment. He calmly took off his spectacles, wiped the sweat from his thick brows with his sleeve, and unclipped the small shovel hanging from his belt. He took out a cigarette from his breast pocket and lit it, carefully extinguishing the match.

Silently he watched my attempt to loosen the rope, which was rubbing the skin off my leg. Then he took a small jackknife out of his trouser pocket, opened it, and moving closer held my leg with one hand, and with the other carefully cut the rope. He rolled it up and flung it over the embankment with a sweeping gesture.

I smiled in an attempt to express my gratitude, but he did not smile back. We now sat, he drawing at his cigarette and I observing the bluish smoke drifting upward in loops.

I began to think of the many ways there were of dying. Until now, only two ways had impressed me.

I recalled well the time, in the first days of the war, when a bomb hit a house across the street from my parents' home. Our windows were blown out. We were assaulted by falling walls, the tremor of the shaken earth, the screams of unknown dying people. I saw the brown surfaces of doors, ceilings, walls with the pictures still clinging desperately to them, all falling into the void. Like an avalanche rushing to the street came majestic grand pianos opening and closing their lids in flight, obese, clumsy armchairs, skittering stools and hassocks. They were chased by chandeliers that were falling apart with shrill cries, by polished kitchen pots, kettles, and sparkling aluminum chamber pots. Pages torn out of gutted books fell down, flapping like flocks of scared birds. Bathtubs tore themselves away slowly and deliberately from their pipes, entwining themselves magically in the knots and scrolls of banisters and railings and rain gutters.

As the dust settled, the split house timidly bared its entrails. Limp human bodies lay tossed over the jagged edges of the broken floors and ceilings like rags covering the break. They were just beginning to soak in the red dye. Tiny particles of torn paper, plaster, and paint clung to the sticky red rags like hungry flies. Everything around was still in motion; only the bodies seemed at peace.

Then came the groans and screams of people pinned down by the falling beams, impaled on rods and pipes, partially torn and crushed under chunks of walls. Only one old woman came up from the dark pit. She clutched desperately at bricks and when her toothless mouth opened to speak she was suddenly unable to utter a sound. She was half naked and withered breasts hung from her bony chest. When she reached the end of the crater at the pile of rubble between the pit and the road, she stood up straight for a moment on the ridge. Then she toppled over backwards and disappeared behind the debris.

One could die less spectacularly at the hands of another man. Not long ago, when I lived at Lekh's, two peasants began to fight at a reception. In the middle of the hut they rushed at each other, clutched at each other's throat, and fell on the dirt floor. They bit with their teeth like enraged dogs, tearing off pieces of clothing and flesh. Their horny hands and knees and shoulders and feet seemed to have a life of their own. They jumped about clutching, striking, scratching, twisting in a wild dance. Bare knuckles hit skulls like hammers and bones cracked under stress.

Then the guests, watching calmly in a circle, heard a crushing noise and a hoarse rattle. One of the men stayed on top longer. The other gasped and seemed to be weakening, but still lifted his head and spat in the victor's face. The man on top did not forgive this. He triumphantly blew himself up like a bullfrog and took a wide swing, smashing the other's head in with terrible force. The head did not struggle to rise any more, but seemed to dissolve into a growing pool of blood. The man was dead.

I felt now like the mangy dog that the partisans had killed. They had first stroked his head and scratched him behind the ears. The dog, overwhelmed with joy, yapped with love and gratitude. Then they tossed him a bone. He ran after it, wagging his scruffy tail, scaring the butterflies and trampling flowers. When he seized the bone and proudly lifted it, they shot him.

The soldier hitched up his belt. His movement caught my attention and I stopped thinking for a moment.

Then I tried to calculate the distance to the forest and the time it would take him to pick up his rifle and shoot if I should suddenly escape. The forest was too far; I would die midway on the sandy ridge. At best I might reach the patch of weeds, in which I would still be visible and unable to run fast.

The soldier rose and stretched with a groan. Silence surrounded us. The soft wind blew away the smell of the gasoline and brought back a fragrance of marjoram and fir resin.

He could, of course, shoot me from the back, I thought. People preferred killing a person without looking into his eyes.

The soldier turned toward me and pointing to the forest made a gesture with his hand which seemed to say, "run away, be off!" So the end was coming. I pretended I did not understand and edged toward him. He moved back violently, as if fearing that I might touch him, and angrily pointed to the forest, shielding his eyes with his other hand.

I thought that this was a clever way of tricking me; he was pretending not to look. I stood rooted to the spot. He glanced at me impatiently and said something in his rough tongue. I smiled fawningly at him, but this only exasperated him more. Again he thrust his arm toward the forest. Again I did not move. Then he lay down between the rails, across his rifle, from which he had removed the bolt.

I calculated the distance once more; it seemed to me that this time the risk was small. As I began to move away, the soldier smiled affably. When I reached the edge of the embankment, I glanced back; he was still lying motionless, dozing in the warm sun.

I hastily waved and then leapt like a hare down the embankment straight into the undergrowth of the cool, shady forest. I tore my skin against the ferns as I fled farther and farther until I finally lost my breath and fell down in the moist, soothing moss.

While I lay listening to the sounds of the forest, I heard two shots from the direction of the railroad track. Apparently the soldier was simulating my execution.

Birds awakened and began rustling in the foliage. Right next to me a small lizard leapt out of a root and stared attentively at me. I could have squashed it with a whack of my hand, but I was too tired.

8

After an early autumn destroyed some of the crops, a severe winter set in. First it snowed for many days. The people knew their weather and hastily stored food for themselves and their livestock, plugged any holes in their houses or barns with straw, and secured the chimneys and thatched roofs against the harsh winds. Then the frost came, freezing everything solid under the snow.

No one wanted to keep me. Food was scarce and every mouth was a burden to feed. Besides, there was no work for me to do. One could not even clear manure out of barns which were banked up to the eaves by snow. People shared their shelter with hens, calves, rabbits, pigs, goats, and horses, men and animals warming each other with the heat of their bodies. But there was no room for me.

Winter did not loosen its grip. The heavy sky, filled with leaden clouds, seemed to weigh down on the thatched roofs. Sometimes a cloud darker than the others raced over like a balloon, trailing behind it a mournful shadow that stalked it as evil spirits stalk a sinner. People breathed peepholes onto the ice-frosted windows. When they saw the sinister shadow sweep over the village, they made the sign of the cross and mumbled prayers. It was obvious that the Devil was riding over the countryside on the dark cloud, and as long as he was there one could expect only the worst.

Wrapped in old rags, scraps of rabbit fur and horsehides, I wandered from one village to another, warmed only by the heat of the comet that I made from a can I found on the railway track. I carried on my back a sack full of fuel, which I anxiously replenished at every opportunity. As soon as my sack grew lighter, I would go to the forest, break off branches, tear off some bark, and dig up peat and moss. When the sack was full I continued on my way with a feeling of contentment and security, twirling my comet and delighting in its warmth.

Food was not difficult to find. The endless snowing kept people in their huts. I could safely dig my way into the snowbound barns to find the best potatoes and beetroots, which I later baked in my comet. Even when someone spied me, a shapeless bundle of rags moving sluggishly through the snow, they mistook me for a wraith and only sent the dogs after me. The dogs were reluctant to leave their lairs in the warm huts and waded slowly through the deep snow. When they finally reached me I could easily scare them away with my hot comet. Cold and tired, they returned to the huts.

I wore big wooden shoes bound with long strips of cloth. The width of the footwear, coupled with my light weight, enabled me to move over snow quite well without sinking to my waist. Wrapped up to the eyes, I roamed the countryside freely, meeting no one but ravens.

I slept in the forest, burrowing into a hollow beneath tree roots, with a snowdrift for a roof. I loaded the comet with damp peat and rotten leaves that warmed my dugout with fragrant smoke. The fire lasted through the night.

Finally, after a few weeks of milder winds the snow began to thaw and the peasants began to go outside. I had no choice. Well-rested dogs now roamed about the farmhouses, and I could steal food no more and had to be on my guard every minute. I had to look for some remote village, safely distant from the German outposts.

During my wanderings through the forest, splotches of wet snow often fell on me, threatening to choke my comet. On the second day I was halted by a cry. I crouched behind a bush, afraid to move, listening intently to the rustling trees. I heard the cry again. Above crows flapped their wings, scared by something. Moving stealthily from the cover of one tree to another, I approached the source of the sound. On a narrow, soggy road I saw an overturned cart and horse, but no sign of a person.

When the horse saw me it pricked its ears and tossed its head. I came closer. The animal was so thin that I could see its every bone. Every strand of emaciated muscle hung like wet rope. It looked at me with dim bloodshot eyes that seemed about to close. It moved its head feebly, and a froglike croak rose up in its thin neck.

One of the horse's legs was broken above the fetlock. A sharp splinter of broken bone protruded, and every time the animal moved its leg the bone cut farther through the skin.

Ravens circled over the stricken beast, hovering upwind and downwind, persistently keeping their watch. Now and then one of them would perch in the trees and send lumps of wet, thawed snow cascading to the ground with the thud of potato pancakes flapped into a pan. At every sound the horse wearily lifted its head, opened its eyes, and looked about.

Seeing me walk around the cart, the horse switched its tail invitingly. I approached him and he put his heavy head on my shoulder, rubbing against my cheek. As I stroked his dry nostrils, he moved his muzzle, nudging me closer.

I bent down to examine his leg. The horse turned his head toward me, as if awaiting my verdict. I encouraged him to take a step or two. He tried, groaning and stumbling, but it was useless. He lowered his head, ashamed and resigned. I grasped his neck, feeling it still pulse with life. I tried to persuade him to follow me; staying in the forest could only mean his death. I spoke to him about the warm stable, the smell of hay, and I assured him that a man could set his bone and heal it with herbs.

I told him about the lush meadows still under snow, only awaiting spring. I admitted that if I succeeded in bringing him back to the local village and returning him to his owner, my relations with the local people might improve. I might even be able to stay on the farm. He listened, squinting at me from time to time to make sure that I was telling the truth.

I stepped back and urged him to walk with a gentle tap of a twig. He swayed, lifting the injured leg high. He hobbled, but finally I persuaded him to move. Progress was slow and painful. The horse occasionally stopped and slumped motionless. Then I would put my arm around his neck, hug him, and lift the broken leg. After a while he would start walking again, as if moved by some recollection, by some thought that had temporarily slipped from his mind. He missed a step, lost his balance, stumbled. Whenever he walked on the broken leg the splintered bone emerged from under the skin, so that he walked in the snow and mud almost on this stump of bare bone. Each of his pained neighs shattered me. I forgot the clogs on my feet and felt for the moment as if I were walking on the jagged edges of my shinbones, heaving a moan of pain with every step.

Exhausted, covered with mud, I reached the village with the horse. We were immediately surrounded by a pack of snarling dogs. I kept them at bay with my comet, singeing the fur of the most vicious ones. The horse stood by impassive, sinking into a torpor.

Many peasants came out of their huts. One of them was the pleasantly surprised owner of the horse, which had bolted two days previously. He chased away the dogs and examined the broken leg, after which he declared that the horse would have to be killed. His only use would be to provide some meat, a hide for tanning, and bones for medicinal purposes. Actually, in that area, the bones were the most valuable item. The treatment for a serious illness consisted of several daily draughts of an infusion of herbs mixed with ground horse bones. Toothache was treated by a compress made of a frog's thigh with some powdered horse teeth. Burnt horse hoofs were certain to cure colds within two days, while the hipbones of a horse, placed on an epileptic's body, helped the patient to avoid seizures.

I stood aside while the peasant checked the horse. My turn came next. The man looked me over carefully and asked me where I had been before and what I had done. I answered as cautiously as possible, anxious to avoid any stories which might arouse his suspicions. He wanted me to repeat what I had said several times and laughed at my unsuccessful attempt to speak the local dialect. He asked me time and again if I were a Jewish or Gypsy orphan. I swore on everything and everybody I could think of that I was a good Christian and an obedient worker. Other men were standing nearby watching me critically. Nevertheless, the farmer decided to take me on as a workhand in the yard and in the fields. I fell to my knees and kissed his feet.

Next morning, the farmer took two big, strong horses out of his stable. He hitched them to a plow and drove them to the crippled horse waiting patiently by a fence. Then he threw a noose over the crippled horse's neck and tied the other end of the rope to the plow. The strong horses twitched their ears and looked with indifference at the victim. He breathed hard and twisted his neck, which was being squeezed by the tight rope. I stood by wondering how I could save his life, how I could convince him that I had no idea that I would be bringing him back to the farm for this . . . When the farmer approached the horse to check the position of the noose, the cripple suddenly turned his head and licked the farmer's face. The man did not look at him, but gave him a powerful, open-handed slap on the muzzle. The horse turned away, hurt and humiliated.

I wanted to throw myself at the farmer's feet and beg for the horse's life, but I caught the animal's reproachful look. He was staring straight at me. I remembered what would happen if a man or animal about to die counted the teeth of the person responsible for his death. I was afraid to utter a word as long as the horse was looking at me with that resigned, terrible look. I waited, but he would not drop his eyes from me.

Suddenly the farmer spat on his hands, grabbed a knotted whip, and lashed the rumps of the two strong horses. They bolted forward violently, the rope grew taut, and the noose tightened on the neck of the condemned. Wheezing hoarsely, he was dragged down and fell like a fence blown over by the wind. They pulled him over the soft ground brutally for a few more paces. When the panting horses stopped, the farmer walked up to the victim and kicked him a few times on the neck and on the knees. The animal did not stir. The strong horses, scenting death, stamped their feet nervously as though trying to avoid the stare of the wide-open, dead eyes.

I spent the rest of the day helping the farmer skin off the hide and cut up the carcass.

Weeks went by and the village left me alone. Some of the boys said occasionally that I should be delivered to the German headquarters, or that the soldiers should be told about the Gypsy bastard in the village. Women avoided me on the road, carefully covering the heads of their children. The men looked me over in silence, and casually spat in my direction.

They were people of slow, deliberate speech who measured their words carefully. Their custom required them to spare words as one spares salt, and a loose tongue was regarded as a man's worst enemy. Fast talkers were thought devious and dishonest, obviously trained by Jewish or Gypsy fortunetellers. People used to sit in a heavy silence broken only infrequently by some insignificant remark. Whenever speaking or laughing, everyone would cover his mouth with a hand to avoid showing his teeth to ill-wishers. Only vodka managed to loosen their tongues and relax their manners.

My master was widely respected and often invited to local weddings and celebrations. Sometimes, if the children were well and neither his wife nor his mother-in-law objected, I was also taken along. At such receptions he ordered me to display my urban language to the guests, and to recite the poems and stories I had learned before the war from my mother and nurses. Compared to the soft, drawling local speech, my city talk, full of hard consonants which rattled like machine-gun fire, sounded like a caricature. Before my performance I was forced by my farmer to drink a glass of vodka at one gulp. I stumbled over feet which tried to trip me and barely reached the center of the room.

I started my show at once, trying to avoid looking at anyone's eyes or teeth. Whenever I recited poetry at great speed, the peasants opened their eyes wide in amazement, thinking that I was out of my mind and that my fast speech was some sort of infirmity.

They were entirely convulsed by the fables and rhymed stories about animals. Listening to stories about a goat traveling across the world in search of the capital of goatland, about a cat in seven-league boots, the bull Ferdinand, Snow White and the Seven Dwarfs, Mickey Mouse, and Pinocchio, the guests laughed, choking on their food and sputtering vodka.

After the performance I was called to one table after another to repeat some poems, and was forced to drink new toasts. When I refused, they poured the liquor down my throat. Usually I was quite drunk by the middle of the evening and hardly knew what was going on. The faces around me began to take on the features of the animals in the stories I recited, like some live illustrations in the children's books which I still remembered. I felt as though I were falling down a deep well with smooth, moist walls coated with spongy moss. At the bottom of the well, instead of water, there was my warm, secure bed where I could safely sleep and forget about everything.

The winter was ending. I went every day with my farmer to fetch wood from the forest. Warm moisture filled the air and swelled the woolly mosses hanging from the boughs of great trees like graying, half-frozen rabbit skins. They were soaked with water, dripping dark drops over the sheets of torn bark. Small streams spilled in every direction, gamboling here and diving there under swampy roots to emerge and playfully continue their erratic childlike scamper.

A neighboring family held a big wedding reception for their handsome daughter. Peasants, dressed in their Sunday best, danced in the barnyard, which had been swept clean and decorated for the occasion. The groom followed ancient tradition by kissing everyone on the mouth. The bride, dizzy from too many toasts, wept and laughed in turns, paying little attention to men who pinched her buttocks or rested their hands on her breasts.

When the room emptied and the guests started dancing, I rushed to the table for the meal I had earned by my performance. I sat in the darkest corner, anxious

to avoid the jeers of drunks. Two men entered the
room with their arms over each other's shoulders in a
friendly hug. I knew them both. They were among the
more prosperous farmers in the village. Each had several cows, a team of horses, and choice pieces of land.

I slid behind some empty barrels in the corner.
The men sat on a bench by the table, still loaded with
food, and talked slowly. They offered each other por-
tions of food and, as was the custom, avoided each
other's eyes and kept grave faces. Then one of them
slowly reached into his pocket. While picking up a
piece of sausage with one hand, he slid out a knife
with a long pointed blade with the other. Then he
plunged it with all his strength into the back of his unsuspecting companion.

Without looking back he left the room munching
the sausage with relish. The stabbed man tried to rise.
He looked around with glassy eyes; when he saw me
he tried to say something, but all that came out of his
mouth was a half-chewed piece of cabbage. Once more
he tried to stand up, but he wobbled and slid gently
between the bench and the table. Making sure that
there was no one else about, and trying in vain to stop
trembling, I scurried out of the half-open door like a
rat and ran to the barn.

In the dusk, village lads were grabbing girls and
pulling them into the barn. On a pile of hay a man
showing his buttocks had a woman spreadeagled on
her back. Drunks stumbled across the threshing yard,
cursing to each other and vomiting, harassing the lov-
ers and waking the snorers. I pried off a board in the
rear of the barn and squeezed through the opening. I
ran to my farmer's barn and quickly scrambled onto
the heap of hay in the stable which was my sleeping
quarters.

The body of the murdered man was not removed
from the house immediately after the wedding. It was
placed in one of the side rooms while the dead man's

family assembled in the main room. Meanwhile, one
of the older village women had bared the left arm of
the corpse and washed it with a brown mixture. The
men and women suffering from goiter entered the
room, one by one, the ugly sacks of inflated flesh hanging under their chins and spreading over their necks.
The old woman brought each of them to the body,
made some involved gestures over the afflicted part,
and then lifted the lifeless hand to touch the swelling
seven times. The patient, pale with fright, had to repeat with her, "Let the disease go where this hand will
be going."

After the treatment the patients paid the dead
man's family for the cure. The corpse remained in the
room. The left hand rested on his chest; a holy candle
had been placed in the stiff right hand. By the fourth
day, when the odor in the room became stronger, a
priest was summoned to the village and burial prepara-
tions started.

Long after the funeral, the farmer's wife still refused to wash the bloodstains from the room of the
murder. They were clearly visible on the floor and table, like a dark rust-colored fungus embedded in the
wood forever. Everyone believed that these stains, tes-
tifying to the crime, would sooner or later draw the
murderer back to the spot against his will and lead to
his death.

However, the murderer, whose face I remembered
very well, frequently dined in the same room where he
had murdered, gorging himself on the ample meals
served there. I could not understand how he could remain unafraid of these bloodstains. I often watched
him with morbid fascination as he walked over them,
imperturbably smoking his pipe or taking a bite of
pickled cucumber after a glass of vodka downed in one
gulp.

At such times I was as tense as a drawn slingshot.
I awaited some shattering event: a dark chasm that

would open under the bloodstains and swallow him without a trace, or a seizure of St. Vitus's dance. But the murderer trod fearlessly over the stains. Sometimes at night I wondered if the stains had lost their power of vengeance. After all, they were somewhat faded now; kittens had dirtied them, and the woman herself, forgetting her resolution, had often mopped the floor.

On the other hand, I knew that the workings of justice were often exceedingly slow. In the village I had heard a tale about a skull which tumbled out of a grave and proceeded to roll down an incline, in between the crosses, carefully avoiding beds of blooming flowers. The sexton tried to stop the skull with a spade, but it evaded him and headed toward the cemetery gate. A forester saw it and also tried to stop it by shooting at it with his rifle. The skull, quite undaunted by all the obstacles, rolled steadily down the road leading to the village. It waited for the opportune moment and then threw itself under the hooves of a local farmer's horses. They bolted, overturned their cart, and killed the driver on the spot.

When people heard about the accident they were curious and investigated the matter further. They discovered that the skull had "jumped" out of the grave of the older brother of the accident victim. Ten years earlier, the older brother was about to inherit the father's property. The younger brother and his wife were obviously envious of his good fortune. Then one night the older brother died suddenly. His brother and sister-in-law decided on a hasty burial, not even allowing the relatives of the deceased to visit the body.

Various rumors about the cause of such a sudden death circulated in the village, yet nothing definite was known. Gradually, the younger brother, who eventually took over the property, prospered in wealth and general esteem.

After the accident by the cemetery gate, the skull

gave up its wandering and rested quietly in the road dust. Close inspection showed that a large rusty nail had been driven deep into the bone.

Thus, after many years, the victim punished the executioner, and justice prevailed. So it was believed that neither rain, nor fire, nor wind could ever wipe out the stain of a crime. For justice hangs over the world like a great sledgehammer lifted by a powerful arm, which has to stop for a while before coming down with terrible force on the unsuspecting anvil. As they used to say in the villages, even a speck of dust shows up in the sun.

While the adults usually left me alone, I had to watch out for the village boys. They were great hunters; I was their game. Even my farmer warned me to keep out of their way. I took the cattle to the edge of the pasture, far away from the other boys. The grass was richer there, but one had to watch the cows constantly to keep them from straying into the adjoining fields and damaging crops. But here I was fairly safe from raids and not too conspicuous. Every now and then some herdsmen crept up on me and sprang a surprise attack. I usually got a beating and had to flee into the fields. I warned them loudly on such occasions that if the cows should damage any crops while I was away, my farmer would punish them. The threat often worked and they would return to their cows.

Still, I was afraid of such attacks and did not have a moment's peace. Every movement of the herdsmen, every huddle, every sign of action toward me filled me with apprehension of some plot.

Their other games and schemes centered around military equipment found in the woods, mostly rifle cartridges and land mines, locally called "soap" because of their shape. To find a cache of ammunition, one had only to walk a few miles into the forest and forage in the underbrush. The weapons had been left by two detachments of partisans who had waged a drawn-out battle there some months earlier. "Soap" cakes were particularly plentiful. Some peasants said that they were left by the fleeing "white" partisans; others swore that they were booty taken from the "reds," which the "whites" could not carry along with all their other equipment.

One could also find broken rifles in the forest. The boys would take out the barrels, cut them to shorter sections, and fashion them into pistols with handles whittled from branches. Such pistols used rifle ammunition, which was also easily found in the bush. The cartridge was detonated by a nail attached to a band of rubber.

Crude though they were, these pistols could be lethal. Two of the village boys were seriously injured when they quarreled and shot each other with such guns. Another homemade pistol exploded in a boy's hand, tearing off all his fingers and an ear. The most pathetic was the paralyzed and crippled son of one of our neighbors. Someone played a practical joke on him by placing several rounds of rifle ammunition at the bottom of his comet. When the unsuspecting boy lit his comet in the morning and swung it between his legs, the cartridges went off.

There was also the "powder up" method of shooting. One took the bullet from the cartridge case and poured out some of the powder. The bullet was then pressed deep into the half-empty case and the rest of the powder was placed on top, covering the bullet. A cartridge doctored in this way was then placed in a slot in a board, or buried in the ground almost to the tip, and aimed in the direction of the target. The powder on top was lit. When the fire reached the primer, the bullet shot a distance of twenty feet or more. The "powder up" experts held contests and made bets on whose bullet would go farthest and on what proportion of powder on top and bottom would prove best. The bolder boys tried to impress girls by shooting the bullet while holding the cartridge. Often the cartridge case or detonator hit a boy or some bystander. The best-looking boy in the village had such a fuse imbedded in a part of his body the very mention of which started everyone laughing. He strolled around mostly alone, avoiding the glance of giggling women.

But such accidents never deterred anyone. Both adults and boys traded constantly in ammunition, "soap," rifle barrels, and bolts, having spent many hours on an inch-by-inch search of the thick undergrowth.

A time fuse was a prize find. It could be traded for a homemade pistol with a wooden stock and twenty rounds of ammunition. A time fuse was necessary to make mines out of soap. All one had to do was stick the fuse into a cake of soap, light it, and quickly run away from the explosion, which would shake the windows of all the houses in the village. There was a big demand for fuses at the time of weddings and baptisms. The explosions were a great additional attraction, and the women shrieked in excitement waiting for the detonation of the mines.

No one knew that I had hidden a time fuse and three soaps in the barn. I had found it in the woods while picking wild thyme for the farmer's wife. The fuse was almost new and had a very long wick.

Sometimes, when there was no one around, I would take out the soaps and the fuse and balance them in my hand. There was something quite extraordinary about these bits of strange substance. The soaps did not burn well by themselves; but when the fuse was placed inside and lit, it did not take long for the flame to crawl along the wick and produce an explosion that could wreck a whole farmhouse.

I tried to visualize the people who invented and made such fuses and mines. They were certain to be German. Didn't they say in the villages that no one could resist the power of the German because he gobbled up the brains of the Poles, Russians, Gypsies, and Jews?

I wondered what gave people the ability to invent such things. Why were the village peasants unable to do it? I wondered what gave people of one color of eyes and hair such great power over other people.

The peasants' plows, scythes, rakes, spinning wheels, wells, and mills turned by sluggish horses or sickly oxen were so simple that even the dullest man could invent them and understand their use and working. But the making of a fuse capable of injecting an overwhelming power into a mine was surely beyond the capacity of even the wisest farmer.

If it was true that the Germans were capable of such inventions, and also that they were determined to clear the world of all swarthy, dark-eyed, long-nosed, black-haired people, then my chances of survival were obviously poor. Sooner or later I would fall into their hands again, and I might not be as lucky as in the past.

I recalled the spectacled German who let me escape into the forest. He was blond and blue-eyed, but he did not appear particularly wise. What sense did it make to stay at a small, derelict station and chase after tiny fry like me? If what the head peasant of the village had said was true, then who was going to make all the inventions when the Germans were busy guarding the little railroad stations? It seemed that even the wisest man could not invent very much at such a miserable station.

I dozed off thinking of the inventions I would like to make. For example, a fuse for the human body which, when lighted, would change old skin for new and alter the color of the eyes and hair. A fuse to place in a pile of construction material that could build a house in a day that would be finer than any in the village. A fuse which could protect anybody from an evil eye. Then nobody would fear me and my life would become easier and more pleasant.

The Germans puzzled me. What a waste. Was such a destitute, cruel world worth ruling?

One Sunday a group of village boys returning from church spotted me on the road. Too late for flight, I feigned indifference, and tried to conceal my fear. Passing by, one of them swung at me and pushed me into a deep, muddy puddle. Others spat straight into my eyes, laughing with each good hit. They demanded some "Gypsy tricks." I tried to break away and run, but the circle tightened around me. Taller than I, they closed over me like a living net trapping a bird. I was afraid of what they might do. Looking down at their heavy Sunday boots, I realized that being barefoot, I could run faster than they. I singled out the largest boy, picked up a heavy stone, and smashed it in his face. The face crumpled and sagged under the blow; the boy fell down bleeding. The others recoiled with shock. In that moment I leapt over the boy and fled across the fields to the village.

When I reached home I looked for the farmer to tell him what had happened and to seek his protection. He had not yet returned from the church with the family. Only the old toothless mother-in-law was wandering around the yard.

My legs went weak under me. A crowd of men and boys approached from the village. They waved clubs and sticks, coming closer with increasing speed.

This had to be my end. The father or brothers of the wounded boy were surely in the crowd and I could expect no mercy. I dashed into the kitchen, shoveled a few glowing coals into my comet, and rushed to the barn, closing the door behind me.

My thoughts were scattering like scared chickens. The crowd would take me into its hands at any moment.

Suddenly I remembered the fuse and the mines. I dug them up quickly. With trembling fingers I stuck the fuse between the tightly lashed soaps and lighted it with the comet. The end of the fuse hissed, and the red spot started crawling slowly along the wick toward the soaps. I pushed it all under a pile of broken plows and harrows in a corner of the barn and frantically pried off a board in the back wall.

The crowd was already in the farmyard and I could hear their shouts. I grabbed the comet and scrambled out of the hole into the thick wheat behind the barn. I plunged into it and ran crouching under cover, boring my way to the forest like a mole.

I was perhaps halfway across the field when the ground shuddered from the explosion. I looked back. Two walls sadly leaning against each other were all that remained of the barn. Between them whirled a mass of splintered boards and swirling hay. A cloud of dust mushroomed above.

I rested after reaching the edge of the forest. I was glad to see that there was no fire at my master's farm. All I could hear was the tumult of voices. No one followed me.

I knew I could never go back there. I continued into the forest, looking carefully through the undergrowth where there were still many cartridges, soaps, and fuses to be found.

9

I wandered for several days in the woods and made attempts to approach the villages. The first time I noticed people running from one house to another, shouting and waving their arms. I did not know what had happened, but it seemed wiser to stay away. In the next village I heard shots, which meant that either partisans or Germans were nearby. Discouraged, I continued my trek for another two days. Finally, hungry and exhausted, I decided to try the next village, which seemed quiet enough.

As I emerged from the bushes I nearly walked into a man plowing a small field. He was a giant with enormous hands and feet. Reddish whiskers covered his face, almost up to the eyes, and his long, disheveled hair stood up like a tangle of reeds. His pale gray eyes watched me warily. Trying to imitate the local dialect, I told him that for a place to sleep and a little food I would milk his cows, clean the stable, take the beasts to pasture, chop wood, set snares for game, and cast spells of all kinds against human and animal ills. The peasant listened carefully, and then took me home without saying a word.

He had no children. His wife, after arguing with

some neighbors, agreed to take me in. I was shown a
sleeping place in the stable and told my duties.

The village was poor. The huts were built of logs
plastered on both sides with clay and straw. The walls
were sunk deeply in the ground and supported thatched
roofs crowned with chimneys made of willow and clay.
Only a few of the peasants had barns, and these were
often built back to back to save one wall. Now and
then German soldiers from a nearby railroad station
came to the village to take any food they could find.

When the Germans were approaching and it was
too late to run for the woods, my master hid me in a
skillfully camouflaged cellar beneath the barn. Its entrance was very narrow and it was at least ten feet
deep. I had helped dig it myself, and no one else,
other than the man and his wife, knew of its existence.

It had a well-stocked larder with large lumps of
butter and cheese, smoked hams, strings of sausages,
bottles of homemade liquor, and other delicacies. The
bottom of the cellar was always cool. While the Germans rushed all over the house searching for food, chasing pigs in the fields, clumsily trying to catch chickens,
I sat there absorbing the delicious fragrances. Often the
soldiers stood on the board covering the entrance to the
cellar. I used to hold my nose to avoid sneezing as I
listened to their strange speech. As soon as the sound
of the army trucks died into the distance the man
would pull me up out of the cellar to resume my usual
duties.

The mushroom season had begun. The hungry villagers welcomed it and went into the woods for their
rich harvest. Every hand was needed and my master
always took me along. Large parties of peasants from
other villages roamed the woods in search of the small
growths. My master realized that I looked like a Gypsy
and, anxious not to be denounced to the Germans, he
shaved my black hair. When going out I put on my
head a large old cap that covered half of my face and

made me less conspicuous. Still, I felt uneasy under the suspicious glances of the other peasants, so I tried always to stay close to my master. I felt that I was sufficiently useful to him to be kept for a while.

On the way to the mushroom gathering we crossed the railroad running through the forest. Several times a day great puffing locomotives passed pulling long freight trains. Machine-guns thrust out of the roofs of the cars and rested on a platform in front of the steam engine. Helmeted soldiers scanned the sky and woods with binoculars.

Then a new kind of train appeared on the line. Living people were jammed in locked cattle cars. Some of the men who worked at the station brought news to the village. These trains carried Jews and Gypsies, who had been captured and sentenced to death. In each car there were two hundred of them stacked like cornstalks, arms raised to take up less space. Old and young, men, women, and children, even babies. Often the peasants from the neighboring village were temporarily employed on the construction of a concentration camp and brought back strange tales. They told us that after leaving the train the Jews were sorted into different groups, then stripped naked and deprived of all their possessions. Their hair was cut off, apparently for use in mattresses. The Germans also looked at their teeth, and if there were any gold ones they were immediately pulled out. The gas chambers and ovens could not cope with the great supply of people; thousands of those killed by gas were not burned but simply buried in pits around the camp.

The peasants listened to these stories thoughtfully. They said the Lord's punishment had finally reached the Jews. They had deserved it long ago, ever since they crucified Christ. God never forgot. If He had overlooked the sins of the Jews so far, He had not forgiven them. Now the Lord was using the Germans as His instrument of justice. The Jews were to be de-

nied the privilege of a natural death. They had to
perish by fire, suffering the torments of hell here on
earth. They were being justly punished for the shameful crimes of their ancestors, for refuting the only True
Faith, for mercilessly killing Christian babies and
drinking their blood.

The villagers now gave me even darker looks.
"You Gypsy-Jew," they yelled. "You'll burn yet, bastard, you will." I pretended that this did not concern
me, even when some shepherds caught me and tried
to drag me to a fire and toast my heels, as was God's
will. I struggled, scratching and biting them. I had no
intention of being burned in such an ordinary campfire
when others were incinerated in special and elaborate
furnaces built by the Germans and equipped with engines more powerful than those of the largest locomotives.

I stayed awake at night worrying whether God
would punish me too. Was it possible that God's wrath
was reserved only for people with black hair and eyes,
who were called Gypsies? Why did my father, whom I
still remembered well, have fair hair and blue eyes,
while my mother was dark? What was the difference between a Gypsy and a Jew, since both were dusky and
both were destined for the same end? Probably after
the war only fair-haired, blue-eyed people would be
left in the world. Then what would happen to children
of blond people who might be born dark?

When the trains carrying Jews went by in the daytime or at dusk, the peasants lined up on both sides of
the track and waved cheerfully to the engineer, the
stoker, and the few guards. Through the small square
windows at the top of the locked cars, one could sometimes glimpse a human face. These people must have
climbed on the shoulders of others to see where they
were going and to find out whose voices they heard outside. Seeing the friendly gestures of the peasants the
people in the car must have thought that they them-

selves were being greeted. Then the Jewish faces would disappear and a mass of thin, pale arms would wave desperate signals.

The peasants watched the trains with curiosity, listening intently to the strange humming sound of the human throng, neither groan, cry, nor song. The train went by, and as it pulled away one could still see against the dark background of the forest disembodied human arms waving tirelessly from the windows.

Sometimes at night people traveling on the trains to the crematories would toss their small children through the windows in the hope of saving their lives. Now and then they managed to wrench up the floorboards and determined Jews might force their way through the hole, hitting the crushed stone track-bed, the rails, or the taut semaphore wire. Slashed by the wheels, their mutilated trunks rolled down the embankment into the tall grass.

Peasants wandering along the tracks in daytime would find these remains and quickly strip them of clothes and shoes. Gingerly, lest they get soiled with the diseased blood of the unbaptized, they ripped the linings off the victims' clothes in search for valuables. There were many disputes and fights over the loot. Later the stripped bodies were left on the track, between the rails, where they were found by the German motorized patrol car which passed once a day. The Germans either poured gasoline over the contaminated bodies and burned them on the spot or buried them nearby.

One day word came to the village that several trains with Jews had passed at night, one after another. The peasants finished their mushroom gathering earlier than usual and then we all went to the railroad tracks. We walked along the line on both sides, in single file, peering into the bushes, looking for signs of blood on the signal pole wires and on the edge of the embankment. There was nothing for a few miles.

Then one of the women spotted some crushed branches in a thicket of wild roses. Someone spread the thorny growth and we saw a small boy of about five sprawled on the ground. His shirt and pants were in shreds. His black hair was long and his dark eyebrows arched. He seemed to be asleep or dead. One of the men stepped on his leg. The boy jerked and opened his eyes. Seeing people leaning over him he tried to say something, but pink froth came from his mouth instead and dripped slowly over his chin and neck. Afraid of his black eyes, the peasants quickly moved aside and crossed themselves.

Hearing voices behind him, the boy tried to turn over. But his bones must have been broken, because he only moaned and a large bloody bubble appeared at his mouth. He fell back and closed his eyes. The peasants watched him suspiciously from a distance. One of the women crept forward, grabbed the worn shoes on his feet, and tore them off. The boy moved, groaned, and coughed up more blood. He opened his eyes and saw the peasants, who darted out of his field of vision, crossing themselves in panic. He closed his eyes again and remained motionless. Two men grabbed him by the legs and turned him over. He was dead. They took off his jacket, shirt, and shorts and carried him to the middle of the track. He was left there and the German patrol car could not miss him.

We turned to go home. I glanced back as we went. The boy was lying on the whitish stones of the track. Only the clump of his black hair remained in view.

I tried to think what he had thought before dying. When he was tossed out of the train his parents or his friends no doubt assured him that he would find human help which would save him from a horrible death in the great furnace. He probably felt cheated, deceived. He would have preferred to cling to the warm bodies of his father and mother in the packed car, to feel the pressure and smell the hot tart odors, the presence of other people, knowing that he was not alone, told by everyone that the journey was only a misunderstanding.

Although I regretted the boy's tragedy, at the bottom of my mind lurked a feeling of relief that he was dead. Keeping him in the village would do no one any good, I thought. He would threaten the lives of all of us. If the Germans heard about a Jewish foundling, they would converge on the village. They would search every house, they would find the boy, and they would also find me in my cellar. They would probably assume that I, too, had fallen off the train and would kill both of us together on the spot, punishing the whole village later.

I pulled the cloth cap over my face, dragging my feet at the end of the line. Wouldn't it be easier to change people's eyes and hair than to build big furnaces and then catch Jews and Gypsies to burn in them?

Mushroom gathering was now a daily chore. Baskets of them were drying everywhere, basketfuls were hidden in lofts and barns. More and more grew in the woods. Every morning people dispersed into the forest with empty baskets. Heavily laden bees, carrying nectar from dying flowers, droned lazily in the autumn sun through the windless peace of the thick undergrowth, guarded by the towers of tall trees.

Bending down to pick the mushrooms, people called to each other in cheerful voices each time they found a rich cluster. They were answered by the soft cacophony of birds calling from the thickets of hazel and juniper, from the branches of oaks and hornbeams. Sometimes the sinister cry of an owl was heard, but no one could see it in its deep, hidden hole in some tree trunk. A reddish fox might scurry away into the dense bushes after a feast of partridge eggs. Vipers would crawl nervously, hissing to give themselves courage. A fat hare would bound into the bush with huge leaps.

The symphony of the forest was broken only by the puffing of a locomotive, the rattle of cars, the grinding of the brakes. People stood still, looking toward the tracks. The birds grew silent, the owl drew deeper into its hole, draping its gray cloak about itself with dignity. The hare stood up, raising its long ears high, and then, reassured, resumed its leaps.

In the weeks that followed, until the mushroom season ended, we often walked along the railroad tracks. Occasionally we passed small oblong heaps of black ashes and some charred bones, broken and trodden into the gravel. With pursed lips the men stopped and stared. Many people feared that even the burnt corpses of those jumping off the train might contaminate both men and animals, and they would hastily kick dirt over the ashes.

Once I pretended to pick up a mushroom which had dropped out of my basket and grasped a handful of this human dust. It stuck to my fingers and smelled of gasoline. I looked at it closely but could find no trace of a person. Yet this ash was not like the ash left in kitchen ovens where wood, dried peat, and moss were burned. I became frightened. It seemed to me, as I rubbed the handful of ash in my fingers, that the ghost of the burned person hovered over me, watching and remembering all of us. I knew that the ghost might never leave me, that it might follow me, haunt me at night, seep sickness into my veins and madness into my brain.

After each train had passed I saw whole battalions of ghosts with ugly, vengeful faces coming into the world. The peasants said the smoke from the crematories went straight to heaven, laying a soft carpet at God's feet, without even soiling them. I wondered whether so many Jews were necessary to compensate

God for the killing of His son. Perhaps the world would soon become one vast incinerator for burning people. Had not the priest said that all were doomed to perish, to go "from ashes to ashes"?

Along the embankment, between the rails, we found innumerable scraps of paper, notebooks, calendars, family photographs, printed personal documents, old passports, and diaries. The pictures were of course the most desirable to collect, since few in the village could read. In many of the pictures elderly people sat stiffly in peculiar clothes. In others, elegantly dressed parents stood with their arms on the shoulders of their children, all smiling and wearing clothing of a type that no one in the village had ever seen. Sometimes we found photographs of beautiful young girls, or handsome young men. There were pictures of old men, who looked like apostles, and old ladies with faded smiles. In some, one could see children playing in a park, babies crying, or newlyweds kissing. On the reverse of these were some farewells, oaths, or religious passages scribbled in handwriting obviously shaken by fear or the motion of the train. The words were often washed off by the morning dew or bleached out by the sun.

The peasants eagerly collected these articles. The women giggled and whispered to one another about the pictures of the men, while the men muttered obscene jokes and comments about the pictures of the girls. People in the village collected these photographs, traded them, and hung them in their huts and barns. In some houses there was a picture of Our Lady on one wall, of Christ on another, a crucifix on the third, and pictures of numerous Jews on the fourth. Farmers would come upon their hired hands exchanging pictures of girls, staring excitedly at them, and playing indecently with each other. And it was said that one of the more attractive village girls fell so hopelessly in love with a handsome man in a photograph that she would not look at her fiancé afterwards.

One day a boy brought back news from the mushroom fields of a Jewish girl found by the railroad tracks. She was alive, with only a sprained shoulder and some bruises. They surmised that she had dropped through a hole in the floor when the train slowed down on a curve, and thus escaped more serious injuries.

Everyone turned out to see this marvel. The girl staggered along, half carried by some men. Her thin face was very pale. She had thick eyebrows and very black eyes. Her long, glossy black hair was tied with a ribbon and fell down her back. Her dress was torn, and I could see bruises and scratches on her white body. With her good arm she tried to hold up the injured one.

The men took her to the house of the village head. A curious crowd assembled, looking her over carefully. She did not seem to understand anything. Whenever any of the men came near her she joined her hands as though in prayer and babbled in a language no one could understand. Terrified, she stared about her with eyes that had blue-white eyeballs and jet-black pupils. The village headman conferred with some of the elders of the village, and also with the man nicknamed Rainbow who had found the Jewess. It was decided that, in accordance with official regulations, she would be sent to the German post the next day.

The peasants slowly dispersed to their homes. But some of the bolder ones stayed on, watching the girl and cracking jokes. Half-blind old women spat thrice in her direction and, muttering under their breath, warned their grandsons.

Then Rainbow took the girl by the arm and led her to his hut. Though some thought him odd, he was well liked in the village. He took special interest in heavenly signs, especially rainbows, hence his nickname. In the evenings when he entertained his neighbors he could talk for hours about rainbows. Listening to him from a dark corner, I learned that a rainbow is a long arched stalk, hollow as a straw. One end is immersed in a river or lake and draws the water off. It is then distributed fairly over the countryside. Fishes and other creatures are drawn up with the water, and that is why one finds the same kind of fish in widely separated lakes, ponds, and rivers.

Rainbow's hut adjoined my master's. His barn shared a wall with the barn in which I slept. His wife had died some time ago but Rainbow, still young, could not decide on another mate. His neighbors used to say that those who stared at rainbows too much could not see an ass in front of their faces. An old woman cooked for Rainbow and looked after his children while he worked in the fields and got drunk once in a while for recreation.

The Jewess was to spend the night at Rainbow's home. That evening I was awakened by noises and cries from his barn. At first I was scared. But I found a knothole through which I could see what was happening. In the middle of the cleaned threshing floor the girl was lying on some sacks. Next to her an oil lamp was burning on an old chopping block. Rainbow sat close to her head. Neither moved. Then Rainbow, with a quick movement, pulled the dress off the girl's shoulders. The strap gave way. The girl tried to escape, but Rainbow kneeled on her long hair and held her face between his knees. He leaned closer. Then he tore the other strap off. The girl cried, but became motionless.

Rainbow crawled to her feet, wedging them between his legs, and with a deft jerk pulled off her dress. She tried to rise and hold on to the material with her good hand, but Rainbow pushed her back. She was now naked. The light of the oil lamp threw shadows on her flesh.

Rainbow sat at the girl's side and stroked her

body with his big hands. His bulk hid her face from me, but I could hear her quiet sobbing broken occasionally by a cry. Slowly Rainbow took off his knee boots and breeches, leaving on only a rough shirt.

He straddled the prostrate girl and moved his hands gently over her shoulders, breasts, and belly. She moaned and whined, uttering strange words in her language when his touch grew rougher. Rainbow lifted himself on his elbows, slipped down a little, and with one brutal push opened her legs and fell on her with a thud.

The girl arched her body, screamed, and kept opening and closing her fingers as though trying to grasp something. Then something strange happened. Rainbow was on top of the girl, his legs between hers, but trying to break away. Every time he hoisted himself, she screamed with pain; he also groaned and cursed. He tried again to detach himself from her crotch, but seemed unable to do so. He was held fast by some strange force inside her, just as a hare or fox is caught in a snare.

He remained on top of the girl, trembling violently. After a while he renewed his efforts, but each time the girl writhed in pain. He also seemed to suffer. He wiped the perspiration off his face, swore, and spat. At his next try the girl wanted to help. She opened her legs wider, lifted her hips, and pushed with her good hand against his belly. It was all in vain. An invisible bond held them together.

I had often seen the same thing happen to dogs. Sometimes when they coupled violently, starved for release, they could not break loose again. They struggled with the painful tie, turning more and more away from each other, finally joined only at their rear ends. They seemed to be one body with two heads, and two tails growing in the same place. From man's friend they became nature's freak. They howled, yelped, and shook all over. Their bloodshot eyes, begging for help, gaped with unspeakable agony at the people hitting them with rakes and sticks. Rolling in the dust and bleeding under the blows, they redoubled their efforts to break apart. People laughed, kicked the dogs, threw screeching cats and rocks at them. The animals tried to run away, but each headed in the opposite direction. They ran in circles. In mad rage they tried to bite each other. Finally they gave up and waited for human help.

Then village boys would throw them into a river or pond. The dogs tried desperately to swim, but each kept pulling away from the other. They were helpless, and their heads only emerged from time to time, frothing at the mouth, too weak to bark. As the current carried them away an amused crowd followed along the riverbank, shouting with joy, throwing stones at their heads as they bobbed out of the water.

On other occasions, people who did not intend to lose their dogs in this manner brutally cut them apart, which meant mutilation or slow death from bleeding for the male. Sometimes the animals managed to separate after wandering around for days, falling into ditches, getting caught in fences and brush.

Rainbow renewed his efforts. He appealed loudly to the Virgin Mary for help. He panted and puffed. He made another big heave, trying to tear himself away from the girl. She screamed and started to hit the bewildered man's face with her fist, scratch him with her nails, bite his hands. Rainbow licked the blood off his lip, lifted himself on one arm, and dealt the girl a powerful blow with the other. Panic must have dimmed his brain, for he collapsed on top of her, biting her breasts, arms and neck. He hammered her thighs with his fists, then grabbed her flesh as if trying to tear it off. The girl screamed with a high-pitched steady cry that finally broke off when her throat dried up—and

then it started again. Rainbow went on beating her until he was exhausted.

They lay, one on top of the other, motionless and
silent. The flickering flame of the oil lamp was the only
thing that moved.

Rainbow started crying for help. His shouts
brought first a band of barking dogs, then some alarmed
men with axes and knives. They opened the door of
the barn and, uncomprehending, goggled at the couple
on the floor. In a hoarse voice, Rainbow quickly explained the situation. They closed the door and, not
letting anyone else enter, sent for a witch-midwife who
knew about such things.

The old woman came, kneeled by the locked couple, and did something to them with the help of others.
I could see nothing; I only heard the girl's last piercing
shriek. Then there was silence and Rainbow's barn
grew dark. At dawn I ran to the knothole. Sunshine
was coming in through the slots between the boards,
lighting up sparkling beams of grain dust. On the
threshing floor, close to the wall, a human shape lay
stretched out flat, covered from head to foot with a
horse blanket.

I had to take the cows to pasture while the village
was still asleep. When I returned at dusk I heard the
peasants discussing the previous night's events. Rainbow had taken the body back to the railroad track,
where the patrol was due to pass in the morning.

For several weeks the village had a lively topic of
conversation. Rainbow himself, when he had taken a
few drinks, would tell people how the Jewess had
sucked him in and wouldn't let go of him.

Strange dreams haunted me at night. I heard
moans and cries in the barn, an icy hand touched me,
black strands of lank hair smelling of gasoline stroked
my face. At dawn when I took the cattle to pasture I
looked fearfully at the mists floating over the fields.
Sometimes the wind would push along a tiny shred of

soot, clearly heading in my direction. I shivered and cold sweat poured down my back. The bit of soot circled over my head, looking me straight in the eye, and then drifted high into heaven.

10

German detachments began to search for partisans in the surrounding forests and to enforce the compulsory deliveries. I knew that my stay in the village was reaching its end.

One night my farmer ordered me to flee at once to the forest. He had been informed of a coming raid. The Germans had learned that a Jew was hiding in one of the villages. He was said to have lived there since the outbreak of the war. The entire village knew him; his grandfather used to own a large tract of land and was greatly liked by the community. As they said, though a Jew, he was a decent enough fellow. I left late that evening. It was an overcast night, but the clouds began separating, stars sprang out, and the moon revealed itself in all its eminence. I hid in a bush.

When dawn came I moved toward the waving ears of grain, keeping far from the village. My toes were stinging from the thick scraping blades of grain, but I tried to reach the center of the field. I had to proceed carefully; I did not want to leave behind too many broken stalks that could betray my presence. Finally I found myself fairly deep in the grain. Shivering from the morning cold, I curled into a ball and tried to sleep.

I woke to hear rough voices coming from all directions. The Germans had surrounded the field. I clung to the earth. As the soldiers strode through the field, the crackling of broken stalks became loud.

They almost stepped on me. Startled, they aimed their rifles at me; when I rose, they readied them. There were two of them, young, in new green uniforms. The taller one grabbed me by the ear, and both laughed, exchanging remarks about me. I understood that they were asking whether I was a Gypsy or a Jew. I denied it. This amused them even more; they kept on joking. All three of us walked toward the village, I ahead and they, laughing, directly behind.

We entered the main road. Terrified peasants spied from behind the windows. When they recognized me they disappeared.

Two large brown trucks stood in the center of the village. Soldiers in unbuttoned uniforms squatted around them drinking from canteens. More soldiers were returning from the fields, stacking their rifles and sitting down.

A few of the soldiers surrounded me. They pointed at me, laughed or grew serious. One of them walked up close to me, leaned over, and smiled straight in my face with a warm, loving smile. I was going to smile back when he suddenly punched me very hard in the stomach. I lost my breath and fell, gasping and groaning. The soldiers burst into laughter.

From a nearby hut an officer emerged, noticed me, and approached. The soldiers snapped to attention. I also stood up, alone in the circle. The officer scrutinized me coldly and issued a command. Two soldiers grabbed me by the arms, dragged me to the hut, opened the door, and shoved me inside.

In the center of the room, in semi-darkness, a man lay. He was small, emaciated, dark. His snarled hair hung over his forehead, a bayonet wound split his entire face. His hands were tied behind him, and a deep wound gaped through the cut jacket sleeve.

I crouched in a corner. The man fixed me with shining black eyes. They seemed to look out from under his thick, overhanging eyebrows and come straight at me. They terrified me. I averted my gaze.

Outside engines were being started; boots, weapons, and canteens rattled. Commands rang out and the trucks departed with a roar.

The door opened and peasants and soldiers entered the hut. They dragged the wounded man out by his hands and dumped him on a seat in a cart. His broken knuckles hung limp as on a swaying dummy. We were seated back to back; I faced the shoulders of the drivers; he the rear of the cart and the receding road. A soldier sat with the two peasants who drove the cart. From the peasants' conversation, I gathered that we were being taken to the police station in a nearby town.

For several hours we rode on a well-traveled road bearing the recent tracks of trucks. Later we left the road and drove through the forest, startling birds and hares. The wounded man sagged listlessly. I was not sure if he was alive; I could only feel his inert body lashed by rope to the cart and me.

We halted twice. The two peasants offered some of their meal to the German, who in return doled out a cigarette and a yellow candy to each of them. The peasants thanked him servilely. They took long draughts from the bottles hidden under the box seat and then urinated in the bushes.

We were ignored. I was hungry and weak. A warm resin-scented breeze drifted from the forest. The wounded man moaned. The horses restlessly tossed their heads, their long tails lashing out against the flies.

We moved on. The German on the cart was breathing heavily, as though in sleep. He closed his gaping mouth only when a fly threatened to swoop into it.

Before sunset we rode into a small, densely built-up town. Here and there the houses had brick walls and chimneys. The fences were painted white or blue. Sleeping doves huddled together on the gutterpipes.

As we passed the first few buildings, children playing in the road noticed us. They surrounded our slow cart and stared at us. The soldier rubbed his eyes, stretched his arms, hitched up his trousers, jumped down, and walked alongside the cart, oblivious to his surroundings.

The troop of children increased; children jumped out of every house. Suddenly one of the older and taller boys struck the prisoner with a long birch twig. The wounded man shuddered and drew back. The children became excited and began pelting us with a barrage of rubbish and rocks. The wounded man drooped. I felt his shoulders, glued to mine, wet with sweat. A few stones hit me also; but I was a more elusive target, sitting between the wounded man and the drivers. The children were making great sport of us. We were being pelted with dried lumps of cow dung, rotten tomatoes, reeking little cadavers of birds. One of the young brutes began to concentrate on me. He walked alongside the cart and with a stick methodically hit selected parts of my body. I tried vainly to ball-up enough saliva to spit into his derisive face.

Adults joined the crowd around the cart. They shrieked, "Beat the Jews, beat the bastards," and egged the children on to further attacks. The drivers, unwilling to expose themselves to accidental blows, jumped off the box seat and walked along beside the horses. The wounded man and I now provided excellent targets. A new hail of stones struck us. My cheek was cut, a broken tooth was dangling, and my lower lip was split. I spat blood into the faces of those nearest to me, but they leapt back adroitly to aim other blows.

Some fiend tore whole bundles of ivy and ferns growing along the roadway out by the root and lashed the wounded man and me. The pain burned at my body, the stones were striking me with more precision, and I dropped my chin on my breast, dreading that some stone might strike my eyes.

Suddenly a small, stout priest leapt out of an unprepossessing house as we were passing by. He wore a torn, faded cassock. Flushed with excitement, he burst into the crowd brandishing a cane, and he began to strike at them on the hands, faces, and heads. Panting, perspiring, trembling with exhaustion, he scattered the mob in all directions.

The priest now walked alongside the cart, slowly regaining his breath. With one hand he wiped his brow and with the other clasped mine. The wounded man had evidently fainted, for his shoulders grew cold as he swayed rhythmically like a puppet tied to a stick.

The cart entered the courtyard of the military police building. The priest had to remain outside. Two soldiers untied the rope, took the wounded man off the cart, and laid him down at the wall. I stood nearby.

Soon afterward a tall SS officer in a soot-black uniform sauntered into the courtyard. Never before had I seen such a striking uniform. At the proud peak of the cap glittered a death's-head and crossbones, while lightninglike signs embellished the collar. A red badge bearing the bold sign of the swastika cut across his sleeve.

The officer received a report from one of the soldiers. Then his heels drummed against the flat concrete surface of the courtyard as he strode to the wounded man. With a deft movement of the tip of his shining jackboot he flipped the man's face toward the light.

The man looked hideous—a mangled face with a rammed-in nose and a mouth hidden by torn skin. Shreds of ivy, lumps of earth, and cow dung were sticking to his eye socket. The officer squatted close to this amorphous head which was reflected in the smooth surface of his boot tops. He was questioning or saying something to the wounded man.

The bloody mass moved like a thousand-pound load. The thin, mutilated body pushed itself by its tied hands. The officer edged away. His face was in the sunshine now, and it had a sheer and compelling beauty, the skin almost waxlike, with flaxen hair as smooth as a baby's. Once before, in a church, I had seen such a delicate face. It was painted on a wall, bathed in organ music, and touched only by light from the stained-glass windows.

The wounded man continued rising until he was nearly sitting. Silence lay over the courtyard like a heavy cloak. The other soldiers stood stiffly, gazing at the spectacle. The wounded man breathed hard. Straining to open his mouth, he swayed like a scarecrow in a gust of wind. Sensing the nearness of the officer he listed in his direction.

The officer, disgusted, was about to rise from his squatting position when suddenly the wounded man moved his mouth again, grunted, and then, extremely loudly, uttered a short word that sounded like "pig" and fell back, striking his head on the concrete.

On hearing this the soldiers quivered and looked at each other stupefied. The squatting officer rose and barked a command. The soldiers clicked their heels, cocked their rifles, approached the man, and pumped rapid shots into him. The shattered body shuddered and grew still. The soldiers reloaded and stood at attention.

Nonchalantly the officer approached me, beating a swagger stick against the seam of his freshly pressed breeches. The instant I saw him I could not tear my gaze from him. His entire person seemed to have something utterly superhuman about it. Against the background of bland colors he projected an unfadable black-ness. In a world of men with harrowed faces, with smashed eyes, bloody, bruised and disfigured limbs, among the fetid, broken human bodies, he seemed an example of neat perfection that could not be sullied: the smooth, polished skin of his face, the bright golden hair showing under his peaked cap, his pure metal eyes. Every movement of his body seemed propelled by some tremendous internal force. The granite sound of his language was ideally suited to order the death of inferior, forlorn creatures. I was stung by a twinge of envy I had never experienced before, and I admired the glittering death's-head and crossbones that embel-lished his tall cap. I thought how good it would be to have such a gleaming and hairless skull instead of my Gypsy face which was feared and disliked by decent people.

The officer surveyed me sharply. I felt like a squashed caterpillar oozing in the dust, a creature that could not harm anyone yet aroused loathing and dis-gust. In the presence of his resplendent being, armed in all the symbols of might and majesty, I was gen-uinely ashamed of my appearance. I had nothing against his killing me. I gazed at the ornate clasp of his officer's belt that was exactly at the level of my eyes, and awaited his decision.

The courtyard was silent again. The soldiers stood about obediently waiting for what would happen next. I knew my fate was being decided in some manner, but it was a matter of indifference to me. I placed infinite confidence in the decision of the man facing me. I knew that he possessed powers unattainable by ordi-nary people.

Another quick command rang out. The officer strode off. A soldier shoved me roughly toward the gate. Regretting that the splendid spectacle was over, I walked slowly through the gate and fell straight into the plump arms of the priest, who was waiting out-side. He looked even shabbier than before. His cassock was a miserable thing in comparison with the uniform adorned by the death's-head, crossbones, and lightning bolts.

11

The priest took me away in a borrowed cart. He said that he would find someone in a nearby village to take care of me until the end of the war. Before reaching the village we stopped at the local church. The priest left me in the cart and went alone to the vicarage, where I saw him arguing with the vicar. They gesticulated and whispered agitatedly. Then they both came toward me. I jumped off the cart and bowed politely to the vicar, kissing his sleeve. He looked at me, gave me his blessing, and returned to the vicarage without saying another word.

The priest drove on and finally stopped at the far end of the village at a rather isolated farmhouse. He went in and stayed there so long that I began to wonder if something had happened to him. A huge wolfhound with a sullen, downcast expression guarded the farmyard.

The priest came out, accompanied by a short, thickset peasant. The dog tucked his tail under his hindquarters and stopped growling. The man looked at me and then stepped aside with the priest. I could hear only snatches of their conversation. The farmer was obviously upset. Pointing to me he shouted that one look was enough to tell I was an unbaptized Gypsy bastard. The priest quietly protested, but the man would not listen. He argued that keeping me might expose him to great danger, since the Germans often visited the village, and if they found me it would be too late for any intervention.

The priest was gradually losing his patience. He suddenly took the man by the arm and whispered something into his ear. The peasant became subdued and, cursing, told me to follow him into the hut.

The priest came closer to me and looked into my eyes. We stared at each other in silence. I did not quite know what to do. Trying to kiss his hand I kissed my own sleeve and became confused. He laughed, made the sign of the cross over my head, and departed.

As soon as he was sure that the priest was gone, the man grabbed me by the ear, almost lifting me off the ground, and pulled me into the hut. When I yelled he jabbed me in the ribs with his finger so hard that I became breathless.

There were three of us in the household. The farmer Garbos, who had a dead, unsmiling face and half-open mouth; the dog, Judas, with sly glowering eyes; and myself. Garbos was a widower. Sometimes in the course of an argument neighbors would mention an orphaned Jewish girl whom Garbos took as a boarder from her escaping parents some time ago. Whenever one of Garbos's cows or pigs damaged some of the crops, the villagers would maliciously remind him of this girl. They would say that he used to beat her daily, rape her, and force her to commit depravities until she finally vanished. Meanwhile, Garbos renovated his farm with the money he received for her keep. Garbos listened angrily to such accusations. He would unleash Judas and threaten to set him against the slanderers. Each time the neighbors locked their doors and watched the evil beast through their windows.

No one ever visited Garbos. He always sat alone

in his hut. My job was to look after two pigs, a cow, a dozen hens, and two turkeys.

Without saying a word Garbos used to beat me unexpectedly, and for no reason. He would steal behind me and hit me on the legs with a whip. He would twist my ears, rub his thumb in my hair, and tickle my armpits and feet until I shook uncontrollably. He regarded me as a Gypsy and ordered me to tell him Gypsy stories. But all I could recite were the poems and stories I had learned at home before the war. Listening to them would sometimes infuriate Garbos, for what reason I never knew. He would beat me again or threaten to turn Judas loose on me.

Judas was a constant menace. He could kill a man with one snap of his jaws. The neighbors often reproached Garbos for having unleashed the beast on someone stealing apples. The thief's throat was torn out and he died immediately.

Garbos always incited Judas against me. Gradually the dog must have become convinced that I was his worst enemy. The sight of me was enough to make him bristle like a porcupine. His bloodshot eyes, his nose and his lips quivered, and froth dripped over his ugly fangs. He strained toward me with such force that I was afraid he might break the guard rope, though I also hoped that he would strangle himself on his leash. Seeing the dog's fury and my fear, Garbos would sometimes untie Judas, lead him only by the collar, and make him back me against the wall. The growling, sputtering mouth was only inches from my throat, and the animal's big body shook with savage fury. He nearly choked, frothing and spitting, while the man urged him on with hard words and sharp proddings. He came so close that his warm, moist breath dampened my face.

At such moments life would almost pass out of me, and my blood would flow through my veins with a slow, sluggish drip, like heavy spring honey trickling

through the narrow neck of a bottle. My terror was
such that it nearly transported me to the other world.
I looked at the beast's burning eyes and at the man's
hairy, freckled hand gripping the collar. At any moment the dog's teeth might close over my flesh. Not
wanting to suffer, I would push my neck forward for
the first quick bite. I understood, then, the fox's mercy
in killing geese by severing their necks in one snap.

But Garbos did not release the dog. Instead he sat
down in front of me drinking vodka and marveling
aloud why such as I were permitted to live when his
boys had died so young. He often asked me that question, and I did not know what to reply. When I failed
to answer he would hit me.

I could not understand what he wanted from me
or why he beat me. I tried to keep out of his way. I
did as I was told, but he continued the beatings. At
night, Garbos would sneak into the kitchen, where I
slept, and awake me by yelling into my ear. When I
jumped up with a scream, he laughed, while Judas
struggled on the chain outside, ready to fight. At other
times, when I was sleeping, Garbos would take the dog
quietly into the room, tie its muzzle with rags, and
then throw the animal on top of me in the darkness.
The dog rolled over me while I, overcome by terror,
not knowing where I was or what was happening,
fought against the huge hairy beast that was scratching
me with its paws.

One day the vicar came in a dogcart to see Garbos. The priest blessed us both, and then he noticed
the black and blue welts on my shoulders and neck and
demanded who had beaten me and why. Garbos admitted that he had to punish me for laziness. The vicar
then admonished him mildly and told him to bring me
to the church the next day.

As soon as the priest had left, Garbos took me
inside, stripped me, and flogged me with a willow
switch, avoiding only the visible parts, such as my

face, arms, and legs. As usual, he forbade me to cry; but when he hit a more sensitive spot, I could not stand the pain and let out a whimper. Droplets of sweat appeared on his forehead and a vein started swelling on his neck. He jammed some thick canvas in my mouth and, passing his tongue over his dry lips, continued flogging me.

Early the next morning I started on my way to church. My shirt and pants were sticking to the bloody patches on my back and buttocks. But Garbos warned me that if I whispered a word about the beating, he would set Judas on me in the evening. I bit my lips, swearing that I would not say a word and hoping that the vicar would not notice anything.

In the brightening light of dawn, a crowd of aged women waited in front of the church. Their feet and bodies were swathed in strips of cloth and wraps of odd sorts, and they babbled endless words of prayer while their cold-benumbed fingers shifted the rosary beads. When they saw the priest coming they rose unsteadily, teetering on their knotty canes, and rapidly shuffled to meet him, contesting for priority in kissing his greasy sleeve. I stood aside, trying to remain unnoticed. But those with the best sight stared at me with disgust, called me a vampire or Gypsy foundling, and spat three times in my direction.

The church always overwhelmed me. And yet it was one of the many houses of God scattered all over the world. God did not live in any of them, but it was assumed for some reason that He was present in all of them at once. He was like the unexpected guest for whom the wealthier farmers always kept an additional place at their table.

The priest noticed me and patted my hair warmly. I grew confused as I answered his questions, assuring him that I was now obedient and that the farmer did not have to beat me any more. The priest asked me about my parents, about our prewar home, and about the church which we had attended but which I could not remember very well. Realizing my total ignorance of religion and church observances, he took me to the organist and asked him to explain the meaning of liturgical objects, and to start preparing me for service as an altar boy at morning Mass and vespers.

I began coming to church twice a week. I waited at the back until the old women had crawled to their pews and then I took a back seat, close to the holy water font, which mystified me tremendously. This water looked like any other water. It had no color, no odor; it looked far less impressive than, for example, ground horse bones. Yet its magic power was supposed to far exceed that of any herb, incantation, or mixture that I had ever seen.

I understood neither the meaning of the Mass nor the role of the priest at the altar. All of this to me was magic, more splendid and elaborate than Olga's witchcraft, but just as difficult to fathom. I looked with wonder at the stone structure of the altar, the finery of the cloths hanging from it, the majestic tabernacle in which the divine spirit dwelled. With awe I touched the fancifully shaped objects stored in the sacristy: the chalice with the shining, polished interior where wine changed into blood, the gilded paten on which the priest dispensed the Holy Ghost, the square, flat burse in which the corporal was kept. This burse opened at one side and resembled a harmonica. How poor Olga's hut was by comparison, full of its evil-smelling frogs, rotting pus from human wounds, and cockroaches.

When the priest was away from the church and the organist was busy with the organ in the balcony, I would stealthily enter the mysterious sacristy to admire the humeral veil which the priest used to slip over his head and with a nimble movement slide down his arms and loop around his neck. I would stroke my fingers voluptuously along the alb placed over the humeral, smoothing out the fringes of the alb belt, smelling the ever-fragrant maniple which the priest wore suspended from his left arm, admiring the precisely measured length of the stole, the infinitely beautiful patterns of the chasubles, whose varied colors, as the priest explained to me, symbolized blood, fire, hope, penance, and mourning.

While mumbling her magic incantations, Olga's face had always taken on changing expressions that aroused fright or respect. She rolled her eyes, shook her head rhythmically, and made elaborate movements with her arms and palms. In contrast, the priest, while saying the Mass, remained the same as in everyday life. He merely wore a different robe and spoke a different language.

His vibrant, sonorous voice seemed to buttress the dome of the church, even awakening the sluggish old women sitting in the tall pews. They would suddenly gather their drooping arms and with difficulty raise their wrinkled eyelids, resembling shriveled, heavy, late-cut peapods. The bleak pupils of their dimmed eyes would glance fearfully around, uncertain of where they were, until, finally beginning anew their rumination of the words from an interrupted prayer, they rocked back to sleep like wilted heather swayed by the wind.

The Mass was ending, the old women thronged the aisles, jockeying to reach the priest's sleeve. The organ fell silent. At the door the organist greeted the priest warmly and gave me a sign with his hand. I had to return to work, to sweep the rooms, feed the cattle, prepare the meal.

Every time I came back from the pasture, the henhouse, or the stable, Garbos would take me into the house and practice, at first casually and then more eagerly, new ways of flogging me with a willow cane, or hurting me with his fists and fingers. My welts and cuts, having no chance to heal, turned into open sores, seeping yellow pus. At night I was so terrified of Judas that I could not sleep. Every slight noise, every creaking of the floorboards, would jolt me into attention. I stared into the impenetrable darkness, pressing my body into the corner of the room. My ears seemed to grow to the size of half-pumpkins, straining to catch any movement in the house or yard.

Even when I finally dozed off my sleep was disturbed by dreams of dogs howling through the countryside. I saw them lifting their heads to the moon, sniffing in the night, and I sensed my approaching death. Hearing their calls, Judas would sneak up to my bed and when he was quite close he would jump on me at Garbos's command and maul me. The touch of his nails would make rising blisters on my body and the local man-of-cures would have to burn them out with a red-hot poker.

I would wake up screaming and Judas would start barking and jumping at the walls of the house. Garbos, half awake, would rush into the kitchen thinking thieves had broken into the farm. When he realized that I had yelled for no reason, he beat and kicked me until he was out of breath. I remained on the mat, bloody and bruised, afraid to fall asleep again and risk another nightmare.

In the daytime I went around in a daze and was beaten for neglecting my work. Sometimes I would fall asleep on the hay in the barn while Garbos looked for me everywhere. When he found me idling, it started all over again.

I came to the conclusion that Garbos's seemingly unmotivated fits of rage must have some mysterious cause. I recalled the magic incantations of Marta and Olga. They were meant to influence diseases and such things that had no obvious connection with the magic itself. I decided to observe all the circumstances accompanying Garbos's attacks of fury. Once or twice I thought I had detected a clue. On two consecutive occasions I was beaten immediately after scratching my head. Who knows, perhaps there was some connection between the lice on my head, which were undoubtedly disturbed in their normal routine by my searching fingers, and Garbos's behavior. I immediately stopped scratching, even though the itching was unbearable. After two days of leaving the lice alone I was beaten again. I had to speculate anew.

My next guess was that the gate in the fence leading to the clover field had something to do with it. Three times after I went through that gate Garbos called me to him and slapped me when I approached him. I concluded that some hostile spirit was crossing my path at the gate and inciting Garbos against me. I decided to avoid the evil one at the gate by scrambling over the fence. This hardly improved matters. Garbos could not understand why I took time to climb over a high fence instead of taking the short route through the gate. He thought I was mocking him on purpose and I got an even worse beating.

He suspected me of malice and tormented me ceaselessly. He amused himself by jabbing a hoe handle between my ribs. He threw me into beds of nettles and thorny bushes, and afterwards laughed at the way I scratched the stings on my skin. He threatened that if I continued to be disobedient he would hold a mouse on my belly as husbands did to unfaithful wives. This terrified me more than anything else. I visualized a mouse under a glass cup on top of my belly button. I could feel the indescribable agony as the trapped rodent gnawed its way through my navel and into my entrails.

I pondered various ways of casting a spell on Garbos, but nothing seemed feasible. One day, when he tied my foot to a stool and tickled it with an ear of rye, I recalled one of old Olga's stories. She had told me of a moth with a death's-head pattern on its body that was similar to the one I had seen on the uniform of the German officer. If one caught such a moth and breathed on it three times the death of the oldest member of the household would shortly follow. That is why young married couples, awaiting their inheritance from living grandparents, spent many nights chasing after these moths.

After that I made a habit of wandering about the house at night when Garbos and Judas were asleep, opening windows to let the moths in. They came in swarms, starting an insane dance of death around the flickering flame, colliding with each other. Others flew into the flame and were burnt alive or stuck in the melting wax of the candle. It was said that Divine Providence had changed them into various creatures and in every new incarnation they had to endure the sufferings most appropriate to their species. But I was little concerned with their penance. I was looking for just one moth, though I had to wave my candle in the window and invite them all in. The light of the candle and my movements startled Judas and his barking woke up Garbos. He sneaked up behind me. Seeing me, candle in hand, jumping all over the room with a swarm of flies, moths, and other insects, he was convinced that I was practicing some sinister Gypsy rite. On the following day I received exemplary punishment.

But I did not give up. After many weeks, just before dawn, I finally caught the desired moth with the strange markings. I breathed on it carefully three times and then let it go. It fluttered around the stove for a few moments and then vanished. I knew that Garbos had only a few days to live. I looked at him with pity. He had no idea that his executioner was on the way from a strange limbo inhabited by disease, pain, and death. Perhaps it was already in the house, waiting eagerly to cut the thread of his life as a sickle cuts a frail stalk. I did not mind being beaten as I stared intently at his face, looking for the signs of death in his eyes. If he only knew what was awaiting him.

However, Garbos continued to look quite strong

and healthy. On the fifth day, when I began to suspect that death was neglecting its duties, I heard Garbos cry out in the barn. I rushed there, hoping to find him breathing his last and calling for the priest, but he was only bending over the dead body of a small turtle he had inherited from his grandfather. It had been quite tame and lived in its own corner of the barn. Garbos was proud of this turtle because it was the oldest creature in the whole village.

Eventually I exhausted all the possible means of bringing about his end. Garbos in the meantime invented new ways of persecuting me. Sometimes he hung me by the arms on a branch of the oak tree, leaving Judas loose underneath. Only the appearance of the priest in his dogcart caused him to discontinue that game.

The world seemed to close over my head like a massive stone vault. I thought of telling the priest what was going on, but I was afraid he would just admonish Garbos and give him a chance to beat me again for complaining. For a while I planned to escape from the village, but there were many German outposts in the neighborhood and I was afraid that, if I was caught by them again, they would take me for a Gypsy bastard, and then who knows what might happen to me.

One day I heard the priest explaining to an old man that for certain prayers God granted from one hundred to three hundred days of indulgence. When the peasant failed to understand the meaning of these words, the priest went into a long exposition. From all this I understood that those who say more prayers earn more days of indulgence, and that this was also supposed to have an immediate influence on their lives; in fact, the greater the number of prayers offered, the better one would live, and the smaller the number, the more troubles and pain one would have to endure.

Suddenly the ruling pattern of the world was revealed to me with beautiful clarity. I understood why some people were strong and others weak, some free and others enslaved, some rich and others poor, some well and others sick. The former had simply been the first to see the need for prayer and for collecting the maximum number of days of indulgence. Somewhere, far above, all these prayers coming from earth were properly classified, so that every person had his bin where his days of indulgence were stored.

I saw in my mind the unending heavenly pastures full of bins, some big and bulging with days of indulgence, others small and almost empty. Elsewhere I could see unused bins to accommodate those who, like myself, had not yet discovered the value of prayer.

I stopped blaming others; the fault was mine alone, I thought. I had been too stupid to find the governing principle of the world of people, animals, and events. But now there was order in the human world, and justice too. One had only to recite prayers, concentrating on the ones carrying the greatest number of days of indulgence. Then one of God's aides would immediately note the new member of the faithful and allocate to him a place in which his days of indulgence would start accumulating like sacks of wheat piled up at harvest time. I was confident in my strength. I believed that in a short while I would collect more days of indulgence than other people, that my bin would fill quickly, and that heaven would have to assign me a larger one; and even that would overflow, and I would need a bigger one, as big as the church itself.

Feigning casual interest, I asked the priest to show me the prayer book. I quickly noted the prayers marked with the largest number of indulgence days and asked him to teach them to me. He was somewhat surprised by my preference for some prayers and indifference to others, but he agreed and read them to me several times. I made an effort to concentrate all the powers of my mind and body in memorizing them. I soon knew them perfectly. I was ready to start a new life. I had all that was needed and gloried in the knowledge that the days of punishment and humiliation would soon be past. Until now I had been a small bug that anyone might squash. From now on the humble bug would become an unapproachable bull.

There was no time to lose. Any spare moment could be used for one more prayer, thus earning additional days of indulgence for my heavenly account. I would soon be rewarded with the Lord's grace, and Garbos would not torment me any more.

I now devoted my entire time to prayers. I rattled them off quickly, one after another, occasionally slipping in one that carried fewer days of indulgence. I did not want heaven to think that I neglected the more humble prayers completely. After all, one could not outwit the Lord.

Garbos could not understand what had happened to me. Seeing me continuously mumbling something under my breath and paying little attention to his threats, he suspected that I was casting Gypsy spells on him. I did not want to tell him the truth. I was afraid that in some unknown manner he might forbid me to pray or, even worse, as a Christian of older standing than myself, use his influence in heaven to nullify my prayers or perhaps divert some of them to his own undoubtedly empty bin.

He started to beat me more often. Sometimes when he asked me something and I was in the middle of a prayer I would not answer him immediately, anxious not to lose the days of indulgence which I was just earning. Garbos thought I was getting impudent and wanted to break me down. He was also afraid that I might get bold enough to tell the priest about the beatings. Thus my life was spent alternately praying and being beaten.

I muttered prayers continuously from dawn to dusk, losing count of the days of indulgence I was earning, but almost seeing their pile constantly rising until some of the saints, stopping on their strolls through the heavenly pastures, looked approvingly at the flocks of prayers soaring up from earth like sparrows—all coming from a small boy with black hair and black eyes. I visualized my name being mentioned at the councils of angels, then at those of some minor saints, later at those of major saints, and so closer and closer to the heavenly throne.

Garbos thought that I was losing respect for him. Even when he was beating me harder than usual, I did not lose time but continued collecting my days of indulgence. After all, pain came and went, but the indulgences were in my bin forever. The present was bad precisely because I had not known earlier about such a marvelous way of improving my future. I could not afford to lose any more time; I had to make up for lost years.

Garbos was now convinced that I was in a Gypsy trance which could bring no good. I swore to him that I was only praying, but he did not believe me.

His fears were soon confirmed. One day a cow broke through the barn door and went into a neighbor's garden, causing considerable damage. The neighbor was furious and rushed into Garbos's orchard with an ax and cut down all the pear and apple trees in revenge. Garbos was sleeping dead drunk, and Judas was helplessly straining at his chain. To complete the disaster a fox got into the henhouse the next day and killed some of the best laying hens. That same evening, with one stroke of his paw, Judas massacred Garbos's pride, a fine turkey he had purchased recently at great expense.

Garbos broke down completely. He got drunk on homemade vodka and revealed to me his secret. He would have killed me long ago had he not been afraid of St. Anthony, his patron. He knew, too, that I had counted his teeth and that my death would cost him many years of his life. Of course, he added, if Judas should kill me accidentally, then he would be perfectly safe from my spells and St. Anthony would not punish him.

In the meantime the priest was sick at the vicarage. He apparently caught a cold in the chilly church. He was lying in a fevered and hallucinatory state in his room, talking to himself or to God. I once took the vicar some eggs, a gift from Garbos. I climbed on the fence to see the vicar. His face was pale. His older sister, a short, buxom woman with her hair piled in a bun, was fussing about the bed and the local wise woman was letting his blood and applying leeches which grew plump as soon as they fastened on his body.

I was astonished. The priest must have accumulated an extraordinary number of days of indulgence during his pious life, and yet here he was lying sick like anybody else.

A new priest arrived at the vicarage. He was old, bald, and had a very thin, parchmentlike face. He wore a violet band on his cassock. When he saw me returning with the basket he called me and asked me where I, with my swarthy looks, had come from. The organist, seeing us together, quickly whispered some words to the priest. He gave me his blessing and walked away.

The organist then told me that the vicar did not want me to make myself too conspicuous at church. Many people came there, and although the priest believed that I was neither a Gypsy nor a Jew, the suspicious Germans might take a different view and the parish would suffer severe reprisals.

I quickly rushed to the church altar. I started reciting prayers desperately, and again only those with the greatest number of days of indulgence attached to them. I had little time left. Besides, who knows, perhaps prayers at the altar itself, under the tearful eye of God's Son and the motherly gaze of the Virgin Mary, might carry greater weight than those said elsewhere.

They might have a shorter route to travel to heaven, or they might possibly be carried by a special messenger using a faster conveyance, like a train on rails. The organist saw me alone in the church and reminded me again about the new priest's warning. So I bade farewell regretfully to the altar and all its familiar objects.

Garbos was waiting for me at home. As soon as I entered he dragged me to an empty room in the corner of the house. There at the highest point of the ceiling two large hooks had been driven into the beams, less than two feet apart. Leather straps were attached to each as handles.

Garbos climbed on a stool, lifted me high, and told me to grab a handle with each hand. Then he left me suspended and brought Judas into the room. On his way out he locked the door.

Judas saw me hanging from the ceiling and immediately jumped up in an effort to reach my feet. I brought my legs up and he missed them by a few inches. He started another run and tried again, still missing. After a few more tries he lay down and waited.

I had to watch him. When freely hanging, my feet were no more than six feet above the ground and Judas could easily reach them. I did not know how long I would have to hang like this. I guessed that Garbos expected me to fall down and be attacked by Judas. This would frustrate the efforts I had been making all these months, counting Garbos's teeth, including the yellow, ingrown ones at the back of his mouth. Innumerable times when Garbos was drunk with vodka and snored openmouthed I had counted his loathsome teeth painstakingly. This was my weapon against him. Whenever he beat me too long I reminded him of the number of his teeth; if he did not believe me he could check the count himself. I knew every one of them, no matter how wobbly, how putrefied, or how nearly hidden under the gums. If he killed me he would have very few years left to live. However, if I fell down into the waiting fangs of Judas, Garbos would have a clear conscience. He would have nothing to fear, and his patron, St. Anthony, might even give him absolution for my accidental death.

My shoulders were becoming numb. I shifted my weight, opened and closed my hands, and slowly relaxed my legs, lowering them dangerously near to the floor. Judas was in the corner pretending to be asleep. But I knew his tricks as well as he knew mine. He knew that I still had some strength left and that I could lift my legs faster than he could leap after them. So he waited for fatigue to overcome me.

The pain in my body raced in two directions. One went from the hands to the shoulders and neck, the other from the legs to the waist. They were two different kinds of pain, boring toward my middle like two moles tunneling toward each other underground. The pain from my hands was easier to endure. I could cope with it by switching my weight from one hand to the other, relaxing the muscles and then taking the load up again, hanging on one hand while blood returned to the other. The pain from my legs and abdomen was more persistent, and once it settled in my belly it refused to leave. It was like a woodworm that finds a cozy spot behind a knot in the timber and stays there forever.

It was a strange, dull, penetrating pain. It must have been like the pain felt by a man Garbos mentioned in warning. Apparently this man had treacherously killed the son of an influential farmer and the father had decided to punish the murderer in the old-fashioned manner. Together with his two cousins the man brought the culprit to the forest. There they prepared a twelve-foot stake, sharpened at one end to a fine point like a gigantic pencil. They laid it on the ground, wedging the blunt end against a tree trunk. Then a strong horse was hitched to each of the victim's feet, while his crotch was leveled with the waiting point. The horses, gently nudged, pulled the man against the spiked beam, which gradually sank into the tensed flesh. When the point was deep into the entrails of the victim, the men lifted the stake, together with the impaled man upon it and planted it in a previously dug hole. They left him there to die slowly.

Now hanging under the ceiling I could almost see the man and hear him howling into the night, trying to raise to the indifferent sky his arms which hung by the bloated trunk of his body. He must have looked like a bird knocked out of a tree by a slingshot and fallen flabbily onto a dried-out, pointed stalk.

Still feigning indifference, Judas woke up below. He yawned, scratched behind his ears, and hunted the fleas in his tail. Sometimes he glanced slyly at me, but turned away in disgust when he saw my hunched legs.

He only fooled me once. I thought he had really gone to sleep and straightened out my legs. Judas instantly bounced off the floor, leaping like a grasshopper. One of my feet did not jerk up fast enough and he tore off some skin at the heel. The fear and pain almost caused me to fall. Judas licked his chops triumphantly and reclined by the wall. He watched me through the slits of his eyes and waited.

I thought I could not hold on any longer. I decided to jump down and planned my defense against Judas, though I knew that I wouldn't even have time to make a fist before he would be at my throat. There was no time to lose. Then suddenly I remembered the prayers.

I started shifting weight from one hand to the other, moving my head, jerking my legs up and down. Judas looked at me, discouraged by this display of strength. Finally he turned toward the wall and remained indifferent.

Time went by and my prayers multiplied. Thousands of days of indulgence streaked through the thatched roof toward heaven.

Late in the afternoon Garbos came into the room.

He looked at my wet body and the pool of sweat on the floor. He took me off the hooks roughly and kicked the dog out. All that evening I could neither walk nor move my arms. I lay down on the mattress and prayed. Days of indulgence came in hundreds, in thousands. Surely by now there were more of them in heaven for me than grains of wheat in the field. Any day, any minute, notice of this would have to be taken in heaven. Perhaps even now the saints were considering some radical improvement of my life.

Garbos hung me up every day. Sometimes he did it in the morning and sometimes in the evening. And had he not been afraid of foxes and thieves and needed Judas in the yard, he would have done it at night too.

It was always the same. While I still had some strength the dog stretched out on the floor calmly, pretending to sleep or casually catching fleas. When the pain in my arms and legs became more intense, he grew alert as though sensing what was going on inside my body. Sweat poured from me, running in rivulets over my straining muscles, hitting the floor with regular plip-plops. As soon as I straightened my legs Judas invariably leapt at them.

Months went by. Garbos needed me more around the farm because he was often drunk and didn't want to work. He hung me up only when he felt he had no particular use for me. When he sobered up and heard the hungry pigs and the lowing cow he took me off the hooks and put me to work. The muscles of my arms became conditioned by the hanging and I could endure it for hours without much effort. Although the pain that came to my belly began later now, I got cramps which frightened me. And Judas never missed a chance to leap at me, though by now he must have doubted he would ever catch me off guard.

Hanging on the straps I concentrated on my prayers to the exclusion of all else. When my strength ebbed I told myself that I should be able to last another ten or twenty prayers before I dropped down. After these were recited I made another promise of ten or fifteen prayers. I believed that something could happen at any moment, that every extra thousand days of indulgence could save my life, perhaps at this very instant.

Occasionally, to divert my attention from the pain and from my numb arm muscles, I teased Judas. First I swung on my arms as though I were about to fall down. The dog barked, jumped, and raged. When he went to sleep again I would wake him with cries and the smacking of lips and grinding of teeth. He could not understand what was happening. Thinking that this was the end of my endurance, he leapt about madly, knocking into the walls in the darkness, overturning the stool standing by the door. He grunted with pain, heaved heavily, and finally rested. I took the opportunity to straighten my legs. When the room resounded to the snoring of the fatigued beast, I saved strength by setting prizes for myself for endurance: straightening one leg for every thousand days of indulgence, resting one arm for every ten prayers, and one major shift of position for every fifteen prayers.

At some unexpected moment I would hear the clatter of the latch and Garbos would enter. When he saw me alive he would curse Judas, kick and beat him until the dog cried and whimpered like a puppy.

His fury was so tremendous that I wondered if God Himself had not sent him at this moment. But when I looked at his face, I could find no trace of the divine presence.

I was now beaten less often. The hanging took up a lot of time and the farm required attention. I wondered why he went on hanging me up. Did he really expect the dog to kill me when it had failed to do so all these times?

After each hanging I took a while to recover. Muscles stretched like yarn on the spinning wheel refused to retract to their normal span. I moved with difficulty. I felt like a stiff, frail stem trying to support the burden of a sunflower blossom.

When I was slow at my work Garbos used to kick me and say that he would not shelter an idler, and threaten to send me to the German outpost. I tried to work harder than ever to convince him of my usefulness, but he was never satisfied. Whenever he got drunk he put me on the hooks with Judas waiting patiently below.

The spring passed. I was already ten years old and I had accumulated who knows how many days of indulgence for each day of my life. A great church feast was approaching and people in the villages were busy preparing festive clothes. The women made wreaths of wild thyme, sundew, linden, apple flowers, and wild carnations which would be blessed in the church. The nave and the altars of the church were decorated with green branches of birch, poplar, and willow. After the feast, these branches would acquire great value. They would be planted in vegetable beds, in cabbage, in hemp, and flax fields, to ensure rapid growth and protection against pests.

On the day of the feast Garbos went to the church early in the morning. I remained at the farm bruised and aching from my last beating. The broken echo of tolling church bells rolled over the fields and even Judas stopped lounging in the sun and listened.

It was Corpus Christi. It was said that on this fete day the bodily presence of the Son of God would make itself felt in the church more than on any other feast. Everybody went to church that day: the sinners and the righteous, those who prayed constantly and those who never prayed, the rich and the poor, the sick and the well. But I was left alone with a dog that had no chance of achieving a better life, even though it was one of God's creatures.

I made a quick decision. The store of prayers

which I had accumulated could surely rival those of many younger saints. And even though my prayers had not produced perceptible results, they must have been noticed in heaven, where justice is the law.

I had nothing to fear. I started on my way to the church, walking along the untilled strips which separated the fields from each other.

The churchyard was already overflowing with an unusually colorful throng of people and their gaily decorated carts and horses. I crouched in a hidden corner, waiting for an opportune moment to slip into the church by one of the side doors.

Suddenly the vicar's housekeeper spotted me. One of the altar boys selected for the day had fallen sick with poisoning, she said. I had to go immediately into the vestry, change, and take his place at the altar. The new priest had ordered it himself.

A hot wave swept over me. I looked at the sky. At last someone up there had noticed me. They saw my prayers lying in a huge heap like potatoes piled high at harvest time. In a moment I would be close to Him, at His altar, within the protection of His vicar. This was only a beginning. From now on a different, easier life would begin for me. I had seen the end of terror that shakes one until it squeezes the stomach empty of vomit, like a punctured poppy pod blown open by the wind. No more beatings from Garbos, no more hangings, no more Judas. A new life lay before me, a life as smooth as the yellow fields of wheat waving under the gentle breath of the breeze. I ran to the church.

It was not easy to get inside. The garish crowd overflowed around the churchyard densely. Someone saw me immediately and drew attention to me. The peasants rushed at me and began to scourge me with osier branches and horsewhips, the older peasants laughing so hard that they had to lie down. I was dragged under a cart and then tied to the tail of a horse. I was held fast between the shafts. The horse neighed and reared and kicked me once or twice before I succeeded in freeing myself.

I reached the vestry trembling, and my body ached. The priest, impatient at my delay, was ready to proceed; the ministrants had also finished dressing. I shook with nervousness as I put on the altar boy's sleeveless mantle. Whenever the priest looked away the other boys tripped me up or poked me in the back. The priest, puzzled by my slowness, became so furious that he shoved me roughly; I fell on a bench, bruising my arm. Finally everything was ready. The doors of the vestry opened and in the stillness of the crowded, expectant church we took our places at the foot of the altar, three of us on each side of the priest.

The Mass proceeded in all its splendor.

The priest's voice was more melodious than usual; the organ thundered with its thousand turbulent hearts; the altar boys carried out solemnly their meticulously inculcated functions.

I was suddenly jabbed in the ribs by the altar boy standing next to me. He gestured nervously toward the altar with his head. I stared uncomprehendingly as blood pounded in my temples. He gestured again, and I noticed that the priest himself was throwing me expectant glances. I was supposed to do something, but what? I panicked, I lost my breath. The acolyte turned toward me and whispered that I must carry the missal.

Then I realized that it was my duty to transfer the missal from one side of the altar to the other. I had seen this done many times before. An altar boy would approach the altar, grasp the missal together with the base on which it stood, walk backward to the center of the lowest step in front of the altar, kneel holding the missal in his hands, then rise and carry the missal to the other side of the altar, and finally return to his place.

Now it was my turn to perform all this.

I felt the gaze of the entire crowd on me. At the

same time the organist, as if to attach deliberate importance to this scene of a Gypsy assisting at the altar of God, suddenly hushed the organ.

Absolute silence held the church.

I mastered the trembling of my legs and climbed the steps to the altar. The missal, the Holy Book filled with sacred prayers collected for the greater glory of God by the saints and learned men throughout the centuries, stood on a heavy wooden tray with legs tipped by brass balls. Even before I laid my hands on it I knew that I would not have strength enough to lift it and carry it to the other side of the altar. The book itself was too heavy, even without the tray.

But it was too late to withdraw. I stood on the altar platform, the lean flames of the candles flickering in my eyes. Their uncertain flutter made the agony-racked body of the crucified Jesus seem almost lifelike. But when I examined His face, it did not seem to be gazing; the eyes of Jesus were fixed somewhere downward, below the altar, below us all.

I heard an impatient hiss behind me. I placed my sweaty palms under the cool tray of the missal, breathed deeply, and straining to the utmost, raised it. I cautiously stepped back, feeling the edge of the step with my toe. Suddenly, in an instant of time as brief as the prick of a needle, the weight of the missal grew overwhelming and tipped me backward. I staggered and could not regain my balance. The ceiling of the church reeled. The missal and its tray tumbled down the steps. An involuntary shout sprang from my throat. Almost simultaneously my head and shoulders struck against the floor. When I opened my eyes angry, red faces were bent over me.

Rough hands tore me up from the floor and pulled me toward the doorway. The crowd parted in stupefaction. From the balcony a male voice shouted "Gypsy vampire!" and several voices took up the chant. Hands clamped my body with excruciating hardness, tearing at my flesh. Outside I wanted to cry and beg for mercy, but no sound came from my throat. I tried once more. There was no voice in me.

The fresh air hit my heated body. The peasants dragged me straight toward a large manure pit. It had been dug two or three years ago, and the small outhouse standing next to it with small windows cut in the shape of the cross was the subject of special pride to the priest. It was the only one in the area. The peasants were accustomed to attending to the wants of nature directly in the field and only used it when coming to church. A new pit was being dug on the other side of the presbytery, however, because the old pit was completely full and the wind often carried foul odors to the church.

When I realized what was going to happen to me, I again tried to shout. But no voice came from me. Every time I struggled a heavy peasant hand would drop on me, gagging my mouth and nose. The stench from the pit increased. We were very close to it now. Once more I tried to struggle free, but the men held me fast, never ceasing their talk about the event in the church. They had no doubt that I was a vampire and that the interruption of the High Mass could only bode evil for the village.

We halted at the edge of the pit. Its brown, wrinkled surface steamed with fetor like horrible skin on the surface of a cup of hot buckwheat soup. Over this surface swarmed a myriad of small white caterpillars, about as long as a fingernail. Above circled clouds of flies, buzzing monotonously, with beautiful blue and violet bodies glittering in the sun, colliding, falling toward the pit for a moment, and soaring into the air again.

I retched. The peasants swung me by the hands and feet. The pale clouds in the blue sky swam before my eyes. I was hurled into the very center of the brown filth, which parted under my body to engulf me.

Daylight disappeared above me and I began to suffocate. I tossed instinctively in the dense element, lashing out with my arms and legs. I touched the bottom and rebounded from it as fast as I could. A spongy upswell raised me toward the surface. I opened my mouth and caught a dash of air. I was sucked back below the surface and again pushed myself up from the bottom. The pit was only twelve feet square. Once more I sprang up from the bottom, this time toward the edge. At the last moment, when the downswell was about to pull me under, I caught hold of a creeper of the long thick weeds growing over the edge of the pit. I fought against the suction of the reluctant maw and pulled myself to the bank of the pit, barely able to see through my slime-obscured eyes.

I crawled out of the mire and was immediately gripped with cramps of vomiting. They shook me so long that my strength vanished and I slid down completely exhausted into the stinging, burning bushes of thistle, fern, and ivy.

I heard the distant sound of the organ and human singing and I reasoned that after the Mass the people might come out of the church and drown me again in the pit if they saw me alive in the bushes. I had to escape and so I darted into the forest. The sun baked the brown crust on me and clouds of large flies and insects besieged me.

As soon as I found myself in the shade of the trees I started rolling over in the cool, moist moss, rubbing myself with cold leaves. With pieces of bark I scraped off the remaining muck. I rubbed sand in my hair and then rolled in the grass and vomited again.

Suddenly I realized that something had happened to my voice. I tried to cry out, but my tongue flapped helplessly in my open mouth. I had no voice. I was terrified and, covered with cold sweat, I refused to believe that this was possible and tried to convince myself that my voice would come back. I waited a few moments and tried again. Nothing happened. The silence of the forest was broken only by the buzzing of the flies around me.

I sat down. The last cry that I had uttered under the falling missal still echoed in my ears. Was it the last cry I would ever utter? Was my voice escaping with it like a solitary duck call straying over a huge pond? Where was it now? I could envision my voice flying alone under the high-arched, vaulting ribs of the church roof. I saw it knocking against the cold walls, the holy pictures, against the thick panes of colored glass in the windows, which the sun's rays could scarcely penetrate. I followed its aimless wanderings through the dark aisles, where it wafted from the altar to the pulpit, from the pulpit to the balcony, from the balcony to the altar again, driven by the multichorded sound of the organ and the groundswell of the singing crowd.

All the mutes I had ever seen paraded by under my lids. There were not very many of them and their absence of speech made them seem very much alike. The absurd twitching of their faces tried to substitute for the missing sound of their voices, while the frantic movement of their limbs took the place of their unforthcoming words. Other people always looked at them with suspicion; they appeared like strange creatures, shaking, grimacing, dribbling heavily down their chins.

There must have been some cause for the loss of my speech. Some greater force, with which I had not yet managed to communicate, commanded my destiny. I began to doubt that it could be God or one of His saints. With my credit secured by vast numbers of prayers, my days of indulgence must have been innumerable; God had no reason to inflict such terrible punishment on me. I had probably incurred the wrath of some other forces, which spread their tentacles over those God had abandoned for some reason or other.

I walked farther and farther from the church, plunging into the thickening forest. From the black earth that the sun never reached stuck out the trunks of trees cut down long ago. These stumps were now cripples unable to clothe their stunted mutilated bodies. They stood single and alone. Hunched and squat, they lacked the force to reach up toward the light and air. No power could change their condition; their sap would never rise up into limbs or foliage. Large knotholes low on their boles were like dead eyes staring eternally with unseeing pupils at the waving crests of their living brethren. They would never be torn or tossed by the winds but would rot slowly, the broken victims of the dampness and decay of the forest floor.

12

When the village boys who were lying in wait for me in the forest caught me at last, I expected something terrible to happen to me. Instead, I was taken to the head of the village. He made certain that I had no sores or ulcers on my body and that I could make the sign of the cross. Then, after several unsuccessful attempts to place me with other peasants, he handed me over to a farmer called Makar.

Makar lived with his son and daughter on a farmstead set apart from the rest of the settlement. Apparently his wife had died long ago. He himself was not well known in the village. He had arrived only a few years before and was treated as a stranger. But rumors circulated that he avoided other people because he sinned both with the boy he called his son and with the girl he called his daughter. Makar was short and stocky, and had a thick neck. He suspected I only pretended to be mute to avoid betraying my Gypsy speech. Sometimes at night he would rush into the tiny attic in which I slept and try to force a scream of fear from me. I would awake shaking and open my mouth like a baby chick wanting to be fed, but no sound came out. He watched me intently and seemed disappointed. After repeating the test from time to time, he eventually gave up.

His son Anton was twenty years old. He was a redhead with pale eyes and no eyelashes. He was shunned in the village as much as his father. When someone spoke to him he would glance indifferently at the speaker and then turn silently away. They called him the Quail, because he was like that bird in his habit of speaking only to himself and never answering other voices.

There was also the daughter Ewka, a year younger than the Quail. She was tall and blond and thin with breasts like unripe pears and hips that allowed her to squeeze easily between the staves of a fence. Ewka never visited the village either. When Makar went with Quail to sell rabbits and rabbit skins in the neighboring villages, she remained alone. She was visited occasionally by Anulka, the local purveyor of cures.

Ewka was not liked by the villagers. The peasants said she had a ram in her eyes. They laughed at the goiter which was beginning to disfigure her neck, and at her hoarse voice. They said that the cows lost their milk in her presence, and that was why Makar kept only rabbits and goats.

I often heard peasants mutter that Makar's strange family should be turned out of the village and his house burned down. But Makar did not listen to such threats. He always carried a long knife in his sleeve, and he could throw it with such perfect aim that he once pinned a cockroach to a wall at five paces. And Quail held a hand grenade in his pocket. He had found it on a dead partisan, and he always threatened the person and family of anyone who bothered him or his father or sister.

Makar kept a trained wolfhound, which he called Ditko, in the backyard. There were the rabbit cages arranged in rows in the outbuildings surrounding the yard. Only wire netting separated the cages from one another. The rabbits sniffed and communicated while Makar could watch them all at one glance.

Makar was a rabbit expert. In his cages he had many splendid specimens too costly for even the wealthiest farmers. At the farm he had four she-goats and a male goat. The Quail looked after them, milked them, took them out to pasture, and sometimes locked himself up with them in the stable. When Makar came home after a successful sale, both he and his son would get drunk and go to the goats' quarters. Ewka used to hint maliciously that they were enjoying themselves in there. At such times Ditko was tied close to the door to prevent anyone approaching.

Ewka did not like her brother and father. Sometimes she would not leave the house for days, fearing that Makar and Quail would force her to spend the whole afternoon with them in the goats' stable.

Ewka liked to have me around when she was cooking. I helped to peel the vegetables, brought firewood, and carried out the ashes.

Sometimes she asked me to sit close to her legs and kiss them. I used to cling to her slim calves and start kissing them very slowly from the ankles, first with a light touch of the lips and gentle strokes of the hand along the taut muscles, kissing the soft hollow under her knee, up on the smooth white thighs. I gradually lifted her skirt. I was urged on by light taps on my back, and I hastened upward, kissing and half biting the tender flesh. When I reached the warm mound, Ewka's body began to shake spasmodically. She ran her fingers wildly through my hair, caressed my neck and pinched my ears, panting faster and faster. Then she pressed my face hard against herself and after a moment of trance fell back on the bench, all spent.

I also liked what followed next. Ewka sat on the bench, holding me between her open legs, hugging and caressing me, kissing me on my neck and face. Her dry heatherlike hair fell over my face as I looked into her pale eyes and saw a scarlet blush spread from her face to her neck and shoulders. My hands and mouth revived again. Ewka began to tremble and breathe deeper, her mouth turned cold and her shaking hands pulled me to her body.

When we heard the men coming, Ewka would rush to the kitchen, fixing her hair and skirts, while I ran to the rabbit hutches for the evening feeding.

Later, after Makar and his son had gone to sleep, she brought me my meal. I ate it quickly while she lay down naked by my side, eagerly stroking my legs, kissing my hair, hastily removing my clothes. We would lie together and Ewka would press her body tightly to mine, asking me to kiss and suck her, now here, and now there. I followed all her wishes, doing all kinds of things even if they were painful or meaningless. Ewka's motions became spasms, she twitched under me, then scrambled on top, then made me sit on her, grasped me eagerly, dug her nails into my back and shoulders. We spent most of the nights like this, dozing off from time to time, and waking again to yield to her seething emotions. Her whole body seemed to be tormented by secret internal eruptions and tensions. It grew taut like a rabbit skin stretched on a board to dry, and then it relaxed again.

At times Ewka would come for me at the rabbit huts in the daytime, when Quail was alone with the goats and Makar had not yet returned home. We jumped over the fence together and disappeared in the high-growing wheat. Ewka led the way and chose a safe hiding place. We would lie down on the stubbly ground, where Ewka urged me to undress faster, and tugged impatiently at my clothes. I sank onto her and tried to satisfy all her different whims, while the heavy ears of wheat moved over us like the swells of the tranquil pond. Ewka would fall asleep for a few moments. I scanned this golden river of wheat, noticing the bluebottles timidly hovering in the sun's rays.

Higher up the swallows promised good weather with their intricate gyrations. Butterflies circled in carefree pursuit and a lonely hawk hung high in the sky, like an eternal warning, waiting for some unsuspecting pigeon.

I felt secure and happy. Ewka moved in her nap, her hand sought me instinctively, and it bent the wheat stalks on its way to me. I crawled over to her and worked my way between her legs and kissed her.

Ewka tried to make me become a man. She would visit me at night and tickle my parts, painfully pushing in thin straws, squeezing, licking. I was surprised to perceive something I had not known before; things over which I had no control began to happen. It was still spasmodic and unpredictable, sometimes rapid, sometimes slow, but I knew I could not stop the feeling any more.

When Ewka fell asleep at my side, muttering through her dreams, I pondered all those things, listening to the sounds of the rabbits around us.

There was nothing I would not do for Ewka. I forgot my fate of a Gypsy mute destined for fire. I ceased to be a goblin jeered at by herders, casting spells on children and animals. In my dreams I turned into a tall, handsome man, fair-skinned, blue-eyed, with hair like pale autumn leaves. I became a German officer in a tight, black uniform. Or I turned into a bird-catcher, familiar with all the secret paths of the woods and marshes.

In these dreams my artful hands induced wild passions in the village girls, turning them into wanton Ludmilas who chased me through flowery glades, lying with me on beds of wild thyme, among fields of goldenrod.

I clung to Ewka in my dreams, seizing her like a spider, entwining as many legs around her as a centipede has. I grew into her body like a small twig, grafted on a broad-limbed apple tree by a skillful gardener.

There was another recurring dream, bringing a

different kind of vision. Ewka's attempt to make a grown man of me succeeded instantly. One part of my body grew rapidly into a monstrous shaft of incredible size, while the rest remained unchanged. I became a hideous freak; I was locked in a cage and people watched me through bars, laughing excitedly. Then Ewka came naked through the crowd and joined me in a grotesque embrace. I became a horrible growth on her smooth body. The witch Anulka lurked nearby with a big knife, ready to cut me away from the girl, to mutilate me foully and throw me to the ants.

The sounds of dawn ended my nightmares. The hens squawked, the roosters crowed, the rabbits stamped their feet in hunger, while Ditko, annoyed by it all, started growling and barking. Ewka furtively hurried home and I surrendered to the rabbits the grass our bodies had warmed.

Makar inspected the hutches several times daily. He knew all the rabbits by name and nothing escaped his attention. He had some favorite females whose grazing he watched over himself, and he would not leave their cages when they had their litters. One of the females was particularly loved by Makar. She was a white giant with pink eyes and had not had any young. Makar used to take her to the house and keep her there for several days, after which she seemed quite ill. After some of these visits the big white rabbit bled under her tail, refused to eat, and appeared sick.

One day Makar called me over, pointed to her and ordered me to kill her. I could not believe he meant it. The white female was very valuable, for pure white skins were rare. Besides, she was very large and would no doubt prove a fertile breeder. Makar repeated his order, without looking at me or at the rabbit. I hardly knew what to do. Makar always killed the rabbits himself, afraid that I was not strong enough to execute them quickly and painlessly. Skinning and dressing them was my job. Later Ewka made tasty dishes of them. Noticing my hesitation, Makar slapped my face and once again ordered me to kill the rabbit.

She was heavy and I had difficulty dragging her to the yard. She struggled and squealed so that I could not lift her high enough by the hind legs to deal her a lethal blow behind the ears. I had no choice but to kill her without lifting her up. I waited for the right moment and then hit the animal with all my strength. She fell down. To make doubly sure I hit her again. When I thought she was dead I hung her on a special post. I sharpened my knife on a stone and started the skinning.

First, I cut the skin on the legs, carefully separating the tissue from the muscle, anxiously avoiding any damage to the hide. After each cut I pulled the skin down, until I got to the neck. That was a difficult spot, for the blow behind the ears had caused so much bleeding that it made it hard to distinguish between the skin and the muscle. Since any damage to a valuable rabbit skin enraged Makar, I did not dare to think what would happen if I nicked this one.

I started detaching the skin with added care, pulling it slowly toward the head, when suddenly a tremor ran through the hanging body. Cold sweat covered me. I waited a moment, but the body remained still. I was reassured and, thinking it an illusion, resumed my task. Then the body twitched again. The rabbit must have been only stunned.

I ran for the club to kill her, but a horrible shriek stopped me. The partially skinned carcass started to jump and squirm on the post where it was suspended. Bewildered and not knowing what I was doing, I released the struggling rabbit. She fell down and started running immediately, now forward, now backward. With her skin hanging down behind her she rolled on the ground uttering an unending squeal. Sawdust, leaves, dirt, dung, clung to the bare, bloody flesh. She wriggled more and more violently. She lost all sense of direction, blinded by flaps of skin falling over her eyes, catching twigs and weeds with it as with a half pulled-off stocking.

Her piercing shrieks caused pandemonium in the yard. The terrified rabbits went mad in their hutches, the excited females trampled their young, the males fought one another, squealing, hitting their rumps on the walls. Ditko was jumping and straining at his chain. The hens flapped their wings in a desperate attempt to fly away and then collapsed, resigned and humiliated, in the tomatoes and onions.

The rabbit, now completely red, was still running. She dashed through the grass, then returned to the hutches; she tried to struggle through the bean patch. Each time her loose hanging skin caught on some obstacle she halted with a horrid scream and spurted blood.

Makar rushed out of the house finally with an ax in his hand. He ran after the bloody creature and split it in two with one blow. Then he hit the heap of gore again and again. His face was pale yellow and he bellowed horrible curses.

When only a bloody pulp remained of the rabbit, Makar noticed me and came toward me quivering with rage. I did not have time to dodge and a powerful kick in the stomach sent me breathless over the fence. The world seemed to swirl. I was blinded as if my own skin were falling over my head in a black hood.

The kick immobilized me for several weeks. I lay in an old rabbit hutch. Once a day Quail or Ewka brought me some food. Sometimes Ewka came alone, but left without a word when she saw my condition.

One day Anulka, who heard about my injuries, brought me a live mole. She tore it apart before my eyes and applied it to my abdomen until the animal's body turned quite cold. When she finished she was confident that her treatment would make me well quite soon.

I missed Ewka's presence, her voice, her touch, her smile. I tried to get better rapidly, but will power alone was not sufficient. Whenever I tried to stand, a spasm of pain in my belly paralyzed me for minutes. Crawling out of the hutch to urinate was sheer agony, and I often gave up and did it where I slept.

Finally Makar himself looked in and told me that if I did not return to work within two days he would hand me over to the peasants. They were about to deliver some quotas to the railroad station and would gladly turn me over to the German military police.

I began to practice walking. My legs did not obey me and I tired easily.

One night I heard noises outside. I peered through a slot between the boards. Quail was leading the he-goat to his father's room, where an oil lamp burned dimly.

The he-goat was seldom taken out. He was a large, stinking animal, fierce and afraid of no one. Even Ditko preferred not to take him on. The he-goat attacked hens and turkeys and butted his head against fences and tree trunks. Once he chased me, but I hid in the rabbit hutches until Quail led him away.

Intrigued by this unexpected visit to Makar's room, I climbed onto the roof of the hutch, from where I could see into the hut. Soon Ewka came into the room, huddled in a sheet. Makar approached the buck and stroked its under-belly with birch twigs until the animal became sufficiently aroused. Then with a few light blows of the stick he forced the beast to stand up, resting his forelegs on a shelf. Ewka tossed off her sheet and, to my horror, naked she slipped under the goat, clinging to it as though it were a man. Now and then Makar pushed her aside and excited the animal still more. Then he let Ewka couple passionately with the buck, gyrating, thrusting, and then embracing it.

Something collapsed inside me. My thoughts fell apart and shattered into broken fragments like a smashed jug. I felt as empty as a fish bladder punctured again and again and sinking into deep, muddy waters.

All these events became suddenly clear and obvious. They explained the expression I had often heard people use about people who were very successful in life: "He is in league with the Devil."

Peasants also accused one another of accepting help from various demons, such as Lucifer, Cadaver, Mammon, Exterminator, and many others. If the powers of Evil were so readily available to peasants, they probably lurked near every person, ready to pounce on any sign of encouragement, any weakness.

I tried to visualize the manner in which the evil spirits operated. The minds and souls of people were as open to these forces as a plowed field, and it was on this field that the Evil Ones incessantly scattered their malignant seed. If their seed sprouted to life, if they felt welcomed, they offered all the help which might be needed, on the condition that it would be used for selfish purposes and only to the detriment of others. From the moment of signing a pact with the Devil, the more harm, misery, injury, and bitterness a man could inflict on those around him, the more help he could expect. If he shrank from inflicting harm on others, if he succumbed to emotions of love, friendship, and compassion, he would immediately become weaker and his own life would have to absorb the suffering and defeats that he spared others.

These creatures that inhabited the human soul observed keenly not only man's every action, but also his motives and emotions. What mattered was that a man should consciously promote evil, find pleasure in harming others, nurturing and using the diabolical powers granted him by the Evil Ones in a manner calculated to cause as much misery and suffering around him as possible.

Only those with a sufficiently powerful passion

for hatred, greed, revenge, or torture to obtain some objective seemed to make a good bargain with the powers of Evil. Others, confused, uncertain of their aim, lost between curses and prayers, the tavern and the church, struggled through life alone, without help from either God or the Devil.

So far I had been one of those. I felt annoyed with myself for not having understood sooner the real rules of this world. The Evil Ones surely picked only those who had already displayed a sufficient supply of inner hatred and maliciousness.

A man who had sold out to the Evil Ones would remain in their power all his life. From time to time he would have to demonstrate an increasing number of misdeeds. But they were not rated equally by his superiors. An action harming one person was obviously worth less than one affecting many. The consequences of the evil deed were also important. Ruining the life of a young man was certainly more valuable than doing the same to an old man who hadn't long to live anyway. Furthermore, if the wrong done to someone managed to change his character in such a way as to turn him toward evil as a way of life, then a special bonus was due. Thus, simply beating up an innocent man was worth less than inciting him to hate others. But hatreds of large groups of people must have been the most valuable of all. I could barely imagine the prize earned by the person who managed to inculcate in all blond, blue-eyed people a long-lasting hatred of dark ones.

I also began to understand the extraordinary success of the Germans. Didn't the priest explain once to some peasants that even in remote times the Germans delighted in waging wars? Peace had never appealed to them. They did not want to till the soil, they had no patience to wait all year for the harvest. They preferred attacking other tribes and taking crops from them. The Germans probably were noticed then by the

Evil Ones. Eager to do harm, they agreed to sell out wholesale to them. That is why they were endowed with all their splendid abilities and talents. That is why they could impose all their refined methods of wrong-doing on others. Success was a vicious circle: the more harm they inflicted, the more secret powers they secured for evil. The more diabolical powers they had, the more evil they could achieve.

No one could stop them. They were invincible; they performed their function with masterful skill. They contaminated others with hatred, they condemned whole nations to extermination. Every German must have sold his soul to the Devil at birth. This was the source of their power and strength.

Cold sweat drained over me in the dark hutch. I myself hated many people. How many times had I dreamed of the time when I would be strong enough to return, set their settlements on fire, poison their children and cattle, lure them into deadly swamps. In a sense I had already been recruited by the powers of Evil and had made a pact with them. What I needed now was their assistance for spreading evil. After all, I was still very young; the Evil Ones had reason to believe that I had a future to give to them, that eventually my hatred and appetite for evil would grow like a noxious weed, spreading its seed over many fields.

I felt stronger and more confident. The time of passivity was over; the belief in good, the power of prayer, altars, priests, and God had deprived me of my speech. My love for Ewka, my desire to do anything I could for her, also met with its proper reward.

Now I would join those who were helped by the Evil Ones. I had not yet made any real contribution to their work, but in time I could become as prominent as any of the leading Germans. I could expect distinctions and prizes, as well as additional powers enabling me to destroy others in the subtlest ways. People who had contact with me would likewise become infected with evil. They would carry on the task of destruction, and every one of their successes would earn new powers for me.

There was no time to be lost. I had to build up a potential for hatred that would force me to action and attract the attention of the Evil Ones. If they really existed, they could hardly afford to miss an opportunity to make use of me.

I did not feel pain any more. I crawled to the house and peered through the window. In the room the game with the goat was over; the beast was standing calmly in a corner. Ewka was playing with Quail. They were both naked and they took turns lying on each other, jumping like frogs, rolling on the floor, and hugging in the way Ewka had taught me. Makar, also naked, stood by and watched them from above. When the girl started kicking and jerking, while Quail seemed rigid like a fence post, Makar knelt down over them close to his daughter's face and his huge body shielded them from my sight.

I continued watching them for a few moments. The sight dribbled off my numb mind like a drop of freezing water descending an icicle.

I suddenly desired to act and hobbled outside. Ditko, familiar with my movements, only growled and went to sleep. I moved toward Anulka's hut at the far end of the village. I sneaked up to it, looking everywhere for the comet. The hens were startled by my presence and began to cackle. I peered into the small doorway.

The old woman woke up at that moment. I crouched behind a large cask and when Anulka stepped out I uttered an unearthly howl and jabbed her in the ribs with a stick. The old witch ran screaming and calling for help from the Lord and all the saints, stumbling over the poles supporting the tomato plants in the garden.

I slipped into the stuffy room and soon found an

old comet by the stove. I shoveled some burning cinders into the comet and sprinted for the forest. Behind me I heard the shrill voice of Anulka and the alarmed voices of dogs and people slowly responding to her cries.

13

At that time of year it was not very difficult to escape from a village. I often watched the boys attach home-made skates to their shoes and spread pieces of canvas over their heads, and then let the wind push them over the smooth surface of the ice covering the marshes and pastures.

The marshes spread over many miles between the villages. In the autumn the waters rose, submerging the reeds and bushes. Small fish and other creatures multiplied rapidly in the bogs. One could sometimes see a snake, its head raised stiffly, swimming with determination. The marshes did not freeze as quickly as the local ponds and lakes. It was as though the winds and reeds were defending themselves by agitating the water.

In the end, however, ice gripped everything. Only the tips of tall reeds and an odd twig or two protruded here and there, covered by a frosty coating on which snowflakes perched precariously.

The winds came wild and unharnessed. They by-passed human settlements and gained speed over the flat marshlands, swirling with them clouds of powdery snow, pushing along old branches and dried potato stalks, bending the proud heads of taller trees jutting through the ice. I knew there were many different winds and that they fought battles, butting each other, wrestling, trying to win more ground.

I had already made a pair of skates, hoping that someday I would have to leave the village. I attached some thick wire to two long pieces of wood, curved at one end. Then I threaded straps through the skates and attached them firmly to the boots, which I myself also made. These boots consisted of wooden rectangular soles and scraps of rabbit skin, reinforced on the outside with canvas.

I fixed the skates to my boots at the edge of the marshland. I hung the burning comet over my shoulder and spread the sail over my head. The invisible hand of the wind began to push me. I gathered speed with every gust that blew me away from the village. My skates glided over the ice, and I felt the warmth of my comet. I was now in the middle of a vast icy surface. The howling wind drove me along, and dark gray clouds with light edges raced along with me on my journey.

Flying along that endless white plain I felt free and alone like a starling soaring in the air, tossed by every flurry, following a stream, unconscious of its speed, drawn into an abandoned dance. Trusting myself to the frenzied power of the wind, I spread my sail even wider. It was hard to believe that the local people regarded the wind as an enemy and closed their windows to it, afraid that it might bring them plague, paralysis, and death. They always said that the Devil was master of the winds, which carried out his evil orders.

The swelling air was now pushing me with a steady thrust. I flew over the ice, dodging the occasional frozen stalks. The sun was dim, and when I finally stopped my shoulders and ankles were stiff and cold. I decided to rest and warm myself, but when I reached for my comet I found that it had blown out.

Not a spark remained. I sagged with fear, not knowing what to do. I could not return to the village; I did not have the strength for the long struggle against the wind. I had no idea whether there were any farms in the vicinity, whether I could find them before nightfall, and whether they would give me shelter even if I found them.

I heard something that sounded like a chuckle in the whistling wind. I shivered at the thought that the Devil himself was testing me by leading me around in circles, waiting for the moment when I would accept his offer.

As the wind whipped me I could hear other whispers, mutterings, and moans. The Evil Ones were interested in me at last. To train me in hatred they had first separated me from my parents, then taken away Marta and Olga, delivered me into the hands of the carpenter, robbed me of my speech, then given Ewka to the he-goat. Now they dragged me through a frozen wilderness, threw snow in my face, churned my thoughts into confusion. I was in their power, alone on a glassy sheet of ice which the Evil Ones themselves had spread between remote villages. They turned somersaults over my head and could send me anywhere at their whim.

I started walking on my aching feet, oblivious of time. Every step was painful and I had to rest at frequent intervals. I sat on the ice trying to move my freezing legs, rubbing my cheeks, nose, and ears with snow scraped off my hair and clothes, massaging my rigid fingers, trying to find some feeling in my numb toes.

The sun was down to the horizon and its slanting rays were as cold as the moon's. When I sat down the world around me looked like a vast skillet carefully polished by an industrious housewife.

I stretched the canvas over my head, trying to catch every turbulence as I moved straight ahead toward the setting sun. When I had almost given up hope, I noticed the outlines of thatched roofs. A few moments later, when the village was clearly visible, I saw a gang of boys approaching on skates. Without my comet I was afraid of them and tried to cut away at an angle, aiming at the outskirts of the settlement. But it was too late; they had already noticed me.

The group headed in my direction. I started running against the wind, but I was out of breath and could hardly stand on my legs. I sat on the ice grasping the handle of the comet.

The boys came closer. There were ten or more. Swinging their arms, supporting one another, they progressed steadily against the wind. The air threw their voices back; I could hear nothing.

When they were quite close they split into two groups and surrounded me cautiously. I huddled on the ice and covered my face with the canvas sail, hoping they might leave me alone.

They encircled me with suspicion. I pretended not to notice them. Three of the strongest came closer. "A Gypsy," one said, "a Gypsy bastard."

The others stood by calmly, but when I tried to get up they jumped on me and twisted my arms behind my back. The group became excited. They beat me on the face and stomach. Blood froze on my lip and closed one eye. The tallest one said something. The others seemed to agree enthusiastically. Some held me by the legs, others started pulling off my pants. I knew what they wanted to do. I had seen a band of cowherds raping a boy from another village who happened to wander into their territory. I knew that only something unforeseen could save me.

I allowed them to take off my pants, pretending I was exhausted and could not fight any more. I guessed that they would not take off my boots and skates because they were too firmly attached to my feet. Noticing that I was limp and did not resist, they relaxed their grip. Two of the biggest crouched by my bare abdomen and struck me with frozen gloves.

I tensed my muscles, withdrew one leg slightly, and kicked one of the boys bending over me. Something cracked in his head. At first I thought it was the skate, but it was whole when I jerked it out of the boy's eye. Another one tried to grab me by the legs; I kicked him across the throat with the skate. The two boys fell on the ice, bleeding profusely. The rest of the boys panicked; most of them started dragging the wounded boys toward the village, leaving a bloody trail on the ice. Four stayed behind.

These pinned me down with a long pole used for fishing in ice holes. When I ceased struggling they dragged me toward a nearby hole. I resisted desperately at the edge of the water, but they were ready. Two of them widened the hole and then they all heaved together, pushing me under the ice with the pointed end of the pole. They tried to make sure that I could not emerge.

The icy water shut over me. I closed my mouth and held my breath, feeling the painful thrust of the spike pushing me under. I slid underneath the ice, and it rubbed my head, my shoulders, and my bare hands. And then the pointed pole was bobbing at my fingertips, no longer being jabbed into me, for the boys had let go of it.

The cold encased me. My mind was freezing. I was sliding down, choking. The water here was shallow, and my only thought was that I could use the pole to push against the bottom and lift myself to the ice-cut. I grabbed the pole and it supported me as I moved along underneath the ice. When my lungs were nearly bursting and I was ready to open my mouth and swallow anything, I found myself near the ice-cut. With one more push my head popped out and I gulped air that felt like a stream of boiling soup. I caught the sharp rim of the ice, holding on to it in such a way as to be able to breathe without emerging too often. I did not know how far the boys had gone, and I preferred to wait a while.

Only my face was still alive; I could not feel the rest of my body: it seemed to belong to the ice. I made efforts to move my legs and feet.

I peered over the edge of the ice and saw the boys disappearing in the distance, and diminishing with each step they took. When they were far enough away, I climbed to the surface. My clothes froze solid and crackled at every movement. I jumped up and down and stretched my stiff legs and arms and rubbed myself with snow, but warmth returned only for a few seconds and then vanished again. I tied the ragged remains of my pants to my legs and then pulled the pole out of the ice hole and leaned heavily on it. The wind struck me sideways; I had trouble keeping my direction. Whenever I weakened, I put the pole between my legs and pushed on it, as though riding on a stiff tail.

I was slowly moving away from the huts, toward a forest visible in the distance. It was very late afternoon and the brownish disk of the sun was cut by the square shapes of roofs and chimneys. Every gust of wind robbed my body of precious remnants of warmth. I knew that I must not rest or stop even for a moment until I reached the forest. I began to see the pattern of bark on the trees. A frightened hare jumped from under a bush.

When I reached the first trees my head was spinning. It seemed to be midsummer, and the golden ears of wheat were waving over my head and Ewka touched me with her warm hand. I had visions of food: a huge bowl of beef seasoned with vinegar, garlic, pepper and salt; a pot of coarse gruel thickened with pickled cabbage leaves and pieces of succulent fat bacon; evenly cut slices of barley bread soaked in a thick borscht of barley, potatoes, and corn.

I took another few steps over the frozen ground and entered the woods. My skates caught on roots and bushes. I stumbled once and then sat on a tree trunk. Almost immediately I started sinking into a hot bed full of soft, smooth, warmed pillows and eiderdowns. Someone leaned over me, I heard a woman's voice, I was being carried somewhere. Everything dissolved into a sultry summer night, full of intoxicating, moist, fragrant mists.

14

I woke on a wide low bed nestled against the wall and covered with sheepskins. It was hot in the room and the flickering light of a thick candle revealed a dirt floor, chalky-white walls, and a thatched roof. A cross hung from the chimney-piece. A woman sat staring into the high flames of the fire. She was barefoot, in a tight skirt of coarse linen. Her jerkin of rabbit pelts with many holes was unbuttoned to the waist. Noticing that I was awake she approached and sat down on the bed, which groaned under her weight. She lifted my chin and looked attentively at me. Her eyes were watery blue. When she smiled, she did not cover her mouth with her hand as was customary here. Instead, she displayed two rows of yellowish, uneven teeth.

She spoke to me in a local dialect which I could not fully understand. She persisted in calling me her poor Gypsy, her little Jewish foundling. At first she would not believe that I was a mute. Occasionally she looked inside my mouth, rapped my throat, tried to startle me; but she soon stopped when I stayed silent.

She fed me hot thick borscht and carefully inspected my frozen ears, hands, and feet. She told me

her name was Labina. I felt safe and contented with
her. I liked her very much.

In the daytime Labina went out to work as a
domestic to some of the richer peasants, especially to
those with sick wives or too many children. Often she
took me along so I could have a decent meal, although
it was said in the village that I should be delivered to
the Germans. Labina replied to such remarks with a
torrent of curses, shouting that all were equal before
God and that she was no Judas to sell me for silver
coins.

In the evenings Labina used to receive guests in
her hut. Men who managed to get out of their houses
came to her hut with bottles of vodka and baskets of
food.

The hut contained a single enormous bed that
could easily accommodate three people. Between one
edge of this bed and the wall there was a wide space
where Labina had piled sacks, old rags, and sheepskins,
thus providing me with a place to sleep. I always went
to sleep before the guests arrived, but I was often
awakened by their singing and boisterous toasts. But
I pretended to be asleep. I did not wish to risk the
beating Labina often halfheartedly said I deserved.
With eyes nearly closed I would watch what was happening in the room.

A drinking bout would begin and last far into the
night. Usually one man would stay after the others
had left. He and Labina would sit down against the
warm oven and drink from the same cup. When she
would sway uncertainly and lean toward the man, he
would place a huge blackened hand on her flabby
thighs and slowly move it under her skirt.

Labina at first seemed indifferent, then struggled a
little. The man's other hand slid from beneath her
neck down inside her blouse, squeezing her breasts so
hard that she uttered a cry and panted hoarsely. At

times the man kneeled on the floor and pushed his face aggressively into her groin, biting it through the skirt while squeezing her buttocks with both his hands. Often he would strike her groin abruptly with the edge of his hand and she would bend over and moan.

The candle was put out. They would undress in the dark, laughing and cursing, stumbling over the furniture and each other, impatiently shedding their clothing, overturning bottles that would roll across the room. When they tumbled onto the bed I feared it would collapse. While I thought of the rats who lived with us, Labina and her guest tossed about in the bed, wheezing and fighting, calling on God and Satan, the man howling like a dog, the woman grunting like a pig.

Often, in the middle of the night, in the midst of my dreams, I suddenly awoke on the floor between the bed and the wall. The bed quivered above me; shifted by the bodies struggling in convulsive fits. Finally it began to move over the tilted floor toward the center of the room.

Unable to crawl back into the bed from which I fell, I had to sneak under it and push it back against the wall. Then I returned to my pallet. The dirt floor under the bed was cold and moist and covered with cat feces and the remains of birds they had dragged in. As I inched in the dark I tore at thick cobwebs and the frightened spiders ran over my face and hair. Warm little bodies of mice fled to their holes, brushing against me as they passed.

Touching this dark world with my flesh always filled me with revulsion and fear. I would crawl out from under the bed, wipe the cobwebs off my face, and wait shivering for the proper moment to push the bed back toward the wall.

Gradually my eyes adjusted to the darkness. I looked on while the great sweating body of the man mounted the trembling woman. She embraced his fleshy buttocks with her legs which resembled the wings of a bird crushed under a stone.

The peasant groaned and sighed heavily, gathered up the woman's body under his hand, raised himself, and with the back of his hand struck her breasts. They flapped loudly like a wet cloth being beaten against a rock. He swooped down on her and flattened her to the bed. Labina, crying incoherently, struck his back with her hands. Sometimes the man lifted the woman, forced her to kneel on the bed leaning on her elbows, and he mounted her from the back, beating her rhythmically with his belly and thighs.

I looked on with disappointment and disgust at the two intertwined, twitching human frames. So that's what love was: savage as a bull prodded with a spike; brutal, smelly, sweaty. This love was like a brawl in which man and woman wrested pleasure from each other, fighting, incapable of thought, half stunned, wheezing, less than human.

I recalled the moments I had passed with Ewka. How differently I treated her. My touch was gentle; my hands, my mouth, my tongue, hovered consciously over her skin, soft and delicate like gossamer floating in windless warm air. I continually sought out new sensitive places unknown even to her, bringing them to life with my touch, as rays of sunshine revive a butterfly chilled by the cool air of the autumn night. I remembered my elaborate efforts and how they released within the girl's body some yearnings and tremors that otherwise would have been imprisoned there forever. I freed them, wanting her only to find pleasure in herself.

The loves of Labina and her guests were soon over. They were like short spring thundershowers that wet the leaves and grass but never reach the roots. I remembered how my games with Ewka never really ceased but only dimmed when Makar and Quail intruded into our lives. They continued long into the night like a peat fire whipped gently by the wind. Yet even this love was extinguished as fast as burning logs are smothered with a shepherd's horse blanket. As soon as I became temporarily incapable of playing with her, Ewka forgot me. To the warmth of my body, the tender caress of my arms, the gentle touch of my fingers and my mouth, she preferred a stinking hairy goat and his loathsome deep penetration.

Finally the bed stopped quivering and the slackened carcasses, sprawling there like slaughtered cattle, settled into sleep. Then I pushed the bed back to the wall, climbed over it, and lay down in my cold corner, pulling all the sheepskins over me.

On rainy afternoons Labina grew melancholic and talked about her husband, Laba, who was no longer alive. Many years ago Labina had been a beautiful girl whom the richest peasants wooed. But against reasoned advice she fell in love with and married Laba, the poorest farmhand in the village, known also as the Handsome One.

Laba indeed was handsome, tall as a poplar, nimble as a top. His hair shone in the sun, his eyes were bluer than the fairest sky, and his complexion was as smooth as a child's. When he looked at a woman her blood ran fire and lustful thoughts raced through her head. Laba knew that he was good-looking and that he aroused admiration and lust in women. He liked to parade about the woods and bathe in the pond naked. He would glance into the bushes and know that he was being watched by young virgins and married women.

But he was the poorest farmhand in the village. He was hired by the rich peasants and had to endure many humiliations. These men knew that Laba was desired by their wives and daughters, and they would humble him for it. They also bothered Labina, knowing that her penniless husband depended on them and could only look on helplessly.

One day Laba did not return home from the field. He did not return the next day, or the day after. He vanished like a stone dropped to the bottom of a lake.

It was thought that he was drowned or sucked in by a swamp, or that some jealous suitor had knifed him and buried him at night in the forest.

Life went on without Laba. Only the saying, "handsome as Laba," survived in the village.

A lonely year without Laba passed. People forgot him, and only Labina believed that he was still alive and would return. One summer day, when the villagers rested in the short shadows of the trees, a cart pulled by a fat horse emerged from the forest. On the cart lay a large chest covered by a cloth, and next to it walked Handsome Laba in a beautiful leather jacket slung Hussar-fashion over his shoulders, in trousers of the finest cloth and in tall shining boots.

The children ran among the huts, carrying the news, and men and women swarmed toward the road. Laba greeted them all with a nonchalant wave, while wiping the sweat off his brow and prodding the horse.

Labina was already waiting in the doorway. He kissed his wife, unloaded the enormous chest, and entered the hut. The neighbors gathered in front admiring the horse and cart.

After waiting impatiently for Laba and Labina to reappear, the villagers began to jest. He had rushed to her like a buck to a goat, they said, and cold water should be poured over them.

Suddenly the doors of the hut opened and the crowd gasped with astonishment. On the threshold stood Handsome Laba in a suit of unimaginable splendor. He wore a striped silk shirt with a stark white collar round his tanned neck and a garish tie. His soft flannel suit begged to be touched. A satin handkerchief stuck out of his breast pocket like a flower. To this was added a pair of black lacquered boots and, as a crowning glory, a gold watch hanging from his breast pocket.

The peasants gaped in awe. Nothing like this had happened in the history of the village. Usually the inhabitants wore homespun jackets, trousers sewed together from two lengths of cloth, and boots of rough-tanned leather nailed to a thick wooden sole. Laba extracted from his chest innumerable colorful jackets of unusual cut, trousers, shirts, and patent-leather shoes, shining with such luster they could serve as mirrors, and handkerchiefs, ties, socks, and underclothes. Handsome Laba became the supreme object of local interest. Unusual stories went around about him. Various surmises were made about the origin of all these priceless objects. Labina was showered with questions she could not answer, for Laba gave only vague replies, contributing even more to the growth of the legend.

During church services no one looked at the priest or the altar. They all watched the right-hand corner of the nave where Handsome Laba sat stiffly with his wife in his black satin suit and flowered shirt. On his wrist he wore a glittering watch, at which he would glance ostentatiously. The priest's vestments, once the very acme of ornateness, now seemed as dull as a wintry sky. The people sitting near Laba delighted in the unusual fragrances that wafted from him. Labina confided that they derived from a number of little bottles and jars.

After the Mass the crowd moved into the court-yard of the presbytery and ignored the vicar, who tried to attract their attention. They waited for Laba. He walked toward the exit with a loose, confident stride, his heels loudly tapping the church floor. The people respectfully gave way to him. The richest peasants approached and greeted him familiarly, and invited him to their homes for dinners in his honor. Without inclining his head Laba casually shook the hands outstretched to him. Women barred his way and, heedless of Labina's presence, hiked their skirts up so their thighs showed and pulled at their dresses to make their breasts more prominent.

Handsome Laba no longer worked in the fields. He even refused to help his wife in the house. He passed his days bathing in the lake. He hung his multi-colored clothing on a tree near the shore. Nearby excited women watched his naked muscular body. It was said that Laba allowed some of them to touch him in the shadow of the bushes and that they were ready to commit shameful acts with him, for which a terrible retribution might be exacted.

In the afternoon, when the villagers returned from the fields sweating and gray with dust, they passed Handsome Laba sauntering the other way, carefully stepping on the firmest part of the road so as not to soil his shoes, adjusting his tie, and polishing his watch with a pink handkerchief.

In the evenings horses would be sent for Laba and he would drive off to receptions, often in places dozens of miles away. Labina stayed home, half dead with exhaustion and humiliation, caring for the farm, the horse, and her husband's treasures. For Handsome Laba time had stopped, but Labina aged rapidly, her skin sagging and her thighs growing flabby.

A year passed.

One autumn day Labina returned from the fields, expecting to find her husband in the attic with all his treasures. The attic was Laba's exclusive realm and he carried on his breast along with a medallion of the Holy Virgin the key to the large padlock securing its door. But now the house was absolutely still. No smoke poured from the chimney, and there was no sound of Laba singing as he changed into one of his warmer suits.

Labina, frightened, rushed into the hut. The door to the attic was open. She climbed up to it. What she saw stunned her. On the floor lay the chest with its lid torn off and its whitish bottom visible. A body dangled above the chest. Her husband now hung on the large hook where his suits used to hang. Handsome Laba, swaying like a slowed-down pendulum, was suspended by a floral-patterned necktie. There was a hole in the roof through which the thief had carried away the contents of the chest. The thin rays of the setting sun illuminated the pallid face of Handsome Laba and the bluish tongue sticking out of his mouth. All around iridescent flies murmured.

Labina guessed what had happened. When Laba had returned from bathing in the lake to put on his parade suit, he found the hole in the attic roof and the empty chest. All his fine clothes were gone. Only a single necktie remained, lying like a severed flower in the trampled straw.

Laba's reason for living had disappeared with the contents of his chest. There was an end to weddings at which no one looked at the groom, an end to burials at which Handsome Laba would meet the worshipful gaze of the crowd as he stood above the open grave, an end to proud self-display in the lake and the touch of eager female hands.

With a careful, deliberate movement which no one else in the village could imitate, Laba had put on his necktie for the last time. Then he had pulled the emptied chest toward him and reached for the hook in the ceiling.

Labina never discovered how her husband had acquired his treasures. He never referred to the period of his absence. No one knew where he had been, what he had done, what price he had paid for all those goods. All the village knew was what the loss of his things cost him.

Neither the thief nor any of the stolen objects was ever found. While I was still there rumors circulated that the thief was a cuckolded husband or fiancé. Oth-

ers believed that some insanely jealous woman was responsible. Many people in the village suspected Labina
herself. When she heard of this accusation her face
grew livid, her hands shook, and a rancid smell of
bitterness came from her mouth. Her fingers clawed,
she would hurl herself at the accuser, and the onlookers would have to separate them. Labina would return
home, drink herself into a stupor, and hold me close
to her breast, weeping and sobbing.

During one of these fights, her heart burst. When
I saw several men carrying her dead body to the hut, I
knew I had to flee. I filled my comet with smoldering
embers, grabbed the precious necktie hidden under
the bed by Labina, the necktie on which Handsome
Laba had hung himself, and left. It was common belief
that the rope of a suicide brings good luck. I hoped I
would never lose the necktie.

15

The summer was nearly over. Sheaves of wheat were stacked in the fields. The peasants worked as hard as they could, but they did not have enough horses or oxen to bring in the harvest quickly.

A high railroad bridge spanned the cliffs of a big river near the village. It was guarded by heavy guns set in concrete pillboxes.

At night when high-flying airplanes droned in the sky, everything on the bridge was blacked out. In the morning life resumed. Soldiers in helmets manned the guns, and from the highest point of the bridge the angular form of the swastika, woven into its flag, twisted in the wind.

One hot night gunfire was heard in the distance. The muffled sound washed over the fields, alarming men and birds. Flashes of lightning twinkled far away. People assembled in front of their houses. The men, smoking their corncob pipes, watched the manmade lightning and said: "The front is coming." Others added: "The Germans are losing." Many arguments broke out.

Some of the peasants said that when the Soviet commissars came they would distribute the land fairly to everyone, taking from the rich and giving to the poor. It would be the end of the exploiting landlords, of corrupt officials and brutal policemen.

Others violently disagreed. Swearing on their holy crosses they shouted that the Soviets would nationalize everything right down to wives and children. They looked at the glare in the eastern sky and shouted that the coming of the Reds meant that people would turn away from the altar, forget the teaching of their ancestors, and give themselves up to sinful lives until God's justice made them pillars of salt.

Brother fought against brother, fathers swung axes against sons in front of their mothers. An invisible force divided people, split families, addled brains. Only the elders remained sane, scurrying from one side to the other, begging the combatants to make peace. They cried in their squeaky voices that there was enough war in the world without starting one in the village.

The thunder beyond the horizon was coming nearer. Its roll cooled the quarrels. People suddenly forgot about Soviet commissars or divine wrath in their rush to dig pits in their barns and cellars.

They hid stores of butter, pork, and calves' meat, rye, and wheat. Some secretly dyed sheets red for use as flags to greet the new rulers, while others hid away in safe places crucifixes, the figures of Jesus and Mary, and icons.

I did not understand all of it, but I sensed the urgency in the air. No one paid any attention to me any more. I wandered among the huts, hearing sounds of digging, nervous whispers, and prayers. As I lay in the fields with my ear to the ground, I could hear a thudding sound.

Was it the Red Army coming? The throbbing in the earth was like a heartbeat. I was wondering why, if God could make sinners into pillars of salt so easily, salt was so expensive. And why didn't He turn some sinners into meat or sugar? The villagers certainly needed these as much as salt.

I lay on my back looking at the clouds. They floated by in such a way that I myself seemed to be floating. If it was true that women and children might become communal property, then every child would have many fathers and mothers, innumerable brothers and sisters. It seemed to be too much to hope for. To belong to everyone! Wherever I might go, many fathers would stroke my head with firm, reassuring hands, many mothers would hug me to their bosoms, and many older brothers would defend me against dogs. And I would have to look after my smaller brothers and sisters. There seemed to be no reason for the peasants to be so afraid.

The clouds dissolved into one another, becoming now darker, now lighter. Somewhere high above them God directed it all. I understood now why He could hardly spare time for a small black flea like me. He had vast armies, countless men, animals, and machines battling beneath Him. He had to decide who was to win and who was to lose; who was to live and who was to die.

But if God really decided what was to happen, why did the peasants worry about their faith, the churches, and the clergy? If the Soviet commissars really intended to destroy the churches, desecrate the altars, kill the priests, and persecute the faithful, the Red Army would not have the remotest chance of winning the war. Even the most overworked God could not overlook such a menace to His people. But then would not that mean that the Germans, who also demolished churches and murdered people, would prove the winners? From God's point of view it seemed to make more sense if everyone lost the war, since everyone was committing murder.

"Common ownership of wives and children," the

peasants said. It sounded rather puzzling. Anyway, I thought, with a little goodwill the Soviet commissars might perhaps include me among the children. Although I was smaller than most eight-year-old boys, I was almost eleven now and it disturbed me that the Russians might classify me as an adult or, at least, not regard me as a child. In addition, I was a mute. I also had trouble with food, which sometimes came up from my stomach undigested. I surely deserved to become common property.

One morning I noticed unusual activity on the bridge. Helmeted soldiers were swarming over it, dismantling the cannon and machine-guns, hauling down the German flag. As large trucks went westward from the other side of the bridge, the harsh sound of the German songs faded. "They are running away," said the peasants. "They have lost the war," whispered the bolder ones.

Next day at noon a band of mounted men rode up to the village. There were a hundred of them, perhaps more. They seemed to be one with their horses; they rode with marvelous ease, without any set order. They wore green German uniforms with bright buttons and forage caps pulled down over their eyes.

The peasants instantly recognized them. They screamed in terror that the Kalmuks were coming and the women and children must hide before they could be seized. For months in the village many terrible tales had been told about these riders, usually referred to as Kalmuks. The peasants said that when the once invincible German Army had occupied a large area of Soviet land it was joined by many Kalmuks, mostly volunteers, deserters from the Soviets. Hating the Reds, they joined the Germans who permitted them to loot and rape in the manner of their war customs and manly traditions. This is why the Kalmuks were sent to villages and towns that were to be punished for some noncompliance and, particularly, to those towns that lay in the path of the advancing Red Army.

The Kalmuks rode at full gallop, bent over their horses, using their spurs and uttering hoarse cries. Under their unbuttoned uniforms one could see bare brown skin. Some rode without saddles, some carried heavy sabers at their belts.

Wild confusion seized the village. It was too late for flight. I looked at the horsemen with keen interest. They all had black oily hair which glistened in the sun. Almost blue-black, it was even darker than mine, as were also their eyes and their swarthy skins. They had large white teeth, high cheekbones, and wide faces that looked swollen.

For a moment, as I looked at them, I felt great pride and satisfaction. After all, these proud horsemen were black-haired, black-eyed, and dark-skinned. They differed from the people of the village as night from day. The arrival of these dark Kalmuks drove the fair-haired village people almost insane with fear.

In the meantime the riders pulled up their horses between the houses. One of them, a squat man in a fully buttoned uniform and an officer's cap, shouted orders. They jumped off their horses and tied them up to fences. From their saddles they took pieces of meat that had been cooked by the heat of horse and rider. They ate this blue-gray meat with their hands and drank out of gourds, coughing and spluttering as they swallowed.

Some were already drunk. They rushed into the huts and grabbed the women who were not hidden. The men tried to defend them with their scythes. A Kalmuk cut down one of them with a single stroke of his saber. Others tried to run away but were stopped by bullet shots.

The Kalmuks scattered throughout the village. The air was filled with screams from every quarter. I rushed into the middle of a small thick cluster of raspberry bushes right in the center of the square and flattened myself like a worm.

As I watched carefully, the village exploded in panic. Men tried to defend the houses which Kalmuks had already entered. More shots rang out and a man wounded in the head ran around in circles blinded by his own blood. A Kalmuk cut him down. The children scattered wildly, stumbling over ditches and fences. One of them ran into the bushes where I was hiding but, seeing me, ran out again to be trampled by galloping horses.

The Kalmuks were now dragging a half-naked woman out of a house. She struggled and screamed, trying in vain to catch her tormentors by the legs. A group of women and girls was being rounded up with horsewhips by some laughing riders. The fathers, husbands and brothers of the women ran about begging for mercy, but were chased away with horsewhips and sabers. A farmer ran through the main street with his hand cut off. Blood was spurting from the stump while he kept looking for his family.

Nearby the soldiers had forced a woman to the ground. One soldier held her by the throat while others pulled her legs apart. One of them mounted her and moved on top of her to shouts of encouragement. The woman struggled and cried. When the first was done the others assaulted her in turn. The woman soon grew limp and did not fight back any more.

Still another woman was brought out. She screamed and begged, but the Kalmuks stripped her and threw her on the ground. Two men raped her at once, one in the mouth. When she tried to twist her head aside or close her mouth she was lashed with a bullwhip. Finally she weakened and submitted passively. Some other soldiers were raping from the front and from the back two young girls, passing them from one man to the next, forcing them to perform strange movements. When the girls resisted, they were flogged and kicked.

The screams of raped women were heard in all the houses. One girl somehow managed to escape and ran out half naked, with blood streaming down her thighs, howling like a whipped dog. Two half-naked soldiers ran after her, laughing. They chased her around the square amidst the laughter and jokes of their comrades. Finally they caught up with her. Weeping children looked on.

New victims were being caught all the time. The drunken Kalmuks became more and more aroused. A few of them copulated with each other, then competed in raping women in odd ways: two or three men to one girl, several men in rapid succession. The younger and more desirable girls were nearly torn apart, and some quarrels broke out among the soldiers. The women sobbed and prayed aloud. Their husbands and fathers, sons and brothers, who were now locked in the houses, recognized their voices and responded with maddened shrieks.

In the middle of the square some Kalmuks displayed their skill in raping women on horseback. One of them stripped off his uniform, leaving only his boots on his hairy legs. He rode his horse in circles and then neatly lifted off the ground a naked woman brought to him by the others. He made her sit astride the horse in front of him, and facing him. The horse broke into a faster trot, the rider pulled the woman closer making her lean her back against the horse's mane. At every lunge of the horse he penetrated her afresh, shouting triumphantly each time. The others greeted his performance with applause. The rider then deftly turned the woman around so that she faced forward. He lifted her slightly and repeated his feat from the back while clutching her breasts.

Encouraged by the others, another Kalmuk jumped on the same horse, behind the woman and with his back to the horse's mane. The horse groaned under the load and slowed down, while the two soldiers raped the fainting woman simultaneously.

Other feats followed. Helpless women were passed from one trotting horse to another. One of the Kalmuks tried to couple with a mare; others aroused a stallion and tried to push a girl under it, holding her up by her legs.

I crept deeper into the bushes, overwhelmed by dread and disgust. Now I understood everything. I realized why God would not listen to my prayers, why I was hung from hooks, why Garbos beat me, why I lost my speech. I was black. My hair and eyes were as black as these Kalmuks'. Evidently I belonged with them in another world. There could be no mercy for such as me. A dreadful fate had sentenced me to have black hair and eyes in common with this horde of savages.

Suddenly a tall white-haired old man came out of one of the barns. The peasants called him "The Saint" and perhaps he thought of himself as such. He held with both hands a heavy wooden cross and he wore on his white head a wreath of yellowed oak leaves. His sightless eyes were lifted to the sky. His bare feet, deformed by age and disease, sought a path. The words of a psalm came in a mournful dirge from his toothless mouth. He was pointing the cross at his unseen enemies.

The soldiers sobered for a moment. Even the drunken ones eyed him uneasily, visibly disturbed. Then one of them ran up to the old man and tripped him. He fell down and lost his grip on the cross. The Kalmuks jeered and waited. The old man tried with stiff movements to raise himself, groping for the cross. His bony, gnarled hands searched the ground patiently while the soldier flipped the cross away with his foot as he got close to it. The old man crawled around babbling and moaning softly. Finally he was exhausted and breathed heavily with a hoarse wheeze. The Kalmuk lifted the heavy cross and stood it upright. It balanced for a second, and then toppled onto the prone figure. The old man moaned and ceased to move.

A soldier threw a knife at one of the girls who was trying to crawl away. She was left bleeding in the dirt; no one paid any attention to her. Drunken Kalmuks handed women spattered with blood from one to another, beating them, forcing them to perform odd acts. One of them rushed into a house and brought out a small girl of about five. He lifted her high so that his comrades could see her well. He tore off the child's dress. He kicked her in the belly while her mother crawled in the dust begging for mercy. He slowly unbuttoned and took down his trousers, while still holding the little girl above his waist with one hand. Then he crouched and pierced the screaming child with a sudden thrust. When the girl grew limp he threw her away into the bushes and turned to the mother.

In the doorway of a house some half-naked soldiers were fighting a powerfully built peasant. He stood on the threshold swinging an ax in wild fury. When the soldiers finally overcame him, they dragged a fear-numbed woman out of the house by her hair. Three soldiers sat on the husband, while the others tortured and raped his wife.

Then they dragged out two of the man's youthful daughters. Seizing a moment when the Kalmuks' grip on him loosened, the peasant jumped up and dealt a sudden blow to the nearest one. The soldier fell down, his skull crushed like a swallow's egg. Blood and white pieces of brain resembling the meat of a cracked nut spilled through his hair. The enraged soldiers surrounded the peasant, overpowered him, and raped him. Then they castrated him in front of his wife and daughters. The frantic woman rushed to his defense, biting and scratching. Roaring with delight, the Kalmuks held her fast, forced her mouth open, and pushed the bloody scraps of flesh down her throat.

One of the houses caught fire. In the resulting commotion some peasants ran for the forest, dragging with them half-conscious women and stumbling children. The Kalmuks, firing at random, trampled some of the people with their horses. They captured new victims whom they tortured on the spot.

I hid in the raspberry bushes. Drunken Kalmuks were wandering around, and my chances of remaining there unnoticed were dwindling. I could not think any more; I was frozen with terror. I closed my eyes.

When I opened them again I saw one of the Kalmuks staggering in my direction. I flattened myself on the ground even more, and nearly stopped breathing. The soldier picked some raspberries and ate them. He took another step into the bush and trod on my outstretched hand. The heel and the nails of his boot dug into my skin. The pain was excruciating but I did not move. The soldier leaned on his rifle and urinated calmly. Suddenly he lost his balance, stepped forward, and stumbled over my head. As I jumped up and tried to run he grabbed me and struck me in the chest with the butt of his rifle. Something cracked inside. I was knocked down, but I managed to trip the soldier. As he fell I ran zigzagging away toward the houses. The Kalmuk fired, but the bullet ricocheted off the ground and whizzed by. He fired again but missed. I tore off a board from one of the barns, climbed in and hid in the straw.

In the barn I could still hear the cries of people and animals, rifle shots, the crackling of burning sheds and houses, the neighing of horses, and the raucous laughter of the Kalmuks. A woman moaned softly from time to time. I burrowed deeper into the straw, though every movement hurt me. I wondered what had broken inside my chest. I put my hand against my heart; it was still beating. I did not want to be a cripple. Despite the noise, I dozed off, exhausted and frightened.

I woke with a start. A powerful explosion rocked

the barn; some beams fell, and clouds of dust obscured everything. I heard scattered rifle fire and the continuous rattle of machine-guns. I peered out cautiously and saw horses panicking and galloping away and half-naked Kalmuks, still drunk, trying to jump on them. From the direction of the river and from the forest I could hear the gunfire and the roar of engines. An airplane with a red star on its wings flew low over the village. The cannonade ceased after a while, but the noise of the engines grew louder. It was obvious the Soviets were near; the Red Army, the commissars had arrived.

I dragged myself out, but the sudden pain in my chest nearly knocked me over. I coughed and spat out some blood. I struggled to walk and soon reached the hill. The bridge was gone. The big explosion must have blown it up. Tanks were crawling slowly from the forest. They were followed by helmeted soldiers, strolling casually as if on a Sunday afternoon walk. Closer to the village some Kalmuks were hiding behind the haystacks. But when they saw the tanks they came out, still staggering, and raised their hands. They threw away their rifles and revolver belts. Some fell to their knees begging for mercy. The Red soldiers rounded them up systematically, prodding them with bayonets. In a very short time most of them were captured. Their horses calmly grazed nearby.

The tanks had stopped, but new formations of men kept arriving. A pontoon appeared on the river. Sappers examined the ruined bridge. Several planes flew overhead, dipping their wings in greeting. I was somehow disappointed; the war seemed to be over.

The fields around the village were now filled with machines. Men set up tents and field kitchens and strung out telephone wires. They sang and spoke a language that resembled the local dialect, though it was not quite intelligible to me. I guessed it was Russian.

The peasants watched the visitors uneasily. When

some of the Red soldiers showed their Kalmuk-like Uzbek or Tartar faces the women screamed and recoiled with fear, even though the faces of the recent arrivals were smiling.

A group of peasants marched into the field carrying red flags with clumsily painted hammers and sickles. The soldiers greeted them with cheers and the regimental commander came out of his tent to meet the delegation. He shook hands and invited them inside. The peasants were embarrassed, and took off their caps. They had not known what to do with the flags and finally deposited them outside the tent before entering.

Beside a white truck with a red cross painted on its roof, a white-coated doctor and his orderlies were treating the wounded women and children. A crowd circled the ambulance, curious to see everything that was being done.

Children followed the soldiers, asking for sweets. The men embraced them, and played with them.

At noon the village learned that the Red soldiers had hanged all the captured Kalmuks by the legs from the oak trees along the river. Despite the pain in my chest and my hand I dragged myself there, following a crowd of curious men, women, and children.

One could see the Kalmuks from afar; they were hanging from the trees like sapless, overgrown pinecones. Each had been hanged from a separate tree, dangling by his ankles, his hands tied behind his back. Soviet soldiers with friendly smiling faces walked around calmly rolling cigarettes from pieces of newspaper. Although the soldiers did not allow the peasants to come near, some of the women, recognizing their tormentors, began to curse and throw chunks of wood and dirt at the limp hanging bodies.

Ants and flies crawled all over the strung-up Kalmuks. They crept into their open mouths, into their noses and eyes. They set up nests in their ears; they swarmed over their ragged hair. They came in thousands and fought for the best spots.

The men swung in the wind and some of them revolved slowly like sausages smoking in a fire. Some shuddered and uttered a hoarse shriek or whisper. Others seemed lifeless. They hung with wide unblinking eyes, and the veins on their necks swelled monstrously. The peasants lit a bonfire nearby, and whole families watched the hanging Kalmuks, recalling their cruelties and rejoicing over their end.

A gust of wind shook the trees. The bodies swung shivering in widening circles. The watching peasants made the sign of the cross. I looked around for death, for I felt its breath in the air. It had the face of dead Marta as it romped among the oak branches, brushing the hanging men gently, entwining them with cobwebby threads which it spun out from its translucent body. It whispered treacherous words into their ears; it caressingly trickled a chill through their hearts; it strangled their throats.

It was nearer to me than ever. I could almost touch its airy shroud, gaze into its misty eyes. It stopped in front of me, preening itself coquettishly and hinting at another meeting. I was not afraid of it; I hoped it would take me along to the other side of the forest, to the fathomless marshes where branches dip into the steaming caldrons bubbling with sulphurous fumes, where one hears at night the thin dry clatter of coupling ghosts and the shrill wind in the treetops, like a violin in a distant room.

I reached out my hand, but the ghost vanished among the trees with their burden of rustling leaves and heavy crop of hanging corpses.

Something seemed to burn inside me. My head was spinning, and I was covered with sweat. I walked toward the riverbank. The moist breeze cooled me and I sat down on a log.

The river was wide here. Its swift current carried timber, broken branches, strips of sackcloth, bunches of straw in wildly swirling eddies. Now and again the bloated body of a horse floated by. Once I thought I saw a bluish, rotted human corpse hovering just under the surface. For a moment the waters were clear. Then came a mass of fish killed by the explosions. They rolled over, flowed along upside down, and crowded together, as if there were no longer room for them in this river, to which the rainbow had brought them long ago.

I was shivering. I decided to approach the Red soldiers, though I was not sure how they would look upon people with black, bewitching eyes. As I passed by the array of hanging bodies I thought I recognized the man who had hit me with his rifle butt. He was swinging in wide circles, openmouthed and fly-ridden. I turned my head up to get a better view of his face. A pain again pierced my chest.

16

I was released from the regimental hospital. Weeks had
gone by. It was the autumn of 1944. The pain in my
chest had disappeared, and whatever had been broken
by the butt of the Kalmuk's rifle was now healed.

Contrary to what I had feared, I was allowed to
stay with the soldiers, but I knew that this was temporary. I expected to be left in some village when the
regiment went into the front line. In the meantime it
was encamped by the river, and nothing suggested an
early departure. It was a communications regiment,
composed mainly of very young soldiers and recently
recruited officers, who had been boys when the war began. The cannon, machine-guns, trucks, telegraphic and
telephonic equipment were all brand-new and well oiled
and as yet untested by war. The tent canvas and the
men's uniforms had not yet had time to fade.

The war and the front line were already far away
in enemy territory. The radio reported daily new defeats of the German Army and of its exhausted allies.
The soldiers listened carefully to the reports, nodded
their heads with pride, and went about their training.
They wrote lengthy letters to their relatives and friends,
doubting that they would have a chance to go into bat-

tle before the war ended, for the Germans were being routed by their older brothers.

Life in the regiment was calm and well ordered. Every few days a small biplane landed on the temporary airfield, bringing mail and newspapers. The letters brought news from home, where people were beginning to rebuild the ruins. Pictures in the newspapers showed bombed Soviet and German cities, smashed fortifications, and the bearded faces of German prisoners in endless lines. Rumors of the approaching end of the war circulated more and more frequently among the officers and soldiers.

Two men looked after me most of the time. They were Gavrila, a political officer of the regiment, who was said to have lost his entire family in the first days of the Nazi invasion, and Mitka, known as "Mitka the Cuckoo," a sharpshooting instructor and a crack sniper.

I also enjoyed the protection of many of their friends. Every day Gavrila used to spend time with me in the field library. He taught me to read. After all, he said, I was already over eleven. Russian boys of my age not only could read and write, but they could even fight the enemy when necessary. I did not want to be taken for a child: I studied industriously, watching the ways of the soldiers and imitating their behavior.

Books impressed me tremendously. From their simple printed pages one could conjure up a world as real as that grasped by the senses. Furthermore, the world of books, like meat in cans, was somehow richer and more flavorful than the everyday variety. In ordinary life, for example, one saw many people without really knowing them, while in books one even knew what people were thinking and planning.

I read my first book with Gavrila's assistance. It was called *Childhood* and its hero, a small boy like myself, lost his father on the first page. I read this book several times and it filled me with hope. Its hero did not have an easy life either. After his mother's death he was left quite alone, and yet despite many difficulties he grew up to be, as Gavrila said, a great man. He was Maxim Gorky, one of the greatest of all Russian writers. His books filled many shelves in the regimental library and were known to people all over the world.

I also liked poetry. It was written in a form resembling prayers, but was more beautiful and more intelligible. On the other hand, the poems did not guarantee days of indulgence. But one did not have to recite poetry as penance for sins; poetry was for pleasure. The smooth, polished words meshed with each other like oiled millstones ground to a fine fit. But reading was not my principal occupation. My lessons with Gavrila were more important.

From him I learned that the order of the world had nothing to do with God, and that God had nothing to do with the world. The reason for this was quite simple. God did not exist. The cunning priests had invented Him so they could trick stupid, superstitious people. There was no God, no Holy Trinity, no devils, ghosts, or ghouls rising from graves; there was no Death flying everywhere in search of new sinners to snare. These were all tales for ignorant people who did not understand the natural order of the world, did not believe in their own powers, and therefore had to take refuge in their belief in some God.

According to Gavrila, people themselves determined the course of their lives and were the only masters of their destinies. That is why every man was important, and why it was crucial that each know what to do and what to aim for. An individual might think his actions were of no importance, but that was an illusion. His actions, like those of innumerable others, formed a great pattern which could only be discerned by those at the summit of society. Thus some apparently random stitches of a woman's needle contributed to the beautiful floral pattern as it finally appeared on a tablecloth or bedcover.

In accordance with one of the rules of human history, said Gavrila, a man would from time to time spring up from the vast nameless mass of men; a man who wanted the welfare of others, and because of his superior knowledge and wisdom he knew that waiting for divine help would not help matters on earth very much. Such a man became a leader, one of the great men, who guided people in their thoughts and deeds, as a weaver guides his colored threads through the intricacies of the pattern.

Portraits and photographs of such great men were displayed in the regimental library, in the field hospital, in the recreation hall, in the mess tents, and in the soldiers' quarters. I had often looked at the faces of these wise and great men. Many of them were dead. Some had short, resounding names and long bushy beards. The last one, however, was still living. His portraits were larger, brighter, more handsome than those of the others. It was under his leadership, said Gavrila, that the Red Army was defeating the Germans and bringing to the liberated peoples a new way of life which made all equal. There would be no rich and poor, no exploiters and no exploited, no persecution of the dark by the fair, no people doomed to gas chambers. Gavrila, like all the officers and men in the regiment, owed all he had to this man: education, rank, home. The library owed all its beautifully printed and bound books to him. I owed the care of the army doctors and my recovery to him. Every Soviet citizen was in debt to this man for everything he possessed and for all his good fortune.

This man's name was Stalin.

In the portraits and photographs he had a kind face and compassionate eyes. He looked like a loving grandfather or uncle, long unseen, wanting to take you into his arms. Gavrila read and told me many stories about Stalin's life. At my age young Stalin already had fought for the rights of the underprivileged, resisting the centuries-old exploitation of the helpless poor by the pitiless rich.

I looked at the photographs of Stalin in his youth. He had very black, bushy hair, dark eyes, heavy eyebrows, and later even a black mustache. He looked more of a Gypsy than I did, more Jewish than the Jew killed by the German officer in the black uniform, more Jewish than the boy found by the peasants on the railroad tracks. Stalin was lucky not to have lived his youth in the villages where I had stayed. If he had been beaten as a child all the time for his dark features, perhaps he would not have had so much time to help others; he might have been too busy just fending off the village boys and dogs.

But Stalin was a Georgian. Gavrila did not tell me if the Germans had planned to incinerate the Georgians. But as I looked at the people that surrounded Stalin in the pictures I had not the slightest doubt that if the Germans had captured them, they would all have gone to the furnaces. They were all swarthy, black-haired, with dark eyes.

Because Stalin lived there, Moscow was the heart of the whole country and the longed-for city of the working masses of the whole world. Soldiers sang songs about Moscow, writers wrote books about it, poets praised it in verse. Films were made about Moscow and fascinating tales told about it. It seemed that deep under its streets, entombed like gigantic moles, long gleaming trains rushed smoothly along and stopped noiselessly at stations decorated with marble and mosaics finer than those in the most beautiful churches.

Stalin's home was the Kremlin. Many old palaces and churches stood there in one compound behind a high wall. One could see over it the domes resembling huge radishes with their roots pointing toward the sky. Other pictures showed the Kremlin quarters where Lenin, the late teacher of Stalin, used to live. Some of the soldiers were more impressed by Lenin, others by

Stalin, just as some of the peasants spoke more often
about God the Father and others about God the Son.

The soldiers said that the windows of Stalin's
study in the Kremlin were lit late into the night and
that the people of Moscow, along with all the working
masses of the world, looked toward those windows and
found new inspiration and hope for the future. There
the great Stalin watched over them, worked for them
all, devised the best ways of winning the war and de-
stroying the enemies of the working masses. His mind
was filled with concern for all suffering people, even
those in distant countries still living under terrible op-
pression. But the day of their liberation was approaching, and to bring that day nearer Stalin had to work
late into the night.

After I learned all these things from Gavrila, I
often walked in the fields and thought deeply. I regretted all my prayers. The many thousands of days of
indulgence I had earned with them were wasted. If it
were true that there was no God, no Son, no Holy
Mother, nor any of the lesser saints, what had happened to all my prayers? Were they perhaps circling in
the empty heaven like a flock of birds whose nests had
been destroyed by boys? Or were they in some secret
place and, like my lost voice, struggling to get free?

Recalling some of the phrases in those prayers, I
felt cheated. They were, as Gavrila said, filled only with
meaningless words. Why hadn't I realized it sooner?
On the other hand, I found it hard to credit that the
priests themselves did not believe in God and used Him
only to fool other people. And what about the churches,
Roman and Orthodox? Were they also built, as Gavrila
said, merely for the purpose of intimidating people
through God's presumed power, forcing them to support the clergy? But if the priests acted in good faith,
what would happen to them when they suddenly discovered that there was no God, and that above the
highest church dome there was only a boundless sky

where airplanes with red stars painted on their wings flew? What would they do when they discovered that all their prayers were worthless and that everything they did at the altar, and everything they told people from the pulpit, was a fraud?

The discovery of that terrible truth would strike them down with a blow worse than a father's death or the last glimpse of his lifeless body. People had always been comforted by their belief in God, and they usually died before their children. Such was the law of nature. Their only consolation was the knowlédge that, after their death, God would guide their children through their lives on this earth, just as the children found their only solace in the thought that God would greet their parents beyond the grave. God was always in people's minds, even when He Himself was too busy to listen to their prayers and keep track of their accumulated days of indulgence.

Eventually Gavrila's lessons filled me with a new confidence. In this world there were realistic ways of promoting goodness, and there were people who had dedicated their whole lives to it. These were the Communist Party members. They were selected from the whole population and given special training, set particular tasks to perform. They were prepared to endure hardship, even death, if the cause of the working people required it. The Party members stood at that social summit from which human actions could be seen not as meaningless jumbles, but as part of a definite pattern. The Party could see farther than the best sniper. That was why every member of the Party not only knew the meaning of events, but also shaped them and directed them toward new aims. That was why no Party member was ever surprised at anything. The Party was to the working people what the engine is to a train. It led others toward the best goals, it pointed out shortcuts to an improvement of their lives. And Stalin was the engineer at the throttle of this engine.

Gavrila always returned hoarse and exhausted from Party meetings which were long and tempestuous. The Party members evaluated each other at these frequent meetings; each of them would criticize the others and himself, give praise where due, or point out shortcomings. They were particularly aware of events around them, and they always endeavored to forestall the harmful activities of people under the influence of priests and landlords. Through their constant watchfulness the members of the Party became tempered like steel. Among the Party members there were young and old, officers and enlisted men. The strength of the Party, as Gavrila explained, lay in its ability to rid itself of those who, like a jammed or crooked wheel on a cart, impeded progress. This self-purging was done at the meetings. It was there that members acquired the necessary toughness.

There was about it something immensely captivating. One looked at a man dressed like everyone else, working and fighting as they all did. He seemed to be just another soldier in a great army. But he might be a member of the Party; in a pocket of his uniform, over his heart, he might be carrying his Party card. Then he changed in my eyes as did sensitized paper in the darkroom of the regimental photographer. He became one of the best, one of the chosen, one of those who knew more than the others. His judgment carried more force than a box of explosives. Others grew silent when he spoke, or spoke more carefully when he listened.

In the Soviet world a man was rated according to others' opinion of him, not according to his own. Only the group, which they called "the collective," was qualified to determine a man's worth and importance. The group decided what could make him more useful and what could reduce his usefulness to others. He himself became the composite of everything others said about him. Learning to know a man's inner character was a never-ending process, Gavrila said. There was no way of knowing that at its bottom, as in a deep well, there might not lurk an enemy of the working people, an agent of the landlords. That is why a man had to be continually watched by those around him, by his friends and enemies alike.

In Gavrila's world the individual seemed to have many faces; one of them might be slapped while another was being kissed, and yet another went temporarily unnoticed. At every moment he was measured by yardsticks of professional proficiency, family origin, collective or Party success, and compared with other men who might replace him at any time or who might be replaced by him. The Party looked at a man simultaneously through lenses of different focus, but unvarying precision; no one knew what final image would emerge.

To be a Party member was indeed the goal. The path to that summit was not easy, and the more I learned about the life of the regiment the more I realized the complexity of the world in which Gavrila moved.

It seemed that to reach the pinnacle a man must climb simultaneously many ladders. He might have been already halfway up on the professional ladder while just starting out on the political one. He might have been ascending one and descending the other. Thus his chances of reaching the summit altered, and the peak, as Gavrila said, was often one step forward and two steps back. Besides, even after reaching this peak, one might easily fall and have to start the climb all over again.

Because a person's rating depended in part on one's social origin, one's family background counted even if one's parents were not living. A man had a better chance of ascending the political ladder if his parents were industrial workers rather than peasants or office clerks. This shadow of their family trailed people relentlessly, just as the concept of original sin hounded even the best Catholic.

I was filled with apprehension. Though I could not remember my father's exact occupation, I recalled the presence of cook, maid, and nurse, who would surely be classified as victims of exploitation. I also knew that neither my father nor my mother had been a worker. Would it mean that, just as my black hair and eyes were held against me by the peasants, my social origin could handicap my new life with the Soviets?

On the military ladder one's position was determined by rank and function in the regiment. A veteran Party member had to obey explicitly the orders of his commander, who might not even be a Party member. Later at a Party meeting he could criticize this same commander's activities and, if his charges were supported by other Party members, he might cause the transfer of the commander to a lower post. Sometimes the reverse was true. A commander might punish an officer who belonged to the Party, and the Party might further demote the officer in its hierarchy.

I felt lost in this maze. In the world into which Gavrila was initiating me, human aspirations and expectations were entangled with each other like the roots and branches of great trees in a thick forest, each tree struggling for more moisture from the soil and more sunshine from the sky.

I was worried. What would happen to me when I grew up? How would I look when seen through the many eyes of the Party? What was my deepest core: a healthy core like that of a fresh apple, or a rotten one like the maggoty stone of a withered plum?

What would happen if the others, the collective, decided that I was best suited for deep-water diving, for example? Would it matter that I was terrified of water because every plunge reminded me of my near-drowning under the ice? The group might think that it had been a valuable experience, qualifying me to train for diving. Instead of becoming an inventor of fuses I would have to spend the rest of my life as a diver, hating the very sight of water, panic-stricken before each dive. What would happen in that case? How can an individual, Gavrila asked, presume to put his judgment ahead of that of the many?

I absorbed Gavrila's every word, writing questions which I wanted answered on the slate he had given me. I listened to the soldiers' conversations before and after the meetings; I eavesdropped on the meetings through the canvas walls of the tent.

The life of these Soviet grownups was not very easy. Maybe it was just as hard as wandering from one village to the next, and being taken for a Gypsy. A man had many paths from which to choose, many roads and highways across the country of life. Some were dead ends, others led to swamps, to dangerous traps and snares. In Gavrila's world only the Party knew the right paths and the right destination.

I tried to memorize Gavrila's teaching, not to lose a single word. He maintained that to be happy and useful one should join the march of the working people, keeping in step with the others in the place assigned in the column. Pushing too close to the head of the column was as bad as lagging behind. It could mean loss of contact with the masses, and would lead to decadence and degeneracy. Every stumble could slow down the whole column, and those who fell risked being trampled on by the others . . .

17

In the late afternoon crowds of peasants came from the villages. They brought fruit and vegetables in exchange for the rich canned pork sent to the Red Army all the way from America, for shoes, or for a piece of tent canvas suitable for making into a pair of trousers or a jacket.

As the soldiers were finishing their afternoon duties, one heard accordion music and singing here and there. The peasants listened intently to the songs, barely understanding their words. Some of the peasants joined boldly and loudly in the song. Others appeared alarmed, suspiciously watching the faces of their neighbors who displayed such sudden and unexpected affection for the Red Army.

Women came from the villages in increasing numbers, together with their men. Many of them flirted openly with the soldiers, trying to lure them in the direction of their husbands or brothers who were trading a few steps away. Ashen-haired and light-eyed, they pulled down their ragged blouses and hiked up their worn skirts with a casual air, swinging their hips as they strolled around. The soldiers came closer, bringing from their tents bright cans of American pork and beef, packets of tobacco and paper for rolling cigarettes. Disregarding the presence of the men, they looked deep into the women's eyes, accidentally brushing against their buxom bodies and breathing in their odor.

Soldiers occasionally sneaked out of the camp and visited the villages to continue trade with the farmers and meet village girls. The command of the regiment did its best to prevent such planned secret contacts with the population. The political officers, the battalion commanders, and even the divisional newssheets warned the soldiers against such individual escapades. They pointed out that some of the wealthier farmers were under the influence of the nationalist partisans who roamed the forests in an attempt to slow down the victorious march of the Soviet Army and to prevent the approaching triumph of a government of workers and peasants. They indicated that men from other regiments returned from such excursions severely beaten, and that some had disappeared altogether.

One day, however, a few soldiers disregarded the risk of punishment and managed to slip out of the camp. The guards pretended not to notice. Life in the camp was monotonous and the soldiers, waiting for departure or action, were desperate for some entertainment. Mitka the Cuckoo knew about this outing of his friends and he might even have gone with them if he had not been crippled. He often said that since the Red Army soldiers risked their lives for these local people by fighting the Nazis, there was no reason to avoid their company.

Mitka had been looking after me ever since I entered the regimental hospital. Thanks to his feeding I gained weight. Mitka fished out of the great caldron the best pieces of meat, and skimmed the fat off the soup for me. He also assisted at my painful injections, boosting my courage before medical examinations. Once when I got indigestion from overeating, Mitka sat with me for two days, holding my head when I vomited and wiping my face with a wet cloth.

While Gavrila taught me serious things, explaining the role of the Party, Mitka introduced me to poetry and sang me songs, strumming an accompaniment on his guitar. It was Mitka who took me to the regimental cinema and carefully explained the films. I went with him to watch the mechanics repairing the engines of the powerful Army trucks, and it was Mitka who took me to see the sharpshooters in training.

Mitka was one of the best liked and respected men in the regiment. He had a fine military record. On special Army days one could see decorations on his faded uniform which would be the envy of regimental or even divisional commanders. Mitka was a Hero of the Soviet Union, the highest military honor, and was one of the most decorated men in the whole division.

His feats as a sharpshooter were described in newspapers and books for children and adults. He was featured several times in newsreels seen by millions of Soviet citizens on collective farms and in factories. The regiment took great pride in Mitka; he was photographed for the divisional newssheets and interviewed by correspondents.

Soldiers often told tales at the evening campfire about the dangerous missions he had undertaken only a year earlier. They discussed endlessly his heroic actions in the rear of the enemy, where he parachuted in alone and then sniped at officers and couriers of the German Army with extraordinary long-range marksmanship. They marveled at the way Mitka managed to return from behind the lines, only to be sent out again on another dangerous mission.

During such talks I swelled with pride. I sat next to Mitka, leaning on his strong arm, listening intently to his voice, so as not to miss a word of what he was

saying or the questions of others. If the war lasted until
I was old enough to serve, perhaps I could become a
sharpshooter, a hero about whom working people
talked at their meals.

Mitka's rifle was the object of constant admiration. Yielding to requests, he would take it out of its
sheath, blowing off invisible specks of dust on the
sights and stock. Trembling with curiosity, young soldiers bent over the rifle with the reverence of a priest
at an altar. Old soldiers with large, horny hands picked
up the weapon with its softly polished stock as a mother picks up a baby from its cradle. Holding their breath
they examined the crystal-clear lenses of the telescopic
sight. It was through this eye that Mitka saw the
enemy. These lenses brought the targets so close to
him that he could see the faces, gestures, smiles. It
helped him to aim unerringly at the spot beneath the
metal bars where the German heart was beating.

Mitka's face darkened as the soldiers admired his
rifle. He instinctively touched the pained, stiffened side
of his body in which the fragments of a German bullet
were still embedded. That bullet had ended his career
as a sniper a year ago. It tormented him daily. It
changed him from Mitka the Cuckoo, as he had been
known before, into Mitka the Master, as he was now
more often called.

He was still the regimental sharpshooting instructor, and he taught young soldiers his art, but that was
not what his heart craved. At night I sometimes saw
his wide-open eyes staring at the triangular roof of the
tent. He was probably reliving those days and nights
when, hidden in branches or in ruins far behind enemy
lines, he had waited for the right moment to pick off
an officer, a staff messenger, an airman, or a tank
driver. How many times he must have looked the
enemy in the face, followed their movements, measur-
ing the distance, setting his sights once more. With each

one of his well-aimed bullets he strengthened the Soviet Union by removing one of the enemy's officers.

Special German squads with trained dogs had searched for his hiding places, and the manhunts had covered wide circles. How many times he must have thought he would never return! Yet I knew that these must have been the happiest days of Mitka's life. Mitka would not trade these days when he was both judge and executioner for any others. Alone, guided by the telescopic sights of his rifle, he deprived the enemy of their choicest men. He recognized them by their decorations, by the insignia of their rank, by the color of their uniforms. Before pulling the trigger he must have asked himself if this man was worthy of death by a bullet from Mitka the Cuckoo's rifle. Perhaps he should wait for a choicer victim: a captain instead of a lieutenant, a major instead of a captain, a pilot instead of a tank gunner, a staff officer instead of a battalion commander. Every one of his shots could bring death not only to the enemy, but also to himself, thus robbing the Red Army of one of its finest soldiers.

Thinking about it all, I admired Mitka more and more. Here, lying on a bed a few feet from me, was a man who worked for a better and safer world, not by praying at church altars, but by excelling in his aim. The German officer in the magnificent black uniform, who spent his time killing helpless prisoners or deciding the fate of small black fleas like me, now appeared pitifully insignificant in comparison with Mitka.

When the soldiers who had slipped out of the camp to the village did not return, Mitka became worried. The hour of the night inspection was approaching and their absence might be discovered at any moment. We were sitting in the tent. Mitka paced nervously, rubbing his hands, moist with emotion. They were his closest friends: Grisha, a good singer, whom Mitka accompanied on his accordion; Lonka, who came from the same city; Anton, a poet, who could recite better than anyone else; and Vanka who, Mitka claimed, had once saved his life.

The sun had set and the guard had been changed. Mitka kept looking at the phosphorescent dial of his watch, which he had won as war loot.

There was a commotion among the guards outside. Someone shouted for a doctor as a motorcycle sputtered at top speed across the camp toward headquarters.

Mitka rushed out, pulling me along with him. Others also came running behind.

Many soldiers were already assembled at the guard line. Several soldiers covered with blood knelt or stood surrounding four motionless bodies laid on the ground. We learned from their incoherent words that they had attended a feast at a nearby village and had been attacked by some drunken peasants who had become jealous of their women. The peasants had outnumbered and disarmed them. Four of the soldiers had been killed with axes and others badly wounded.

The deputy commander of the regiment arrived, followed by other senior officers. The soldiers made way for them, and stood at attention. The wounded men tried in vain to rise. The deputy commander, pale but composed, listened to the report of one of the injured men and then issued his orders. The wounded were immediately taken to the hospital. Some of them could walk slowly, supporting one another and wiping blood from their faces and from their hair with their sleeves.

Mitka crouched at the feet of the dead men, staring silently at their butchered faces. Other soldiers stood by visibly upset.

Vanka lay on his back, his white face turned to the surrounding onlookers. In the dim light of a lantern one could see streaks of congealed blood on his chest. Lonka's face had been split in two by a terrible blow from an ax. Splintered skull bones were mixed with hanging ribbons of neck muscles. The battered, bloated faces of the other two were barely recognizable.

An ambulance drove up. Mitka angrily clutched my arm while the bodies were taken away.

The tragedy was brought up in the evening report. The men swallowed hard, listening to new orders forbidding any contact with the hostile local population and prohibiting any action which could further aggravate its relations with the Red Army.

That night Mitka kept whispering and muttering to himself, beat his head with his fist, and then sat in brooding silence.

Several days passed. Regimental life was returning to normal. The men mentioned the names of the dead less frequently. They began to sing again and prepared for the visit of a field theater. But Mitka was not well, and someone else replaced him in his training duties.

One night Mitka woke me up before dawn. He told me to dress quickly and said no more. When I was ready I helped him to bind his feet and to pull on his boots. He groaned with pain but moved in haste. When he was dressed he made sure the other men were asleep and then pulled out his rifle from behind the bed. He took the weapon out of its brown case and slung it over his shoulder. He carefully replaced the empty case behind the bed, locking it to look as though the rifle was still inside. Then he uncovered the telescope and slipped it into his pocket together with a small tripod. He checked his cartridge belt and took a pair of field glasses off the hook and looped the strap around my neck.

We silently slipped out of the tent, past the field kitchen. When the men on guard had marched by, we ran quickly toward the bushes, crossed the adjoining field, and were soon outside the encampment.

The horizon was still swathed in nocturnal mist. The white streak of a country lane crept between the dim layers of fog which hung over the fields.

Mitka wiped the sweat off his neck, hitched his belt, and patted me on the head as we hurried toward the woods.

I did not know where we were going or why. But I guessed that Mitka was doing something on his own, something he was not supposed to do, something that might cost him his position in the Army and in public esteem.

And yet, realizing it all, I was filled with pride to be the person chosen to accompany him, and help a Hero of the Soviet Union in his mysterious mission.

We walked fast. Mitka was obviously tired as he limped and pulled up his rifle which kept slipping off his shoulder. Whenever he stumbled he muttered curses which he usually forbade other soldiers to use and, realizing I had heard them, ordered me to forget them at once. I nodded in agreement, though I would have given much to have my speech back so that I could repeat these magnificent Russian curses, which were as juicy as ripe plums.

We cautiously bypassed a sleeping village. No smoke rose from the chimneys, the dogs and the roosters were silent. Mitka's face stiffened and his lips became dry. He opened a flask of cold coffee, took a gulp and gave me the rest. We hurried on.

It was daylight by the time we entered the forest, but the woods were still gloomy. The trees stood stiffly like sinister monks in black habits guarding the glades and clearings with the broad sleeves of their branches. At one point the sun found a tiny opening at the top of the trees and the rays shone through the open palms of chestnut leaves.

After some reflection Mitka selected a tall sturdy tree close to the fields on the edge of the forest. The trunk was slippery, but there were knots and broad boughs grew fairly low. Mitka first helped me onto one of the boughs and then handed me the long rifle, the binoculars, the telescope, and the tripod, all of which I hung delicately on the branches. Then it was my turn to help him up. When Mitka, groaning and puffing, and wet with sweat, reached me on the branch, I climbed to the next one. Thus, helping each other, we managed to get almost to the top of the tree with the rifle and all the equipment.

After a moment's rest, Mitka deftly bent back some branches which obscured our view, cut some of them, and tied others. We soon had a reasonably comfortable and well-concealed seat. Unseen birds fluttered in the foliage.

Growing accustomed to the height, I discerned the outlines of buildings in the village just ahead of us. The first puffs of smoke were beginning to rise into the sky. Mitka attached the telescope to his rifle and fixed the tripod firmly. He sat back and carefully placed the rifle on its support.

He spent a long time scanning the village through the binoculars. Then he handed them to me and began to adjust the telescopic sight of the rifle. Through the binoculars I surveyed the village. Their image amazingly enlarged, the houses seemed to be just in front of the woodland. The picture was so sharp and clear that I could almost count the straws in the thatched roofs. I could see hens pecking in the yards and a dog lazing in the thin sunshine of the early morning.

Mitka asked me for the binoculars. Before handing them back I had another quick glimpse of the village. I saw a tall man leaving a house. He stretched his arms, yawned, and looked at the cloudless sky. I could see that his shirt was wide open in front, and there were big patches on the knees of his pants.

Mitka took the binoculars and placed them beyond

my reach. Intently he studied the scene through his
telescope. I strained my eyes but, without the glasses,
could see only the dwarfed houses far below.

A shot rang out. I started and birds fluttered in
the thicket. Mitka raised his red, perspiring face and
muttered something. I reached for the binoculars. He
smiled apologetically and held back my hand.

I resented Mitka's refusal, but could guess what
had happened. In my imagination I saw the farmer
keeling over, reaching above his head with his hands,
as if seeking support from an invisible handhold as he
slumped on the threshold of his house.

Mitka reloaded the rifle, placing the used cartridge
case in his pocket. He calmly inspected the village
through the binoculars, whistling softly through tight
lips.

I tried to visualize what he saw there. An old
woman wrapped in brown rags walking out of the
house, looking at the sky, crossing herself, and at the
same moment catching sight of the man's body lying on the ground. As she approached it with clumsy,
waddling steps and bent down to turn his face toward
her, she noticed the blood and ran screaming toward
the neighboring houses.

Startled by her cries, men pulling on their trousers
and women only half awake started running out of
the houses. The village soon swarmed with people rushing to and fro. The men bent over the body, gesturing
wildly and looking helplessly in all directions.

Mitka moved slightly. He had his eye glued to the
telescopic sight and was pressing the butt of his rifle
to his shoulder. Drops of perspiration glistened on his
forehead. One of them broke away, rolled into his
bushy eyebrows, emerged at the base of his nose and
started along the diagonal ridge of his cheek on its way
to his chin. Before it reached his lips, Mitka fired
three times in quick succession.

I closed my eyes and saw the village again, with

the three bodies sliding to the ground. The remaining peasants, unable to hear the shots at that distance, scattered in panic, looking around in bewilderment and wondering where the shots were coming from.

Fear gripped the village. The families of the dead sobbed wildly and dragged the bodies by their hands and feet toward their houses and barns. Children and older people, unaware of what was happening, milled aimlessly about. After a few moments everyone disappeared. Even the shutters were closed.

Mitka examined the village again. There must have been no one left outside, for his inspection took some time. Suddenly he put aside the binoculars and seized the rifle.

I wondered. It was perhaps some young man sneaking between the houses, trying to evade the sniper and get quickly back to his hut. Not knowing where the bullets came from, he stopped now and then and stared about him. As he reached a row of wild rosebushes, Mitka fired again.

The man stopped as though nailed to the ground. He bent one knee, tried to bend the other, and then just toppled into the rosebushes. The thorny branches shook uneasily.

Mitka leaned on his rifle and rested. The peasants were all in their houses and none dared to come out.

How I envied Mitka! I suddenly understood a good deal of what one of the soldiers had said in a discussion with him. Human being, he said, is a proud name. Man carries in himself his own private war, which he has to wage, win or lose, himself—his own justice, which is his alone to administer. Now Mitka the Cuckoo had meted out revenge for the death of his friends, regardless of the opinions of others, risking his position in the regiment, and his title of Hero of the Soviet Union. If he could not revenge his friends, what was the use of all those days of training in the sniper's art, the mastery of eye, hand, and breath? Of what value was the rank of Hero, respected and worshiped by tens of millions of citizens, if he no longer deserved it in his own eyes?

There was another element in Mitka's revenge. A man, no matter how popular and admired, lives mainly with himself. If he is not at peace with himself, if he is harassed by something he did not do but should have done to preserve his own image of himself, he is like the "unhappy Demon, spirit of exile, gliding high above the sinful world."

I also understood something else. There were many paths and many ascents leading to the summit. But one could also reach the summit alone, with the help at most of a single friend, the way Mitka and I had climbed the tree. This was a different summit, apart from the march of the working masses.

With a kind smile Mitka handed me the binoculars. I peered eagerly at the village, but saw nothing except tightly shut houses. Here and there a hen or a turkey strutted. I was just about to hand the glasses back to him when a big dog appeared between the houses. It wagged its tail and scratched its ear with a hind leg. I remembered Judas. He had done just that as he scowled at me hanging on the hooks.

I touched Mitka's arm, pointing to the village with my head. He thought I meant that people were moving and he concentrated on the telescopic sight. Seeing no one, he looked at me questioningly. I told him with signs that I wanted him to kill the dog. He showed surprise and refused. I asked him again. He refused, looking at me with disapproval.

We sat in silence, listening to the fearful rustle of the leaves. Mitka surveyed the village again, then he folded the tripod and removed the telescopic sight. We started down slowly; Mitka sometimes muttered from pain as he hung by his arms searching for a foothold below.

He buried the spent cartridges under the moss

and removed all traces of our presence. Then we walked toward the camp, where we could hear engines being tested by mechanics. We got back in unnoticed.

In the afternoon, when the other men were on duty, Mitka quickly cleaned the rifle and the sight and replaced them in their sheaths.

That evening he was mild and cheerful as before. In a sentimental voice he sang ballads about the beauty of Odessa, about gunners who, with a thousand batteries, were avenging the mothers who had lost their sons in the war.

The soldiers sitting near sang the chorus. Their voices carried loud and clear. From the village came the faint, steady tolling of the funeral bells.

18

It took me several days to become reconciled to the idea of leaving Gavrila, Mitka, and all my other friends in the regiment. But Gavrila was very firm in explaining that the war was ending, that my country had been fully liberated from the Germans and that, according to regulations, lost children had to be delivered to special centers where they would be kept until it was determined if their parents were still alive.

I looked at his face while he was telling me all these things and held back my tears. Gavrila also felt uneasy. I knew that he and Mitka had discussed my future, and if there had been any other solution they would have found it.

Gavrila promised that if no relatives claimed me within three months after the end of the war, he would take care of me himself and would send me to a school where they would teach me to speak again. In the meantime he urged me to be brave and to remember everything I had learned from him and to read *Pravda,* the Soviet newspaper, every day.

I was given a bag full of gifts from the soldiers and books from Gavrila and Mitka. I put on a Soviet Army uniform which was made especially for me by the regimental tailor. In a pocket I found a small wooden pistol with a picture of Stalin on one side and Lenin on the other.

The moment of parting had come. I was going away with sergeant Yury, who had some military business in the town where there was a center for lost children. This industrial city, the country's largest, was where I had lived before the war.

Gavrila made certain that I had all my things and that my personal file was in good order. He had assembled in it all the information I had given him concerning my name, previous place of residence, and the details I remembered about my parents, my hometown, our relatives and friends.

The driver started the engine. Mitka patted me on the shoulder and urged me to uphold the honor of the Red Army. Gavrila hugged me warmly, and the others shook hands with me in turn as though I were a grownup. I wanted to cry but I kept my face straight and laced tight like a soldier's boot.

We started for the station. The train was packed with soldiers and civilians. It stopped often at broken-down signals, went on and stopped again between stations. We passed bombed-out towns, deserted villages, abandoned cars, tanks, guns, airplanes with their wing and tail surfaces cut away. On many stations ragged people ran along the tracks, begging for cigarettes and food, while half-naked children stared openmouthed at the train. It took us two days to reach our destination.

All the tracks were being used by military transports, Red Cross carriages, and open cars loaded with army equipment. On the platforms crowds of Soviet soldiers and ex-prisoners in a variety of uniforms jostled along with limping invalids, shabby civilians, and blind people who tapped the flagstones with their canes. Here and there nurses directed emaciated people in striped clothes; the soldiers looked at them in sudden silence —those were the people saved from the furnaces who were returning to life from the concentration camps.

I clutched Yury's hand and looked into the gray faces of these people, with their feverishly burning eyes shining like pieces of broken glass in the ashes of a dying fire.

Nearby a locomotive pushed a gleaming railcar to the center of the station. A foreign military delegation emerged in colorful uniforms and medals. An honor guard quickly formed and a military band struck up an anthem. The smartly uniformed officers and the men in striped concentration camp clothes passed without a word within a few feet of each other on the narrow platform.

New flags were flying over the main station building and loudspeakers blared music interrupted from time to time by hoarse speeches and greetings. Yury looked at his watch. We made our way to the exit.

One of the military drivers agreed to take us to the orphans' home. The streets of the city were full of convoys and soldiers, the sidewalks swarmed with people. The orphanage occupied several old houses on a side street. Innumerable children peered from the windows.

We spent an hour in the lobby; Yury read a newspaper and I feigned indifference. Finally the woman principal came over and greeted us, taking the folder with my documents from Yury. She signed some papers, gave them to Yury, and placed her hand on my shoulder. I firmly shook it off. The epaulets on a uniform were not meant for a woman's hands.

The moment of parting arrived. Yury pretended to be cheerful. He joked, straightened the forage cap on my head, and tightened the string round the books with Mitka's and Gavrila's inscriptions which I carried under my arm. We hugged each other like two men. The principal stood by.

I clutched the red star attached to my left breast pocket. A gift from Gavrila, it had Lenin's profile on it. I now believed that this star, leading millions of workers throughout the world to their goal, could also bring me good luck. I followed the principal.

Walking along crowded corridors we passed the open doors of classrooms, in which lessons were in progress. Here and there children were scuffling and shouting. Some boys, seeing my uniform, pointed their fingers at me and laughed. I turned away. Someone threw an apple core; I ducked and it hit the principal.

I had no peace for the first few days. The principal wanted me to give up my uniform and wear ordinary civilian clothes sent to the children by the International Red Cross. I nearly hit a nurse on the head when she tried to take away the uniform. I slept with my tunic and trousers folded under my mattress for safekeeping.

After a while my long-unwashed uniform began to smell, but I still refused to part with it even for a day. The principal, annoyed by this insubordination, called two nurses and had them take it away by force. A jubilant crowd of boys witnessed the struggle.

I broke from the clumsy women and ran out into the street. There I accosted four quietly strolling Soviet soldiers. I signaled with my hands that I was a mute. They gave me a piece of paper on which I wrote that I was the son of a Soviet officer who was at the front and that I was waiting for my father at the orphanage. Then I wrote in careful language that the principal was the daughter of a landlord, that she hated the Red Army, and that she, together with the nurses exploited by her, beat me daily because of my uniform.

As I expected, my message aroused the young soldiers. They followed me inside, and while one of them systematically smashed the flowerpots in the principal's carpeted office, the others chased the nurses, slapping them and pinching their bottoms. The frightened women yelled and screamed.

After that the staff let me alone. Even the teachers ignored my refusal to learn reading and writing in my mother-tongue. I wrote in chalk on the blackboard that my language was Russian, the speech of a land where there was no exploitation of the one by the many and where teachers did not persecute their pupils.

A large calendar hung over my bed. I crossed off every day with a red pencil. I did not know how many more days were left to the end of the war still being waged in Germany, but I was confident that the Red Army was doing its best to bring the end nearer.

Every day I sneaked out of the orphanage and bought a copy of *Pravda* with the money Gavrila had given me. I read hastily all the news about the latest victories and I looked carefully at the new pictures of Stalin. I felt reassured. Stalin looked fit and youthful. Everything was going well. The war would end soon.

One day I was summoned for a medical examination. I refused to leave my uniform outside the office and I was examined carrying it under my arm. After the examination I was interviewed by some sort of social commission. One of its members, an older man, read all my papers carefully. He approached me in a friendly manner. He mentioned my name and asked me whether I had any idea where my parents were planning to go when they had left me. I pretended not to understand. Someone translated the question into Russian, adding that he seemed to think that he had known my parents before the war. I wrote nonchalantly on a slate that my parents were dead, killed by a bomb. The members of the commission gave me suspicious looks. I saluted stiffly and walked out of the room. The inquisitive man had upset me.

There were five hundred of us at the orphanage. We were divided into groups, and attended lessons in small dingy classrooms. Many of the boys and girls were crippled and acted very strangely. The classrooms were crowded. We were short of desks and blackboards. I was sitting next to a boy about my own age who kept muttering incessantly, "Where is my daddy, where is my daddy?" He looked around as if he expected his daddy to emerge from under a desk and pat him on his sweaty forehead. Directly behind us was a girl who had lost all her fingers in an explosion. She stared at the fingers of other children, which were as lively as worms. Noticing her glance they quickly hid their hands as if afraid of her eyes. Farther away there was a boy with part of his jaw and arm missing. He had to be fed by others; the odor of a festering wound emanated from him. There were also several partly paralyzed children.

We all looked at one another with loathing and fear. One never knew what one's neighbor might do. Many of the boys in the class were older and stronger than I. They knew that I could not speak, and consequently believed that I was a moron. They called me names and sometimes beat me up. In the morning when I came to the classroom after a sleepless night in the crowded dormitory I felt trapped, fearful and apprehensive. The anticipation of disaster increased. I was as taut as the elastic in a slingshot, and the slightest incident would throw me off balance. I was afraid not so much of being attacked by other boys as of seriously injuring someone in self-defense. As they often told us in the orphanage, that would mean jail, and the end of my hopes of returning to Gavrila.

I could not control my movements in a scuffle. My hands acquired a life of their own and could not be torn away from an opponent. Besides, for a long time after a fight I could not calm down, pondering what had happened and getting excited again.

I was also unable to run away. When I saw a group of boys coming toward me I immediately stopped. I tried to convince myself that I was avoiding being hit from behind and that I could better gauge the strength and intentions of the enemy. But the truth was that I could not run away even when I wanted to. My legs became strangely heavy, with the weight distributed in an odd manner. My thighs and calves grew leaden, but my knees were light and sagged like soft pillows. The memory of all my successful escapes did not seem to help much. A mysterious mechanism bound me to the ground. I would stop and wait for my assailants.

All the time I thought of Mitka's teachings: a man should never let himself be mistreated, for he would then lose his self-respect and his life would become meaningless. What would preserve his self-respect and determine his worth was his ability to take revenge on those who wronged him.

A person should take revenge for every wrong or humiliation. There were far too many injustices in the world to have them all weighed and judged. A man should consider every wrong he had suffered and decide on the appropriate revenge. Only the conviction that one was as strong as the enemy and that one could pay him back double, enabled people to survive, Mitka said. A man should take revenge according to his own nature and the means at his disposal. It was quite simple: if someone was rude to you and it hurt you like a whiplash, you should punish him as though he had lashed you with a whip. If someone slapped you and it felt like a thousand blows, take revenge for a thousand blows. The revenge should be proportionate to all the pain, bitterness, and humiliation felt as a result of an opponent's action. A slap in the face might not be too painful for one man; for another it might cause him to relive the persecution he had endured through hundreds of days of beating. The first man could forget about it in an hour; the second might be tormented for weeks by nightmarish recollections.

Of course the opposite also held true. If a man hit you with a stick but it only hurt like a slap, take revenge for a slap.

Life at the orphanage was full of unexpected attacks and brawls. Nearly everyone had a nickname.

There was a boy in my class called the Tank because
he pummeled with his fists anyone who stood in his
way. There was a boy labeled Cannon because he threw
heavy objects at people for no particular reason. There
were others: the Saber, who slashed his enemy with
the edge of his arm; the Airplane, who knocked you
down and kicked you in the face; the Sniper, who
hurled rocks from a distance; the Flamethrower, who
lit slow-burning matches and tossed them into clothing
and satchels.

The girls also had their nicknames. The Grenade
used to lacerate the faces of her enemies with a nail
hidden in her palm. Another, the Partisan, small and
unobtrusive, crouched on the ground and tripped passersby with a neat leg snatch, while her ally, the Tor-
pedo, would hug a prostrate opponent as though trying
to make love, and then deal him a professional knee
kick in the groin.

The teachers and attendants could not handle this
group, and they often kept out of the way of the brawls,
fearing the stronger boys. Sometimes there were more
serious incidents. The Cannon once threw a heavy boot
at a young girl who apparently had refused to kiss him.
She died a few hours later. On another occasion the
Flamethrower set fire to the clothes of three boys and
locked them in a classroom. Two of them were taken
to the hospital with severe burns.

Every fight drew blood. Boys and girls battled for
their lives and could not be separated. At night even
worse things happened. Boys would assault girls in
dark corridors. One night several boys raped a nurse
in the basement. They kept her there for hours, inviting other boys to join them, exciting the woman in the
elaborate ways they had learned in various places during the war. She was finally reduced to a state of insane
frenzy. She screamed and yelled all night until the ambulance came and took her away.

Other girls invited attention. They stripped and

asked boys to touch them. They discussed blatantly the sexual demands which scores of men had made on them during the war. There were some who said they could not go to sleep without having had a man. They ran out into the parks at night and picked up drunken soldiers.

Many of the boys and girls were quite passive and listless. They stood against the walls, mostly silent, neither crying nor laughing, staring at some image which they alone could see. It was said that some of them had lived in ghettos or concentration camps. Had it not been for the end of the occupation, they would have died long since. Others had apparently been kept by brutal and greedy foster-parents who had exploited them ruthlessly and flogged them for the slightest sign of disobedience. There were also some who had no particular past. They had been placed in the orphanage by the army or the police. No one knew their origins, the whereabouts of their parents, or where they had spent the war. They refused to tell anything about themselves; they responded to all questions with evasive phrases and indulgent half-smiles suggesting infinite contempt for the questioners.

I was afraid to fall asleep at night because the boys were known to play painful practical jokes on one another. I slept in my uniform with a knife in one pocket and a wooden knuckle-duster in the other.

Every morning I crossed one more day off my calendar. *Pravda* said that the Red Army had already reached the nest of the Nazi viper.

Gradually I became friendly with a boy called the Silent One. He acted as though mute; no one had heard the sound of his voice since he had come to the orphanage. It was known that he could speak, but at some stage of the war he had decided that there was no point in doing so. Other boys tried to force him to speak. Once they even gave him a bloody beating, but did not extract a single sound from him.

The Silent One was older and stronger than I. At first we avoided each other. I felt that by refusing to speak he was mocking boys like me who could not speak. If the Silent One, who was not mute, had decided not to speak, others might think that I too was only refusing to speak but could do so if I wanted to. My friendship with him could only enhance this impression.

One day the Silent One unexpectedly came to my rescue and knocked down a boy who was beating me in the corridor. The next day I felt obliged to fight on his side in a scuffle which broke out during a recess.

After that we sat at the same desk in the rear of the classroom. We first wrote notes to each other, but then learned to communicate by signs. The Silent One accompanied me in expeditions to the railroad station, where we made friends with departing Soviet soldiers. Together we stole a drunken postman's bicycle, went across the city park, still sown with land mines and closed to the public, and watched the girls undressing in the communal bathhouse.

In the evening we sneaked out of the dormitory and roamed through the nearby squares and courtyards, scaring love-making couples, throwing stones through open windows, attacking unsuspecting passersby. The Silent One, taller and stronger, always acted as the striking force.

Every morning we were awakened by the whistle of the train which passed close by, bringing peasants to the city with their produce for the market. In the evening the same train returned to the villages alongside its single track, its lighted windows twinkling between the trees like a row of fireflies.

On sunny days the Silent One and I walked along the track, over the sun-warmed crossties and the sharp pebbles which hurt our bare feet. Sometimes, if there were enough boys and girls from nearby settlements playing close to the tracks, we would put on a show for them. A few minutes before the arrival of the train I would lie down between the tracks, face down, arms folded over my head, my body as flat as possible. The Silent One would assemble an audience while I waited patiently. As the train was approaching, I could hear and feel the thudding roar of the wheels through the rails and ties until I was shaking with them. When the locomotive was almost on top of me I flattened even more, and tried not to think. The hot breath of the furnace swept over me and the great engine rolled furiously above my back. Then the carriages rattled rhythmically in a long line, as I waited for the last one to pass. I remembered when I had played the same game in the villages. It so happened that once, at the very moment of passing over a boy's body, the engineer had released some burning cinders. When the train was gone we found the boy dead, his back and head burned like an overbaked potato. Several boys who had witnessed the scene claimed that the fireman had leaned out of his window, seen the boy, and released the cinders on purpose. I recalled another occasion when the couplings hanging free at the end of the last carriage were longer than usual and they smashed the head of the boy lying between the rails. His skull was staved in like a squashed pumpkin.

Despite these grim recollections, there was something immensely tempting about lying between the rails with a train running above. In the moments between the passing of the locomotive and the last car I felt within me life as pure as milk carefully strained through a cloth. During the short time when the carriages roared over one's body, nothing mattered except the simple fact of being alive. I would forget everything: the orphanage, my muteness, Gavrila, the Silent One. I found at the very bottom of this experience the great joy of being unhurt.

After the train had passed I would rise on trembling hands and weak legs and look around with greater satisfaction than I had ever experienced in exacting the most vicious revenge from one of my enemies.

I tried to preserve that feeling of being alive for future use. I might need it in moments of fear and pain. By comparison with the fear that filled me when I waited for an approaching train, all other terrors appeared insignificant.

I walked off the embankment feigning indifference and boredom. The Silent One was the first to approach me, with a protective, though elaborately casual air. He brushed off bits of gravel and splinters of wood embedded in my clothing. Gradually I subdued the trembling of my hands, legs, and the corners of my parched mouth. The others stood in a circle and watched in admiration.

Later I returned with the Silent One to the orphanage. I felt proud and knew that he was proud of me. None of the other boys dared to do what I had done. They gradually stopped bothering me. But I knew that my performance had to be repeated every few days; otherwise there would surely be some skeptical boy who would disbelieve what I had done and openly doubt my courage. I would press my Red Star to my chest, march to the railroad embankment, and wait for the thunder of an approaching train.

The Silent One and I used to spend a good deal of time on the railroad tracks. We watched the trains go by and sometimes we jumped on the steps of the rear cars, getting off when the train slowed down at the crossing.

The crossing was located a few miles from the city. A long time ago, probably before the war, they had started building a spur which was never finished. The rusty switching points were overgrown with moss, for they had never been used. The unfinished spur line ended a few hundred yards away at the end of a cliff from which a bridge had been planned to extend. We carefully inspected the switching points several times and tried to move the lever. But the corroded mechanism would not budge.

One day we saw a locksmith at the orphanage open a jammed lock simply by soaking oil into it. On the following day the Silent One stole a bottle of oil from the kitchen and in the evening we poured it over the bearings of the switch mechanism. We waited for a while to give the oil a chance to penetrate and then we hung on the lever with all our weight. Something creaked inside and the lever moved with a jolt, while the points switched to the other track with a screech. Scared by our unexpected success we quickly threw the lever back.

After that, the Silent One and I exchanged knowing glances whenever we passed by the fork. This was our secret. And whenever I sat in the shade of a tree and watched a train appear on the horizon, I was overcome by a sense of great power. The lives of the people on the train were in my hands. All I had to do was leap to the switch and move the points, sending the whole train over the cliff into the peaceful stream below. All it needed was one push on the lever . . .

I recalled the trains carrying people to the gas chambers and crematories. The men who had ordered and organized all that probably enjoyed a similar feeling of complete power over their uncomprehending victims. These men controlled the fate of millions of people whose names, faces, and occupations were unknown to them, but whom they could either let live or turn to fine soot flying in the wind. All they had to do was issue orders and in countless towns and villages trained squads of troops and police would start rounding up people destined for ghettos and death camps. They had the power to decide whether the points of thousands of railroad spurs would be switched to tracks leading to life or to death.

To be capable of deciding the fate of many people whom one did not even know was a magnificent sensation. I was not sure whether the pleasure depended only on the knowledge of the power one had, or on its use.

A few weeks later the Silent One and I went to a local marketplace where peasants from the neighboring villages brought their produce and home crafts once a week. We usually managed to snare an apple or two, a bunch of carrots, or even a glass of cream in return for the smiles we lavished on the buxom peasant women.

The market was swarming with people. Farmers loudly hawked their goods, women tried on colorful skirts and blouses, scared heifers mooed, and pigs ran squealing underfoot.

Staring at the gleaming bicycle of a militiaman I stumbled against a tall table with dairy produce on it, knocking it over. Buckets of milk and cream and jugs of buttermilk spilled everywhere. Before I had time to run away a tall farmer, purple with rage, hit me hard in the face with his fist. I fell down, spitting out three teeth together with blood. The man lifted me by the scruff of my neck like a rabbit and went on beating me until the blood spattered over his shirt. Then he pushed aside the gathering crowd of onlookers and jammed me into an empty sauerkraut barrel and kicked it over into a garbage heap.

For a moment I did not know what had happened. I heard the laughter of the peasants; my head was spinning from the beating and the rolling in the barrel. I was choking with blood; I felt my face swelling.

Suddenly I saw the Silent One. Pale and shaking he was trying to get me out of the barrel. The peasants, calling me a Gypsy stray, laughed at his efforts. Afraid of further attacks, he started rolling the barrel with me inside toward a water fountain. Some village boys ran along, trying to trip him and take it away. He warded them off with a club until we finally reached the fountain.

Soaked with water and blood, with splinters sticking in my back and hands, I crawled out of the barrel. The Silent One supported me on his shoulder as I staggered along. We reached the orphanage after a painful walk.

A doctor dressed my cut mouth and cheek. The Silent One waited outside the door. When the doctor left, he contemplated my lacerated face for a long time.

Two weeks later the Silent One woke me at dawn. He was covered with dust and his shirt clung to his perspiring body. I gathered that he must have been out all night. He signaled me to follow him. I dressed quickly and we were soon outside with no one the wiser.

He took me to a derelict hut not far from the railroad crossing where we had oiled the points. We scrambled onto the roof. The Silent One lit a cigarette which he had found on the way and gestured for me to wait. I did not know what it was all about, but I had nothing else to do.

The sun was just beginning to rise. Dew was evaporating from the tar-paper roof and brown worms started to crawl out from under the rain gutters.

We heard the whistle of a train. The Silent One stiffened and pointed with his hand. I watched the train appear in the faraway haze and slowly come nearer. It was market day and many of the peasants took this first morning train which ran through some of the villages before dawn. The carriages were filled. Baskets stuck out of the windows and people hung on to the steps in bunches.

The Silent One drew closer to me. He was sweating and his hands were moist. He licked his drawn lips from time to time. He brushed back his hair. He stared at the train and suddenly he seemed much older.

The train was approaching the crossing. The cramped peasants leaned out of the windows, their blond hair flying in the wind. The Silent One squeezed my arm so hard that I jumped. At the same moment the train's locomotive veered aside, twisting violently as if pulled by some invisible force.

Only the two front cars followed the engine obediently. The others hobbled and then like frisky horses started climbing on one another's backs, falling off the embankment at the same time. The crash came with a tumultuous crunch and screech. A cloud of steam shot up into the sky obscuring everything. Screams and cries came from below.

I was stunned and quivered like a telephone wire struck by a stone. The Silent One sagged. He gripped his knees spasmodically for a while, looking at the dust settling slowly. Then he turned and dashed for the stairs, pulling me along behind him. We quickly returned to the orphanage, avoiding the crowd of people rushing to the scene of the accident. Ambulance bells were clanging in the vicinity.

At the orphanage everyone was still asleep. Before going into the dormitory I took a good look at the Silent One. There was no trace of tension in his face. He looked back at me, smiling softly. If it had not been for the bandage over my face and mouth I would have smiled too.

During the next few days everyone at school talked about the railroad disaster. Black-bordered newspapers listed the names of the casualties; the police were looking for political saboteurs suspected of previous crimes. Over the track cranes were lifting the carriages, which were entangled with one another and twisted out of shape.

On the next market day the Silent One hurried me to the marketplace. We pushed through the crowd. Many of the stands were empty and cards with black crosses informed the public of the deaths of their owners. The Silent One looked at them and signified his pleasure to me. We were heading for the stand of my tormentor.

I looked up. The familiar shape of the stand was there, with its jugs of milk and cream, bricks of butter wrapped in cloth, some fruit. From behind them, as in a puppet show, popped up the head of the man who had knocked out my teeth and pushed me into a barrel.

I looked at the Silent One in anguish. He was staring at the man in disbelief. When he caught my glance he grabbed my hand and we quickly left the market. As soon as we reached the road, he fell down on the grass and cried as though in terrible pain, his words muffled by the ground. It was the only time that I had heard his voice.

19

Early in the morning one of the teachers called me out. I was being summoned to the office of the principal. At first I thought it must be news from Gavrila, but on the way I began to have my doubts.

The principal was waiting for me in her office, accompanied by the member of the Social Commission who thought he had known my parents before the war. They greeted me cordially and asked me to sit down. I noticed that they were both rather nervous, though they tried to conceal it. I looked anxiously around, and heard voices in an adjoining office.

The man from the Commission went into the other room and talked to someone in there. Then he opened the door wide. A man and a woman stood inside.

They seemed somehow familiar, and I could hear my heart beating under the star of my uniform. Forcing an expression of indifference, I scrutinized their faces. The resemblance was striking; these two could be my parents. I clutched my chair while thoughts raced through my mind like ricocheting bullets. My parents . . . I didn't know what to do; admit that I recognized them or pretend that I didn't?

They came closer. The woman bent over me. Her

face was suddenly creased by tears. The man, nervously adjusting the spectacles on his moist nose, supported her on his arm. He also was shaking with sobs. But he quickly overcame them and addressed me. He spoke to me in Russian and I noted that his speech was as fluent and beautiful as Gavrila's. He asked me to unbutton my uniform: on my chest, on the left side, there should be a birthmark.

I knew I had the birthmark. I hesitated, wondering whether to expose it. If I did, everything would be lost; there would be no doubt that I was their son. I pondered for a few minutes, but I felt sorry for the crying woman. I slowly unbuttoned my uniform.

There was no way out of the situation, no matter how one looked at it. Parents, as Gavrila often told me, had a right to their children. I was not yet grown up: I was only twelve. Even if they did not want to, it was their duty to take me away.

I looked at them again. The woman smiled at me through the tear-smudged powder on her face. The man excitedly rubbed his hands together. They did not look like people who would beat me. On the contrary, they seemed frail and ailing.

My uniform was now open and the birthmark plainly visible. They bent over me, crying, hugging and kissing me. I was undecided again. I knew that I could run away anytime, jump on one of the crowded trains and ride it until no one could trace me. But I wanted to be found by Gavrila, and therefore it was wise not to run away. I knew that rejoining my parents meant the end of all my dreams of becoming a great inventor of fuses for changing people's color, of working in the land of Gavrila and Mitka, where today was already tomorrow.

My world was becoming cramped like the attic of a peasant's shed. At all times a man risked falling into the snares of those who hated and wanted to persecute him, or into the arms of those who loved and wished to protect him.

I could not readily accept the idea of suddenly becoming someone's real son, of being caressed and cared for, of having to obey people, not because they were stronger and could hurt me, but because they were my parents and had rights which no one could take away from them.

Of course, parents had their uses when a child was very small. But a boy of my age should be free from any restriction. He should be able to choose for himself the people whom he wished to follow and learn from. Yet I could not decide to run away. I looked at the tearful face of the woman who was my mother, at the trembling man who was my father, uncertain whether they should stroke my hair or pat my shoulder, and some inner force restrained me and forbade me to fly off. I suddenly felt like Lekh's painted bird, which some unknown force was pulling toward his kind.

My mother remained with me alone in the room; my father went out to take care of the formalities. She said that I would be happy with her and my father, that I could do anything I wanted. They would make me a new uniform, an exact copy of the one I was wearing.

As I listened to all this, I recalled the hare which Makar once caught in a trap. He was a fine large animal. One could sense in him a drive for freedom, for powerful leaps, playful tumbles, and swift escapes. Locked in a cage he raged, stamped his feet, beat against the walls. After a few days Makar, furious over his restlessness, threw a heavy tarpaulin over him. The hare struggled and fought under it, but finally gave up. Eventually he became tame and ate from my hand. One day Makar got drunk and left the door of the cage open. The hare jumped out and started toward the meadow. I thought he would plunge into the tall grass

with one huge leap and never be seen again. But he
seemed to savor his freedom and just sat down, with
ears pricked up. From the distant fields and woods
came sounds that only he could hear and understand,
smells and fragrances that only he could appreciate. It
was all his own; he had left the cage behind.

Suddenly there was a change in him. The alert
ears flopped, he sagged somehow, and grew smaller. He
jumped once and his whiskers perked up, but he did
not run away. I whistled loudly in the hope that it
would bring him to his senses, make him realize that
he was free. He only turned around and sluggishly
as though suddenly aged and shrunken, moved toward
the hutch. On his way he stopped for a while, stood
up, and looked back once again with ears pricked; then
he passed the rabbits gazing at him and jumped into
the cage. I closed the door, though it was unnecessary.
He now carried the cage in himself; it bound his brain
and heart and paralyzed his muscles. Freedom, which
had set him apart from other resigned, drowsy rabbits,
left him like the wind-driven fragrance evaporating
from crushed, dried clover.

My father came back. Both he and my mother
hugged me and looked me over and exchanged some
comments about me. It was time to leave the orphanage. We went to say goodbye to the Silent One. He
glanced suspiciously at my parents, shaking his head,
and refused to greet them.

We went out into the street and my father helped
to carry my books. There was chaos everywhere.
Ragged, dirty, haggard people with sacks on their backs
were returning to their homes, quarreling with those
who had occupied them during the war. I walked between my parents, feeling their hands on my shoulders
and hair, feeling smothered by their love and protection.

They took me to their apartment. This they had
been able to borrow with great difficulty after they had
learned that a boy answering their son's description

was at the local Center, and a meeting could be arranged. At the apartment a surprise awaited me. They had another child, a four-year-old boy. My parents explained to me that he was an orphan whose parents and older sister had been killed. He had been saved by his old nurse, who handed him to my father at some point in their wanderings during the third year of the war. They had adopted him, and I could see that they loved him very much.

This only contributed to my doubts. Would it not be better for me to stay on my own and wait for Gavrila, who would eventually adopt me? I would much prefer to be alone again, wandering from one village to the next, from one town to another, never knowing what might happen. Here everything was very predictable.

The apartment was small, consisting of one room and a kitchen. There was a washroom on the stairs. It was stuffy and we were crowded, getting in one another's way. My father had a heart condition. If anything upset him he grew pale and perspiration covered his face. Then he would swallow some pills. My mother went out at dawn to wait in the endless queues for food. When she returned, she started cooking and cleaning.

The small boy was a nuisance. He insisted on playing whenever I was reading the newspaper reporting the Red Army successes. He would clutch my pants and knock over my books. One day he annoyed me so much that I grabbed his arm and squeezed it hard. Something cracked and the boy screamed madly. My father called a doctor; the bone was broken. That night, when the child was in bed with his arm in a cast, he whimpered quietly and glanced at me in terror. My parents looked at me without a word.

I often left secretly to meet with the Silent One. One day he did not turn up at the appointed time. They told me later at the orphanage that he had been transferred to another city.

Spring arrived. On a rainy day in May the news came that the war was over. People danced in the streets, kissing and hugging one another. In the evening we heard the ambulances throughout the city picking up all the people injured in the brawls which broke out at the drinking parties. During the days that followed I visited the orphanage frequently, hoping to find a letter from Gavrila or Mitka. But there was none.

I read the newspapers carefully, trying to figure out what was happening in the world. Not all the armies were due to return home. Germany was to be occupied and it might be years before Gavrila and Mitka would return.

Life in the city was becoming more difficult. Every day masses of people arrived from all over the country, hoping that it might be easier to make a living in an industrial center than in the country, and that they would be able to earn back all that they had lost. Unable to find work or living quarters, bewildered people tramped the streets, struggled for seats in streetcars, buses, and restaurants. They were nervous, short-tempered, and quarrelsome. It seemed that everyone believed himself chosen by fate merely because he had survived the war, and felt entitled to deference on that account.

One afternoon my parents gave me some money for the cinema. It was a Soviet film about a man and a girl who had a date to meet at six o'clock on the first day after the war.

There was a crowd at the box office and I waited patiently in line for several hours. When my turn came I discovered that I had lost one of my coins. The cashier, seeing that I was a mute, put my ticket aside to be picked up when I brought the rest of the change. I rushed home. Not more than half an hour later I came back with the money and tried to get my ticket at the box office. An attendant told me to stand in line again. I did not have my slate so I tried to explain with signs that I had already stood in line and that my ticket was waiting for me. He did not try to understand. To the amusement of the people waiting outside he took me by the ear and roughly pushed me out. I slipped and fell on the cobblestones. Blood started dripping from my nose onto my uniform. I quickly returned home, put a cold compress on my face, and started plotting my revenge.

In the evening, as my parents prepared for bed, I got dressed. Anxiously they asked me where I was going. I told them in signs that I was simply going for a walk. They tried to convince me that it was dangerous to go out at night.

I went straight to the theater. There were not many people waiting at the box office and the attendant who had thrown me out earlier was idly strolling in the yard. I picked up two good-sized bricks from the street and sneaked up the staircase of a building adjoining the cinema. I dropped an empty bottle from the third-floor landing. As I expected, the attendant came quickly to the spot where it fell. When he bent down to examine it I dropped the two bricks. And then I ran down the steps into the street.

After this incident I went out only at night. My parents tried to protest, but I would not listen. I slept during the day and at dusk I was ready to start my night prowl.

All cats are the same in the dark, says the proverb. But it certainly did not apply to people. With them it was just the opposite. During the day they were all alike, running in their well-defined ways. At night they changed beyond recognition. Men sauntered along the street, or jumped like grasshoppers from the shadow of one streetlamp into the next, taking occasional swigs from the bottles they carried in their pockets. In the dark gaping doorways there were women with open blouses and tight skirts. Men approached them with a staggering gait and then they disappeared together.

From behind the anemic city shrubbery one heard the squeals of couples making love. In the ruins of a bombed house several boys were raping a girl reckless enough to have ventured out alone. An ambulance turned a distant corner with a screech of tires; a fight broke out in a nearby tavern and there was the crash of broken glass.

I was soon familiar with the night city. I knew quiet lanes where girls younger than myself solicited men older than my father. I found places where men dressed in smart clothes with gold watches on their wrists traded in objects the very possession of which could get them years in prison. I found an inconspicuous house from which young men took piles of leaflets to post on government buildings, posters which the militiamen and soldiers tore down in rage. I saw the militia organize a manhunt and I saw armed civilians killing a soldier. In daytime the world was at peace. The war continued at night.

Every night I visited a park near the zoological garden, on the outskirts of the city. Men and women assembled there to trade, drink, and play cards. These people were good to me. They would give me chocolate which was hard to get, and they taught me how to throw a knife and how to snatch one from a man's hand. In return I was asked to deliver small packages to various addresses, avoiding militiamen and plainclothesmen. When I returned from these missions the women drew me to their perfumed bodies and encouraged me to lie down with them and caress them in the ways I had learned with Ewka. I felt at ease among these people whose faces were concealed in the darkness of night. I did not bother anyone, I did not get into anyone's way. They regarded my being mute as an asset which ensured my discretion when I carried out my missions.

But one night it all ended. Blinding searchlights flashed from behind the trees and police whistles shrilled in the silence. The park was surrounded by militiamen and we were all taken to jail. On the way I nearly broke the finger of a militia officer who pushed me too roughly, ignoring the Red Star on my chest.

The next morning my parents came to take me away. I was brought out all dirty and with my uniform in shreds after a sleepless night. I was sorry to leave my friends, the night people. My parents looked at me puzzled but said nothing.

20

I was too thin and not growing. The doctors advised mountain air and a lot of exercise. The teachers said that the city was not a good place for me. In the fall my father took a job in the hills, in the western part of the country, and we left the city. When the first snows came I was sent to the mountains. An old ski instructor agreed to look after me. I joined him in his mountain shelter and my parents saw me only once a week.

We got up early every morning. The instructor kneeled down for prayer while I looked on indulgently. Here was a grown man, educated in the city, who acted like a simple peasant and could not accept the idea that he was alone in the world and could expect no assistance from anyone. Every one of us stood alone, and the sooner a man realized that all Gavrilas, Mitkas, and Silent Ones were expendable, the better for him. It mattered little if one was mute; people did not understand one another anyway. They collided with or charmed one another, hugged or trampled one another, but everyone knew only himself. His emotions, memory, and senses divided him from others as effectively as thick reeds screen the mainstream from the muddy bank. Like the mountain peaks around us, we looked at one another, separated by valleys, too high to stay unnoticed, too low to touch the heavens.

My days passed in skiing down the long mountain trails. The hills were deserted. The hostels had been burnt down, and the people who had inhabited the valleys had been sent away. The new settlers were only beginning to arrive.

The instructor was a calm and patient man. I tried to obey him and was glad when I earned his scant praise.

The blizzard came suddenly, blocking out the peaks and ridges with swirls of snow. I lost sight of the instructor and started on my own down the steep slope, trying to reach the shelter as quickly as possible. My skis bounced over hardened, icy snow and the speed took my breath away. When I suddenly saw a deep gully it was too late to make a turn.

April sunshine filled the room. I moved my head and it did not seem to hurt. I lifted myself on my hands and was about to lie down when the phone rang. The nurse had already gone, but the phone rang insistently again and again.

I pulled myself out of bed and walked to the table. I lifted up the receiver and heard a man's voice.

I held the receiver to my ear, listening to his impatient words; somewhere at the other end of the wire there was someone who wanted to talk with me . . . I felt an overpowering desire to speak.

I opened my mouth and strained. Sounds crawled up my throat. Tense and concentrated I started to arrange them into syllables and words. I distinctly heard them jumping out of me one after another, like peas from a split pod. I put the receiver aside, hardly believing it possible. I began to recite words and sentences, snatches of Mitka's songs. The voice lost in a faraway village church had found me again and filled the whole room. I spoke loudly and incessantly like the peasants and then like the city folk, as fast as I could, enraptured by the sounds that were heavy with meaning, as wet snow is heavy with water, convincing myself again and again and again that speech was now mine and that it did not intend to escape through the door which opened onto the balcony.

ON KOSINSKI

*Jerzy Kosinski has lived through—and now makes
use of—some of the strongest direct experience
that this century has had to offer.*

TIME

To appreciate the violent, ironic, suspenseful, morally de-
manding world of JERZY KOSINSKI's novels, one must
first acknowledge the random succession of pain and joy,
wealth and poverty, persecution and approbation that have
made his own life often as eventful as those of his fictional
creations.

He was born in Poland. When he was six, all but two
members of his once numerous and distinguished family
were lost in the Holocaust of World War II. Abandoned,
suspected of being a Jew or a gypsy, he fled alone from
village to village in Nazi-occupied eastern Europe, working
as a farm hand, gaining his knowledge of nature, animal
life, farming—and survival. At the age of nine, in a trau-
matic confrontation with a hostile peasant crowd he lost
the power of speech, and was unable to talk for over five
years. After the war, he was reunited with his ailing parents
(his father was a scholar of ancient linguistics, his mother
a pianist) and placed in a school for the handicapped.
While on vacation, he regained his voice in a skiing accident, and with renewed self-reliance promptly worked his
way through high school.

During his studies at the state-controlled Stalinist college
and university he was suspended twice and often threatened
with expulsion for his rejection of the official Marxist
doctrine. While a Ph.D candidate in social psychology, he
rose rapidly to become an associate professor and grantee
of the Academy of Sciences, the state's highest research
institution. Attempting to free himself from state-imposed
collectivity, he would spend winters as a ski instructor in
the Tatra Mountains, and summers as a social counselor at
a Baltic sea resort.

Meanwhile, secretly, he plotted his escape. A confident
master of bureaucratic judo, Kosinski pitted himself against

the Establishment. In need of official sponsors, and reluctant to implicate his family, his friends and the academy staff, he created four distinguished—but fictitious—members of the Academy of Sciences to act in that capacity. As a member of the Academy's inner circle and a prize-winning photographer (with many one-man exhibitions to his credit), Kosinski had access to state printing plants, and he was able to furnish each academician with the appropriate official seals, rubber stamps and stationery. His punishment, had he been caught, would have been many years in prison. After two years of active correspondence between his fictitious sponsors and the various government agencies, Kosinski obtained an official passport allowing him to visit the United States under the auspices of an equally fictitious American "foundation." Waiting for his U.S. visa, expecting to be arrested at any time, Kosinski carried a foil-wrapped egg of cyanide in his pocket. "One way or another," he vowed, "they won't be able to keep me here against my will." But his plan worked. On December 20, 1957, Kosinski arrived in New York fluent in several languages though only with a rudimentary knowledge of English, following what he still considers the singular most creative act of his life. "I left behind being an inner emigré trapped in spiritual exile," he says. "America was to give shelter to my real self and I wanted to become its writer-in-residence." He was twenty-four years of age—his American odyssey was about to begin.

He started wandering widely in the United States as a truck driver, moonlighting as a parking lot attendant, a cinema projectionist, a portrait photographer, a limousine and racing-car driver for a black nightclub enterpreneur. "By working in Harlem as a white, uniformed chauffeur I broke a color barrier of the profession," he recalls. Studying English whenever he could in a year he learned it well enough to obtain a Ford Foundation fellowship. Two years later, as a student of social psychology, he wrote the first of his two nonfiction books on collective society. It became an instant bestseller, serialized by *The Saturday Evening Post*, condensed by *Reader's Digest*, and published in 18 languages. He was firmly set on a writing career.

After his publishing debut he met Mary Weir, the widow of a steel magnate from Pittsburgh. They dated for two years and were married after the publication of Kosinski's second nonfiction book.

During his 10 years with Mary Weir (which ended with her death) Kosinski moved with utmost familiarity in the world of heavy industry, big business and high society. He and Mary traveled a great deal—there was a private plane, a 17-crew boat, and houses in Pittsburgh, New York, Hobe Sound, Southampton, Paris, London and Florence. He led a life most novelists only invent in the pages of their novels.

"During my marriage, I had often thought that it was Stendhal or F. Scott Fitzgerald, both preoccupied with wealth they themselves did not have, who deserved to have had my experience. At first, I considered writing a novel about my immediate American experience, the dimension of wealth, power and high society that surrounded me, not the terror, poverty and privation I had seen and experienced so shortly before. But during my marriage I was too much a part of that world to extract from it the nucleus of what I felt. As a writer, I perceived fiction as the art of imaginative projection and so, instead, I decided to write my first novel about a homeless boy in war-torn Eastern Europe, an existence I'd once led and also one that was shared by millions of others like me, yet was still foreign to most Americans. This novel, *The Painted Bird*, was my gift to Mary, and to my new world."

His following novels—*Steps, Being There, The Devil Tree, Cockpit, Blind Date* and *Passion Play*, all links in an elaborate fictional cycle, were inspired by particular events of his life. He would often draw on the experience he had gained when, once a "Don Quixote of the turnpike," he had become a "Captain Ahab of billionaire's row." "Kosinski has enough technical virtuosity to outwrite almost any competitor," wrote *Los Angeles Herald Examiner*, "but few novelists have a personal background like his to draw on." Translated into most major languages, at first his novels have earned Kosinski the status of an international underground culture hero. Official recognition followed: for *The Painted Bird*, the French Best Foreign Book Award; for *Steps*, the National Book Award. He received a Guggenheim fellowship, the Award in Literature of the American Academy and the National Institute of Arts and Letters, as well as the Brith Sholom Humanitarian Freedom Award, and many others.

While Kosinski was constantly on the move, living and writing in various parts of the United States, Europe and Latin America, close calls with death persisted in his life.

On his way from Paris to the Beverly Hills home of his friend, film director Roman Polanski, and his wife, Sharon Tate, Kosinski's luggage was unloaded by mistake in New York. Unable to catch the connecting flight to Los Angeles, Kosinski reluctantly stayed overnight in New York. That very night in Polanski's household the Charles Manson Helter-Skelter gang murdered five people—among them Kosinski's closest friends, one of whom he financially assisted in leaving Europe and settling in the States.

For the next few years Kosinski taught English at Princeton and Yale. He left university life when he was elected president of American P.E.N., the international association of writers and editors. After serving the maximum two terms, he has remained active in various American human rights organizations. He is proud to have been responsible for freeing from prisons, helping financially, resettling or otherwise giving assistance to a great number of writers, political and religious dissidents and intellectuals all over the world, many of whom openly acknowledged his coming to their rescue.

Called by *America* "a spokesman for the human capacity to survive in a highly complex social system," Kosinski has been often labeled by the media an existential cowboy, a Horatio Alger of the nightmare, a penultimate gamesman, the utterly portable man and a mixture of adventurer and social reformer. In an interview for *Psychology Today*, Kosinski said: "And I have no habits that require maintaining—I don't even have a favorite menu—the only way for me to live is to be as close to other people as life allows. Not much else stimulates me—and nothing interests me more."

Traveling extensively, on an average Kosinski wakes up around 8 A.M. ready for the day. Four more hours of sleep in the afternoon allows him to remain mentally and physically active until the early dawn when he retires. This pattern, he claims, benefits his writing, his photography, and practicing of the sports he has favored for years—downhill skiing and polo, which, as an avid all-around horseman, he plays on a team—or one-on-one.

As a novelist and a screenplay writer (he adapted for the screen his novel, *Being There* which starred Peter Sellers, Shirley MacLaine, Melvyn Douglas and Jack Warden, for which he was nominated for the Golden

Globe, won the Writers Guild of America Best Screenplay of the Year Award and won the British Academy of Film and Television Arts Best Screenplay of the Year Award)—Kosinski is frequently interviewed by the press and appears often on television. Thus, he is apt to be recognized, and to obtain private access to public places he sometimes disguises himself; occasionally, he takes part-time employment in businesses and corporations that interest him. In his film-acting debut in *REDS*, a Paramount picture starring Warren Beatty, Diane Keaton, Jack Nicholson and Maureen Stapleton, Mr. Kosinski portrayed the Russian revolutionary leader Grigori Zinoviev.

A critic once said of Kosinski that he "writes his novels so sparsely as though they cost a thousand dollars a word, and a misplaced or misused locution would cost him his life." He was close to the truth: Kosinski takes almost three years to write a novel, and rewrites it a dozen times; later, in subsequence sets of proofs, he condenses the novel's text often by one-third. Kosinski said that "writing fiction is the essence of my life—whatever else I do revolves around a constant thought: could I—can I—would I—should I—use it in my next novel? As I have no children, no family, no relatives, no business or estate to speak of, my books are my only spiritual accomplishment."

"Learning from the best writing of every era—wrote *The Washington Post*—Kosinski develops his own style and technique.... in harmony with his need to express new things about our life and the world we do live in, to express the inexpressible. Giving to himself as well as to the reader the same chance for interpretation, he traces the truth in the deepest corners of our outdoor and indoor lives, of our outer appearance and our inner reality. He moves the borderline of writing to more remote, still invisible and untouchable poles, in cold and in darkness. Doing so, he enlarges the borders of the bearable."